Make You a Man

Dr Mulholland uncrossed his legs and cracked a smile. 'To all effects and purposes, you *are* one of my students, Ms Sawyer. So you will mind your language in my office. Is that clear?'

There was a glint in his eye and she wished she knew him well enough to be in a better position to decipher it. 'Yes,' she said, then added, 'sir.'

He held her gaze for only a moment, but it was long enough for her to gauge that he would like to play teacher and student. Long enough for her brain to flood with memories of dirty daydreams in which he directed her to do obscene things in his prim, neutral voice.

He turned back to his papers. 'I don't want to see any more stocking tops, Ms Sawyer,' he said. 'Put your underclothes on the desk before you leave, please.'

'What?'

He looked up at her and sighed as if she were an idiot nineteen year old. 'I'm confiscating them. Put them on the desk, please.'

'I'm wearing them,' said Claire.

'Well, take them off, girl!' he snapped, rolling his eyes with impatience.

'You expect me to walk out of your office naked?'

'Don't tempt me,' he said.

By the same author

Mixed Signals

Make You a Man
Anna Clare

BLACK LACE

Black Lace books contain sexual fantasies.
In real life, always practise safe sex.

First published in 2005 by
Black Lace
Thames Wharf Studios
Rainville Road
London W6 9HA

Design by Smith & Gilmour, London
Printed and bound by Mackays of Chatham PLC

ISBN 0 352 34006 1

1

Santosh had dealt with some difficult situations in her time. She had interviewed armed terrorists, argued with border guards, been shot at, shelled and ducked 'friendly fire'. Nothing in these situations, however, prepared her for the trauma of dealing with lost luggage at Heathrow airport. It didn't matter how many languages she spoke – she still couldn't master the International Language of Stupid.

'I don't mean to be rude, but please, I need that bag. There's a month's worth of documentary footage in it.'

The girl behind the desk shrugged. 'Sorry. Which plane was it on?'

Given the amount of air traffic that passed through Heathrow on a daily basis, this didn't exactly inspire confidence. 'One of those ones with wings,' Santosh said, tapping the boarding pass on the desk.

'Right.' The girl scanned the boarding pass and nodded knowledgeably. 'Yes, I'm sorry. It's the law or something – we have to check all luggage on flights from that destination. Terrorism, you know.'

'OK, I appreciate that. Do you know when I'll be able to collect my bags?'

'Depends.'

'OK. A rough estimate?'

'Depends. Sorry.'

'Depends on what?'

'Whether there's a bomb on board.'

'I think if there was a bomb on board it would prob- ably have detonated by now, don't you?' asked Santosh.

'For maximum impact you'd want to detonate the charge in the air, which is the usual MO for Al Qaeda.'

The girl looked worried enough to make Santosh remember that she was still dressed in combats and headscarf and probably looked suspiciously like an Islamic militant. 'Oh, don't worry about this,' Santosh assured her, gesturing to her clothes. 'It's just par for the course in Kabul – still not very stable out there. It's fine. I'm a journalist. I'm from Bethnal Green. I'm British. I know all the words to "Land of Hope and Glory".'

She was uncomfortably conscious of the growing queue of fellow irritated travellers behind her and wondered why it was that she could face off against a heavily armed and possibly insane US marine-corps lieutenant but could be reduced to babbling incompetence when confronted by a blank-faced twenty-something called Joanne.

Suddenly Santosh heard screaming. Not the kind of screaming that was more just a general yell of 'down' and made you drop into a foxhole, undergrowth or trench like a stone. This was more the kind of screaming associated with early footage of the Beatles where teen-aged girls had clawed at their own hair and faces in a strange frenzy of hormone-crazed devotion. Joanne, behind the check-in desk, looked animated for the first time and everyone was looking at about four or five human beings who were surrounded by a bunch of black-clad men and women wearing headsets, dark glasses and don't-fuck-with-me expressions.

'Oh my God!'

'Is it Madonna?'

'David and Victoria?'

'Nah, it's gotta be Kylie.'

Santosh wondered what people would say if it turned out to be the Prime Minister or the President of France or the German Chancellor in the midst of the entourage.

She suspected they'd probably go back to whatever they were doing (queuing, being angry, contemplating a visit to Tie Rack without losing their place in the lost luggage queue) in disappointment. As Joanne craned to look, however, Santosh realised she might have found a level on which she could communicate with the girl.

'I'm off the telly,' she said, hopefully.

Joanne tried to look efficient while still trying to get a look at the celebrity in transit. 'That's nice. I'm sorry, Miss Kapoor, but I can't locate your baggage on the computer at the present time due to our database being down.'

Santosh groaned and wondered how on earth she had let herself be talked into stashing the documentary footage in with her knickers in the first place. Clean pants she could live without, but the tapes needed to be edited in time for the deadline.

A sort of Chinese whisper had run through the queue. Apparently the celebrity was someone called Fred Hill, which meant nothing to Santosh but obviously meant a lot to people who managed to stay in the country for more than six months at a time. The bodyguards wheeled efficiently around their charges and moved rapidly towards an exit labelled VIP, fending off flashes from the paparazzi. Santosh was reminded she had promised to meet Claire for dinner the next day and thought that at least Fred Hill, or the putative sighting thereof, would give her something to discuss other than the usual round of old university stories.

When she finally arrived home to find the goldfish missing, she felt incredibly depressed. Most of her friends had mortgages by now, husbands and children. Others, like Claire, had successful careers. It wasn't that Santosh's career wasn't successful – it was. In the last year or two it had been going spectacularly well, but where she was capable of keeping her head under fire, she was equally incapable of coping with a freezer that had turned into a glacier or a mattress that needed turning. She was, by her own admission, a domestic disaster. Claire had always said that it was a lot of chauvinistic bollocks that a woman should be presumed to be a born housekeeper, but it was all very well for Claire to say that. Claire wasn't Indian and didn't have a domestic divinity for a mother. Santosh's guilt about being too tired (or as she saw it, too lazy) to fix a sandwich was compounded by the knowledge that her mother thought nothing of spending an entire day in the kitchen.

Her flat looked like it should belong to one of the students next door rather than a thirty-two-year-old woman who had left home at eighteen. She was so disorganised that her CDs remained stacked in a corner of the floor because, while she had bought a set of flatpack shelves, she had yet to find the time to construct the things.

She was sure the place looked worse than when she'd left it, and she was positive that she'd had goldfish when she left. Rosencrantz and Guildenstern were the only pets she could have according to the terms of her lease and, as far as she could remember, Rosencrantz and Guildenstern were not dead. She was sure she hadn't yet reached a level of scattiness where she would have asked Daniel to feed a pair of dead goldfish.

She didn't have time to contemplate the mystery of the missing goldfish for long before a noise in the bedroom alerted her to someone else's presence in the flat. Daniel had a key, but there was something deeply unnerving about coming home and finding someone else in your flat. Particularly when the goldfish were missing.

Admittedly, it was a pretty bizarre choice of things to burgle, but with the kind of opportunistic thefts that occurred around this area, Santosh supposed anything was possible. Before she had left the country she'd heard of someone two streets away whose house had been broken into but nothing had been stolen except for a sandwich toaster and a plastic marijuana plant. People just nicked what they could grab, she supposed. While she couldn't help but be impressed by the theft of the sandwich toaster, which had smacked of a canny attempt to anticipate the munchies, she had to wonder what kind of schools were educating criminals so dim that they couldn't tell the difference between a plastic cannabis plant and the real thing. The theft of two goldfish, however, remained unfathomable.

She wondered if she could call the police but decided she could handle it herself. Having a gun held to one's head by a trigger-happy US private determined to earn his stripes by bagging a terrorist tended to redefine fear in terms that rendered your average Wandsworth cat-burglar relatively harmless.

Santosh opened the bedroom door, meaning to grab whoever tried to make a run for it when she did so. Her poise was shattered more or less immediately when she saw what was going on in her bedroom. It was Daniel from next door. He was feeding the fish, who both appeared to be clean, healthy and hungry. Daniel was wearing a tight leather corset, fishnet stockings, enormous wedge heels, a pair of studded leather knickers, a curly black frightwig and a pearl choker. Had she owned any such items of clothing, Santosh would have accused him of raiding her knicker drawer. As it was, she didn't. For the past month or so, her idea of 'underwear' had been an extra T-shirt under her flak jacket.

'Oh hi. You're back,' he said, as if all of this was completely normal. He put the lid back on the fish food, sashayed across the bedroom on his four-inch heels and kissed her on the lips while she was too stunned to object. Somewhere along the line, Daniel had formed the impression that they were having a relationship, despite her protestations that you couldn't have a relationship with a woman twelve years your senior who was in the habit of regularly disappearing to far flung and highly dangerous parts of the world.

'Hello,' she said, which seemed like the only intelligent thing she could think of saying. 'You do know you're wearing a basque, don't you?'

He laughed, showing a mouthful of perfect twenty-something teeth. 'Oh yeah. I just popped in to feed the fish. We're having a *Rocky Horror* party. You want to come?'

'I didn't realise there was a jetlagged hack *in* the *Rocky Horror Show*.'

'That's OK. We can rustle you up a costume.'

'Not in my knicker drawer you can't,' she said. 'Do I look like the kind of woman who owns a French maid's outfit?' Or a feather duster, come to that, she added to herself.

'You could be Janet if you've got a white bra and a slip,' he suggested.

'Oh yes,' she sighed. 'The square girl. Probably. Although I'm buggered if I'm going to a party in my underwear.'

'Oh, why not?' Daniel asked, sitting down heavily on the end of her bed. 'You'd look a hundred per cent shaggable.'

She blinked, peeled off her jacket and shook her head. 'No I wouldn't. I'd look ridiculous. Besides, I can't remember the last time I shaved my legs. There's not much call for feminine waxing when you're picking your way around bomb craters.'

He nodded, black curls falling into his eyes and making him blink as they caught on his false lashes. He tugged off the wig, revealing his normal floppy auburn hair, and peered into the mirror as he attempted to restick his eyelash. 'Oh yeah. How did that go?'

'Kabul? Great. Only trouble is, my film footage has been lost by the baggage handlers at Heathrow.'

'You're kidding?'

'I'm not.'

Daniel sighed heavily. 'That's like ... wow.'

'Yeah. It's like ...' She obviously sounded more sarcastic than she meant to because he looked hurt, his red-glossed lower lip stuck out in a pout. She knew she gave him a hard time, mocking his vocabulary and telling him to get a girlfriend of his own age. For all he used the word 'like' as a punctuation mark and drew her into lengthy and frustrating arguments about politics (Daniel was happy enough to protest about tuition fees and the war or land rights for Palestine, but couldn't actually be arsed to get out of bed and vote) he couldn't help being young.

'I'm sorry,' she said. 'But I'm really tired, very smelly, totally jetlagged and enormously pissed off. Not really a party person at all.'

'Yeah, OK,' he said, standing up and putting his wig back on. 'I have to go. I've been planning this for weeks.'

'OK.'

He wobbled and grabbed her shoulder for support. 'How do you women walk in these heels?' he asked.

Santosh indicated her trusty Doc Martens. 'I don't. So I couldn't tell you.'

'Right,' he said, smiling again. He looked preposterous and yet still pretty. In the wedge heels he stood at nearly six and a half feet tall and she was staring straight into the diminutive cleavage that the corset had made of his pectoral muscles.

'Go on and have your party,' she said, as if she were his mother instructing him to go out and play.

'All right. Can I come and see you later?'

'I'll be asleep.'

'I don't mind,' he said. 'I only wanted a cuddle. I've missed you.'

7

She could have whined that she felt no desire to lie around on ceremony waiting for him to come in, but she felt too tired to do even that, so she told Daniel he might do as he pleased.

Santosh showered quickly, nearly dozed off while laboriously drying and plaiting her long hair (at 32 she had still not mustered the courage to defy her mother and get it all cut off) and dropped into bed like a dead thing. She fell asleep to the sound of the kids next door singing 'The Timewarp'.

She stirred at the sound of a loud drunken chorus of 'Rose Tint My World' and was further disturbed by Daniel taking off all his clothes and climbing into bed with her.

'All right, Lara?' he said, affectionately tugging her long black plait. Daniel had nicknamed her Lara Croft because of her hairstyle and her wardrobe full of very little but camouflage, khaki and sturdy boots.

She rolled over, eyes still closed, and her wrapped her arms around his naked body. He was so bloody young – not a scrap of excess fat on him. He had one of those immaculate surfer-dude bodies sculpted by riding the waves all summer, laziness courtesy of Mummy, Daddy and their big house in Cornwall. It seemed that in Britain the poor grew fat on cheap, processed food while the well-off bought organic and had money for gym membership. It was different in many of the places Santosh had been. Daniel's body was one of those well-maintained middle-class ones, smooth and comforting with nicely toned abdominals, thighs still boyishly soft-skinned over the muscle, with a tight little bum and indefatigable twenty-year-old cock. It all added up to a cuddle buddy more satisfying and pleasurable than any teddy bear.

She often thought she should grow up and start seeing

someone her own age, but her reservations vanished whenever she was in bed with Daniel. He was hard and silky all at once, glossy skinned and with the invincible prettiness of youth – irresistible the way a puppy was irresistible. Even if you weren't a dog person, you couldn't help being charmed by the shiny-eyed, soft-coated newness of a young pup.

'How was your party?' she asked. His hair felt softer than usual under her hand, sweaty from the wig and minus the usual lashings of hair gel.

'S'all right,' he muttered, sounding less than enthusi-astic. 'I'd rather be here though.'

'That's nice.'

'Mmm.'

She squeezed his perfectly narrow, fleshless waist in her arms, burying her nose in his shoulder. He smelled of booze, tobacco and hash with a trace of sweat and deodorant. His cock was stiff against her thigh – as usual. Twenty years old and all it took was a slight breeze in the right direction to get him hard.

'Why did you move the fish?' she asked.

'What?'

'The goldfish. What are they doing in here?'

'The vet said I should take them off the windowsill because the sun was growing all this grotty green algae stuff in the tank and it was making them a bit poorly.'

'You took my fish to the vet's?' She rolled over and let Daniel spoon up behind her. 'They're not prize-winning Japanese carp or anything – I only won them in a darts game at a fair.'

'They're still *alive*, Tosh,' Daniel protested.

She smiled in the dark and shoved her bottom back into his lap. 'Stop being right. It makes it impossible for me to argue with you.'

'I know. That's why I do it.' He kissed the back of her shoulder and wrapped his arm around her waist, determined to get his boots under her bed one way or another. Daniel was nothing if not persistent.

It didn't take long for her to fall asleep again – the kind of dead-weight sleep that only jetlag can produce. The ringing phone that woke her eight hours later was a sharp reminder that she was back in London, where phones rang all the time – aggressive and insistent, full of talk about nothing, unlike the vital businesses of life, death, medicines, survival and secrets that pervaded phone calls in the field. Daniel stirred briefly from his sullen, almost-teenage sleep and pulled the pillow over his head. Santosh hoped it might be some news on her baggage, but instead it was Claire.

'Darling, didn't you get my message? Where have you been?'

'Kabul.'

'Right, yes – but apart from that. Are you still on for tonight?'

'Yeah, I think so. What time is it?'

'It's nearly noon. Have you only just got up?'

'Yep,' she answered, unrepentant. 'Sleeping off a long haul flight.' In the company of a naked twenty-year-old. The covers had slipped low on Daniel's back, revealing exactly where his suntan ended. Life was good sometimes.

'Oh right. Of course,' Claire said. She sounded even throatier than Santosh remembered; gravel voiced, chain-smoking and perpetually busy, that was Claire all over. 'Right – let me think, sweetie … I'm just off for lunch with Neil Savage.'

Santosh couldn't resist. She coughed noisily, deliberately not disguising the word: 'Hack.'

'Oh, piss off and take your broadsheet sensibilities with you, darling,' Claire said, amiably. 'I know he's a dreadful arse but you'd be all over him like a rash if he wrote for the sodding *Grauniad*.'

'I bloody wouldn't. He's a semi-literate thug with all the sexual sophistication of a Tory backbencher.' (At this, Daniel removed his head from under the pillow and demanded to know who she was talking about. Santosh covered the phone with her hand and told him. Daniel mouthed the word 'wanker' and settled back down.)

Claire laughed – a sort of Lauren Bacall-esque contralto gurgle. 'Oh God, Tosh, it's so good to have you back in the land of the living. Have to dash. I've got a meeting with Neil, bikini wax and then Justin Vercoe, providing nothing else comes up, so I should be free about seven. How about I meet you in Covent Garden? By The Eternal String Quartet?'

The Eternal String Quartet was a running joke from college days. No matter what time of year or regardless of weather, there was always a string quartet playing in the covered market at Covent Garden.

The meeting was agreed and Claire hurried off the line to the usual sounds of 'must dash', 'terribly busy' and 'love you to death, darling', punctuated by the rasp of a lighter flint as she sucked one cigarette to ashes after the other.

'Your mate's having lunch with Neil Savage?' asked Daniel, yawning and trying not to look impressed.

'Yep. That's PR, baby.'

Daniel rolled his eyes. As a politics student he had very little time for the tabloids. 'He's a tosser. I saw him on *Question Time*.'

'Isn't *Question Time* a bit political for you?' Santosh teased. As a politics student, Daniel had even less time for politics.

'I have political views,' he said, sticking his nose in the air. 'Abolition of the monarchy, scuba lessons to be made compulsory as part of the National Curriculum and Motorhead's "Ace of Spades" to be instituted as the new national anthem.'

She sighed a mock heartfelt sigh and flopped back on the pillows. 'Ah, the lofty ideals of youth.' She ran a fond hand over his chiselled stomach muscles and peeked under the duvet. Not the only thing that was lofty about youth. 'Don't you think "God Save The Queen" would be better?'

'It's racist to the Scots and nobody knows all the words anyway.'

'No, I meant the Sex Pistols' version.'

He laughed. 'Cool. You fancy a joint?'

'Oh God, yeah.'

Daniel was faintly astonished to discover that anyone still had albums on cassette. Yet another uneasy reminder of how young he was. Santosh could see herself in twenty years' time, dressed in a leopard-print catsuit and draped adoringly around a twenty-something Portuguese toy boy. She was fairly certain her mother would kill her but couldn't bring herself to care when she was getting stoned in bed at midday with the Sex Pistols squawking and Daniel naked.

He was just so pretty, oh so pretty; she was vacant and she didn't care.

Besides, he said that he'd missed her and worried about her but had the decency not to say 'I love you', which kept things uncomplicated. He was energetic and generous in bed. At first he had found it difficult to keep from coming too fast when she went down on him, since he was unaccustomed to an experienced older woman's touch rather than the frantic attempts at deep-throating that girls picked up from pornos and mistakenly tried to duplicate. It seemed as though Daniel hadn't had a decent blow job in his life before he'd met her. He would never give much, if anything, away about his previous lovers and Santosh was never sure that he hadn't lied when he had said he wasn't a virgin.

He had learned to control his timing. 'Teach me Tantra,' he had giggled when she first told him to breathe deeply and tell her to slow or stop if he felt himself close to coming. He gasped when she wrapped her lips around his cock but she felt his thighs tense as he braced his body against the pleasure, digging his heels into the mattress.

She shifted her hips on the pillow as she settled into the accustomed top-to-toe position, which she had discovered to be not only enjoyable but instructive in the matter of timing. His hands steered her hips to his mouth and she hitched one thigh higher, moaning around his cock as his tongue began to lap at her clit.

She loved this – an easy, accomplished exchange of pleasure. It was so straightforward, reciprocal. When she tightened her lips and bobbed her head faster between his legs, he burrowed deeper with his tongue and fingers. When he pushed his fingers into her and searched for the spot that made her shiver and buck, that was her cue to cup and cradle his balls, insinuate a digit behind them to the crease between his buttocks, where it was warm and hairy and the spot that made him flinch might be found.

Every action had an equal and opposite reaction. It worked every time, foolproof as a mathematical theorem.

Daniel licked and slurped greedily, wiggling his tongue and hooking his fingers. Her pubic hair felt heavy and bushy with spit and sex; her inner thighs wet and warm from his breath. The tape had long ago clicked to a clunky, old-fashioned halt, and now the soft, liquid sounds of their mouths filled the room. She swirled her tongue over the sensitive head of his prick, urging him to come because she was getting so close now. He cried out, his noise muffled by her swollen sex, but he didn't cede control. She squirmed, impatient to come, but she was determined to hang on, wanting to taste him.

She shifted her finger further back between his legs, caressing and pressing as she found her way to the edge of his arsehole. The heat from his body was like a furnace just there, thicker and muskier than even the heat of his cock. He moved to accommodate her and she felt sweat drip from his thigh onto her face. His fingers shifted deep inside her and his lips and tongue closed over her clit in a deep, full-on, devouring kiss, suckling at her in a way she knew that he meant business and was determined to make her come. She played him at his own game, pushing with her finger until the tip rested in the dent of his anus.

'Come. Please,' he whispered, disengaging his mouth for a second. 'Please.'

She smiled around his cock and teased him, gently pressing her finger back and forth against his hole as if trying to gain entrance. He was sweaty between his thighs and some of her spit had slid down over his balls and between his legs. The wet muscle seemed to give way easily under her fingertip and he didn't seem to be clenching or resisting.

When her finger slipped past the smooth ring of muscle he yelped in shock and she was sure she could feel the heat of his blush between her legs. She was just as astonished at herself for doing this to him. When she pushed deeper and felt how silky and vulnerable he was in there, just like a woman, she couldn't hold back the first shudders of her climax. Daniel had gone ominously quiet, though, his face buried in her bush, his body rigid. She worried for a second that she had somehow offended him, cast a slur on his manhood by invading his bottom, but then he cried out so harshly that he might have been in agony, but obviously wasn't. His hips moved involuntarily, bucking back and forth so that as he fucked her mouth on the way forwards, her finger fucked him on the way back. He was gasping, swearing and coming, his warm salty spunk filling her mouth and giving her what she wanted – the taste of him on her tongue at the moment her orgasm spiralled dizzily out of control.

After they had disengaged somewhat from the sticky tangle they were in, Daniel was the first to speak. 'Whoa!' he said, boyishly. 'That was like, amazing.'

She twisted back round on the bed to face him. 'Did you like that?'

He widened his eyes in a mock-clueless expression. 'Duh ... yeah,' he said, his voice lifting so that the vague noise he was making sounded like a slightly sarcastic question. He really was far too young.

'I can't believe you let me do that.'

'Neither can I.' He blinked and rubbed his eyes like a child. His face was flushed and his full lips red. His eyes were overlarge and made him look babyish, but the length and shape of his nose gave his profile a sense of the strength it would have when he was thirty and unquestionably a man.

'But you liked it?' she asked, leaning over him.

'You can totally do it again sometime,' he said, grinning.

'I might just do that.' She kissed him and squeezed him close in the sticky, sex-scented bed. He was just too irresistible with his smooth body and the touching way his shock of curling red-brown pubes clustered around his wilting cock. She cuddled him for a while, enjoying the soft, satisfied sounds he made, losing track of time until she remembered it was late afternoon and nearly time to be off.

'I could come with you,' he suggested, as she got out of bed.

'You'd be bored rigid,' she said, shocked at the ease

with which she fobbed him off. 'We'll just be bitching about people you don't know.'

'OK,' he said, stretching out and yawning. 'I should probably go and do this essay anyway.'

'Oh stop. You make me feel old, with your essays.'

Daniel stuck his tongue out at her. 'You're not old. You're not far out of uni yourself.'

'Yeah. But there's years of caffeine and late nights between undergrad and doctorate. What's the essay on?'

'The International Monetary Fund's contribution to relieving Third World debt.'

Santosh pulled on a robe and headed for the shower, shaking her head. 'Should be the IMF's contribution to exacerbating Third World debt, if you ask me. Don't know what they're teaching in these schools.'

Daniel followed her into the shower, announcing his intention to change the focus of his essay. He was impossibly malleable, easily influenced by everyone's opinions – another reason she feared getting too close to him. She sent him on his way with a long, deep kiss and a stack of anti-globalisation literature, secure in the knowledge that if she was going to go around corrupting the succulent young flesh of gorgeous twenty-year-olds, then at least she was influencing their minds for the better.

2

Neil Savage liked to describe himself as 'The Last Gentleman of Fleet Street' and cultivated this impression by dressing the part. Suits from Saville Row, shoes from Jermyn Street, tailor-made eau de cologne from Mayfair, accent from Balham. He attempted to hide the accent, naturally, but if there was one thing Claire had always had it was a good ear. She had a way with people in that respect. Her job, as she saw it, was to make silk purses out of the endless procession of sows' ears that reality TV propelled to fame and into her office.

She had spent the morning dealing with the demands of the latest reality show winner, who was depressed that she wasn't getting her fair share of publicity and had required a champagne brunch and much cosseting in order to be persuaded that a few hours at the gym per week and blonde extensions would get her on the magazine covers that she now considered her due.

'Is it not playing ball?' Neil commiserated, putting aside the wine list with conspicuous nonchalance. 'Oh dear. What does it want now?'

'Adulation. Love. The usual,' Claire said. 'Same as the rest of them.'

'Love?' Neil raised his eyebrows and signalled to a passing wine waiter. 'Tell me, is the Chablis up to scratch or have you people been wringing a cat out over the bottle again?'

'The Chablis is 2002, an excellent year, sir,' said the waiter, smiling glassily. 'Pleasingly crisp, citrusy and with a hint of vanilla, sir.'

'Fine. We'll have that.' Neil nodded. The waiter bowed his head and slunk off.

'He *will* get the cat to piss in it now,' Claire said, reaching for her water glass. 'You should never upset anyone who's preparing your lunch.'

'Little shit wouldn't dare,' Neil snorted, lighting up a cigarette. 'Anyhow, what's the deal with your bottom feeder? Has it developed a talent other than screeching and exposing itself on national TV?'

'She was in a reality show, not a talent show. While screeching and exposing yourself isn't exactly a talent, it gains you a great many column inches if you do it on national TV.'

'Fucking hell.' Neil shook his head. 'Why do you take on these idiots?'

'It's my job, darling.' Claire smiled, attempting to look winsome, and carefully tugged the hem of her top under the table, maximising cleavage. Neil and breasts went a long way back. He was clever not to be considered important enough to merit his indiscretions being splashed about, but Claire had listened to enough pole dancers' tittle-tattle to know that Neil Savage was a notorious nork fiend. The bigger the better; silicone and all other imitations accepted.

'Put them away, Claire. You know I can't give you the column inches unless there's a story. The public won't buy it.'

Claire sighed and hitched up her top. 'Oh well, it was worth a try. OK, how do highlights and a significant degree of weight loss grab you?'

'What, on Sarah Riley?'

'Yes.'

Neil blew out smoke and shook his head. 'No dice, poppet. I'm running a national newspaper here. Got more important things to print than some trollop's new hairdo.'

'OK.' Claire snaffled one of his fags and sipped her

mineral water, hoping it hadn't come into contact with a cat. 'What if she had a tit job?'

Neil made a slightly more enthusiastic face. 'Oh yes. New titties – very nice. Is she planning on a little expansion?'

'She might be,' Claire said guardedly, making a mental note to book the clinic and then call Sarah Riley.

'Good, good.' Neil grinned. 'New knockers we can definitely work with. Pregnancy, now that's a guaranteed front page. Particularly if the father is married, famous or both.'

'Hmm.' Claire shook her head. 'No. Don't think she's pregnant.'

'Can you find out?'

'Of course I can find out,' Claire said airily. 'My clients aren't allowed to hide anything from me. It's the only way I can prevent the likes of you from making me look stupid.'

'You baby them,' Neil snorted. 'Sometimes I believe you actually like them.'

'I'm not as hard-boiled as you, darling. I still have a modicum of sincerity left.'

'Yes. You really ought to get that looked at. Shall we order? Much as I adore your fragrant company I don't have all fucking day, dearie.'

Neil had more time on his hands than Claire. Neil had more minions than Claire and his minions were substantially more intelligent and evil than Claire's. Claire also had to deal with the time-consuming business of being a woman in public. While Neil's sartorial splendour was largely due to vanity, as a man he could have got away with sweat-stained armpits, greasy hair and a nose full of blackheads and still been respected as one of the most powerful tabloid editors in the country. Claire realised with fright that the lemon meringue torte she had just scoffed for dessert would mean at least an hour in the gym this evening and she simply didn't have the time. Bad enough she had to dart from lunch to an appointment at the salon and make her phone calls on her back with her legs in the air, naked from the waist down and with a large quantity of bikini wax smeared all over her nether regions.

Fortunately she knew pretty much all of the plastic surgery clinics dotted around the Home Counties. It was yet another aspect of her job to pretend her clients never went anywhere near the places and smuggle them, black-eyed and bandaged or tomato red and blistered, from under the unsculpted noses of Neil's rapacious paparazzi. She called the closest and booked the consultation for that same afternoon while in the process of removing her knickers in the cubicle, and then set about the important business of schmoozing Sarah Riley.

Sarah was busy crying and throwing up her champagne brunch on account of splitting up with her boyfriend – a plumber from Haringey.

'Everything happens for a reason, darling,' Claire said, spreading her legs and looking suspiciously at the new beautician – a large Ukrainian lady named Veronika who looked like she had never waxed her own bikini line, never mind anyone else's. 'I mean, if he was seeing other people then he probably wasn't worth it, was he?'

Sarah gulped and sniffed down the phone. 'No, but I'm humiliated, ain't I? He's been doing it with some slag from the Peppermint bleedin' Hippo.'

Claire flinched as Veronika clumsily smeared hot wax on her bush. 'One second, darling –' She covered the phone with her hand. 'Where is Donatella, anyway?'

'She sick,' Veronika said, brusquely. 'Open wide.'

'I am open wide. If I was open any wider I'd be at the gynaecologist's.'

'You want smooth vagina or no?' Veronika asked, looking menacing.

'Yes,' Claire sighed and returned to the hopelessly blubbing Sarah. 'Listen, Sarah – he wasn't good enough for you, darling. He was never going to adjust to your new lifestyle anyway. I've seen it thousands of times; a woman becomes famous in her own right and the man just can't handle it. He starts making a fool of himself in public because he feels inadequate.'

'Does he?' Sarah sniffled, a note of optimism creeping into her voice.

'Darling, of course he does.' Claire glared at Veronika. Instead of decently turning her back while the wax cooled sufficiently, Veronika was standing there like a white-coated monolith, arms folded and staring between Claire's legs with a look on her face that was worryingly sadistic. 'Unsuccessful men can't handle successful women. He was just along for the ride – you got him into parties, you got him into premieres. It's all you. You don't need him, sweetie.'

'No. I fuckin' don't,' Sarah said, angrily. 'He's a bastard. I hate him. He was always jealous of me.'

'Yes, he was,' Claire soothed. 'And think how much more jealous he's going to be when he's reduced to selling cheap kiss and tells to the tabloids and you're at that next premiere looking fabulous.'

Sarah began to cry again. It was a slow, monotonous sound that steadily built into a Jocasta-like scream, which Claire felt like joining in with as Veronika ripped the wax off her inner thighs and took what felt like most of her pubes with it.

Claire gritted her teeth. 'Sarah? What's wrong?'

More snuffling and howling. It subsided into a low, wet blubbering sound and then Sarah eventually spoke. 'But, I can't.'

'Can't what, sweetie?'

'Can't do it. I can't go out.'

'Of course you can.'

'I can't! I'm so fat!'

'You are not fat,' Claire assured her. Actually Sarah had been packing it on steadily. Endless parties and premieres had led to Sarah amusing her *bouche* more than strictly necessary at the appetiser trays and night after night full of calorific cocktails. She was moving dangerously out of 'girl next door' territory and into Herman Melville. If there were to be a Sarah Riley exercise video this Christmas, then something drastic would have to be done.

'I am! I'm massive!'

Claire winced. Veronika was going to town on stray hairs with *tweezers*. Fucking woman was a sadist. Claire wanted to shoo her away. She had to think on her feet here and it wasn't easy to think on one's feet when said feet were being held in the air by a mad Ukrainian ex-shot-putter with the power to do horrid things to her second favourite organ.

'Darling,' she cooed, emolliently. 'You're a woman. You have curves.'

'I'm a fat fuckin' sow! That's why Kevin left me!'

'You dumped Kevin because he acted like an idiot,' Claire said, carefully placing the ball back in Sarah's court. Sarah would never consent to anything except whining, drinking and eating chocolates if made to feel like the victim. Claire knew. She had been studying the creature on TV for most of the summer, the better to snare her as a client. 'And you are not a fat sow.'

'I want liposuction!' Sarah wailed.

Bingo. Claire smiled to herself, in spite of what Veronika was doing down below. It was so lovely when they played right into her hands. 'Are you sure?' Claire said. 'That's rather drastic. I'm not sure it can be done.'

'I want it! I don't fuckin' care about the cost. I want to

show that bastard up when he goes running to the fucking papers – that fucking slag of his looks like shit and I want to look gorgeous and I want it now! You're supposed to be my bloody agent.'

'Sarah, darling, of course I'm there for you – whatever you want to do in your career.'

'All finish,' Veronika said brusquely, lowering Claire's left leg with an expression of pronounced disdain on her face.

Claire smiled sarcastically at her and continued with her spiel. 'Look, I'm terribly busy at the moment.'

'Huh,' snorted Veronika.

'Buh?' said Sarah.

'But I think ... if I really dash, I might be able to fit you in this afternoon, darling. I know this little place just outside Romford.' Claire swung her legs over the side of the table and inspected the damage. Christ.

'A clinic?' Sarah gulped.

'*Very* discreet. Professional. Reasonably priced. I can't mention who else uses it because I'm not alone right now, but believe me ... A-list, darling. Fucking A-list.'

Sarah whined. 'Th ... this afternoon?'

'Must be,' Claire said firmly. She checked the clock on the wall. Time was running short. She had Justin Vercoe to deal with at four (Justin never got up before two in the afternoon) and there was no way she could blow out Tosh. Not tonight. 'Really. It won't take two ticks. Just the initial consultation.'

'Oh ... OK,' Sarah conceded.

'Excellent. It's the Winstanley Clinic.' She rattled off the address and glowered at Veronika. 'I'll see you there, sweetie.'

'Have a nice day,' Veronika deadpanned, Terminator-style.

'As nice a day as I can have with a fanny like a frozen chicken,' Claire snarled, shouldering her handbag and finding herself forced to adjust her knickers around the chafed bits. 'Thanks for nothing.'

When Claire met her at the clinic, Sarah looked blotchy from crying and was exactly in the state of mind Claire needed her to be in to pull off what would be a spectacular front-page press coup. Claire knew her job – flatter, cajole, pamper, give them what they want and, in the process, coax them unknowingly into doing what you wanted them to do. The trick was letting them think it was all their own idea.

The first stage was already complete. If Sarah was feeling mad enough to have her cellulite liquefied and extracted through a hose, it was only an unnatural progression to wanting to enhance her boobs to go with her new slimline bottom. Claire already had the advantage. The whole nation had seen Sarah's breasts, and they were just breasts – nothing particularly extraordinary about them; a pair of slightly pointed, suntanned tits that sat rather too far apart on her wide ribcage to be strictly fashionable. Claire, on the other hand, had been singularly blessed with what she knew to be a pair of naturally perfect breasts. Despite the round of leg and pant moustache waxing, upper lip electrolysis and highlighting and fluffing of hair she had to endure, Claire was confident about that one facet of her appearance. She knew she'd got it, so she flaunted it; a pair of pink marble boobs that jostled each other in low-cut tops and, when unleashed, had round pink upturned nipples that one lover had dubbed 'puppies' noses'. It helped to flash at least an inch of cleavage and, for her meeting with Neil, Claire had elected for a calculated two inches, putting her in a position to inspire Sarah's envy where it would be most useful to Sarah's career. It was not for nothing that an early PR rival had described Claire as having the jugs of the Venus de Milo and the social conscience of Attila the Hun.

In the waiting room of the clinic, Claire was careful to lean forwards strategically while picking up a magazine bearing, amongst others, the subheadline, SIMPLY THE BREAST. The waiting rooms of plastic surgery clinics were typically cluttered with magazines of the rich, famous and ridiculously photogenic, in order to inspire you to greater extremes of insanity in the consulting room.

'Good lord,' she said, peering at the before and after photos of a teenage actress who had been vociferously denying that her recent growth spurt was anything to do with the surgeon's knife. 'What has she been doing to herself?'

Sarah pudgily squished up on the pale-pink banquette and peered at the photographs. 'Oh, that's the new style,' Sarah said knowledgeably, pointing out the exaggerated silicone cleavage. 'American style. It's the fashion.'

'Is it?' Claire frowned, carefully painting herself as older and out of touch. 'But they look really fake.'

'They're meant to. It's the fashion, innit?'

'What happens when it's not the fashion?' Claire asked.

'You sound like my mum,' Sarah snorted, petulantly.

'Well, it's just a thought, darling,' Claire said. 'I mean, it's all very well someone saying your lipgloss is so last season, but you can alter that in a heartbeat, but what happens when your tits are out of fashion?'

'Tits never go out of fashion,' said Sarah, eyeing Claire's boobs. 'Specially big tits. Men like big tits.' She snorted into a tissue. 'Like Kevin – the fuckin' bastard. Look at him at them bloody lap-dancing clubs. Big tits win every time.'

She started to blub again and Claire petted her and

rubbed her back sympathetically. 'Well, you'll show him, won't you, darling?'

'Yeah. Yeah, I will,' Sarah said, determinedly.

'When you get back out there looking like a million dollars.'

Sarah blew her nose and sat up decisively. 'I want me tits done too,' she said.

'Darling ...' Claire frowned. This was easier than she had ever dreamed possible. 'You get your boobs done and you won't get a second's privacy.'

'I don't care.'

'Every party, every premiere, every night out – photographers will be all over you like flies. Front page.'

'Good. And I'll do all them lad mags an' all. That'll teach him.'

In spite of the aggressive bikini-line waxing, Claire was flying high. She was the fairy godmother who catered to the wants of her clients' inner children. Not their needs – sod their needs. If they needed anything it was a slap and a reality check, but she was not in the business of delivering them. Sarah's inner child was a spoilt, grabby five-year-old incapable of taking no for an answer and whose favourite word was 'now' – which suited Claire's purposes perfectly. Sarah would have been happy to offer her tits to the scalpel and her thighs to the lipo-hose there and then, and the sooner the fucking better. She bitched about having to have an initial consultation and overall health check and complained that she was fine. Claire had to draw a line there and patiently explain to the idiot girl that plastic surgery was still surgery and carried the same risks. The last thing she needed was a client with a botched boob job and disastrous liposuction, which would haul in the headlines for all the wrong reasons and no doubt an infamous bucketmouth like Sarah would blame Claire for the whole sorry fiasco.

Remembering Neil's advice about pregnancy, Claire furtively appropriated the urine sample that Sarah had been obliged to give the consultant and tucked it into her handbag, praying that the seal would hold. She air-kissed and flattered Sarah goodbye and headed back into the city before the rush hour really got underway.

Justin Vercoe was a much more pleasant proposition, as client-meetings went. Justin had started off as a soap actor who was given more than his fair share of story-lines, mainly because he was extremely attractive to women and kept the viewing figures high. Since leaving the soap in the interests of pursuing other acting projects, Justin had turned into a notorious party fixture and coke-hoover and kept the headlines coming in. However, Claire was concerned that his public was tiring of his antics and that he needed another job as soon as possible.

His theatrical agent had not been optimistic, complaining at great length about these youngsters and their lack of classical training. 'They read a bloody idiot board on some soap opera and come out of it thinking they're Marlon Brando. They need a stint in Rep, with the RSC, darling – somewhere they can learn their fucking lines ... pardon my language, poppet, but it galls a man, it really does, when you've trod the boards for years.'

This assessment had been less than helpful, and Claire, harassed and sick of actors who couldn't actually act, had told the agent to send Justin back to LAMDA if that's what it took – although she had phrased it in less polite language and shocked the elderly thespian on the end of the phone into exclaiming that in all his years in the business he had never heard a woman swear like that.

He hadn't heard the worst of it. Claire aimed far worse language at a scaffolder's truck that threatened to take out her front indicator with an ill-secured pole as she circumnavigated a roundabout. She also cursed bikini waxers, particularly mad ex-shot-putters who had no business ripping the hair of civilised people's pudenda.

Claire finalised her strategy for Justin as she tried to drive through the ever-thickening London traffic. A spell in rehab, an extensive health spa treatment and then toss in a few rumours about interest from Hollywood producers. The rumours didn't have to be true – they'd just set the necessary wheels in motion.

The traffic was getting worse. Sarah had held Claire up longer than she would have liked and they were digging up the road about a hundred yards in front. The last thing Claire had wanted was to be stuck at a set of temporary traffic lights with a bikini-line wax job that itched like buggery. She squirmed in the car seat, stuck a hand up her skirt to scratch and realised that the man in the scaffolder's truck was watching her. He wore a hard hat and a fluorescent workman's vest over a sleeveless T-shirt and his arms were muscular and scarred, tanned and tattooed.

'Oi!' she shouted. 'Why don't you tie that pole of yours down, darling?'

He laughed and looked down into the car from the cab of his truck. 'Bit difficult when you keep flashing your drawers at me, love!' he yelled back, over the noise of pneumatic drills and engines. 'Can't get it to stay down, see?'

She rolled her eyes at him but didn't bother pulling her skirt back down over her thighs. There were paint-splatters on his bare arms. He'd probably spent the day pretending to paint a window frame while looking through the glass at women, hoping to catch them getting undressed. Dirty bugger. He looked all sweaty and had one of those tans that were nothing to do with a bottle, a sunbed or holidays in St Tropez.

'Right, you fucker!' Claire called back at him. She loved workmen. They were quick to give it out, but freaked out if you gave them some of their own back. Her knickers were chafing anyway and she was glad to get out of them. He stared open mouthed and laughed as she wriggled out of them in the front seat of the car. She laughed back at him and tossed her knickers at the side of the truck as the lights turned to amber. 'Something to tie your pole down with, wanker!' she shouted, and drove off, considerably more comfortable in the bikini-line department and giggling madly at the look on his face.

It kept her smiling all the way back to the office, even though she was running ten minutes late for Justin's appointment. 'Got stuck in traffic,' she apologised to Donna, her PA. 'Has he been waiting long?'

'He's not here yet,' said Donna, texting something on her mobile. She had inch-long fingernails the colour of malachite but managed to hit every key perfectly. The girl was such an obsessive texter that on more than one occasion Claire had had to reprimand her for using text speak in written correspondence.

'Well, where the fuck is he?' Claire demanded.

'Dunno. Maybe he got stuck in traffic.'

Claire exhaled. 'Never mind,' she said, disdainfully removing Sarah's sample from her handbag and placing it on the desk in front of Donna. 'Pop down to the chemist's and pick up a pregnancy testing kit, will you?'

Donna stared in horror at the sample. 'Is that . . .?'

'Yes.'

'. . . piss?'

'It's not any old piss, darling,' said Claire. 'It's celebrity piss. Football managers have to go through this all the time, you know.'

'I don't care whose piss it is! It's still piss! I ain't touching it!' Donna protested.

'You don't have to touch it,' Claire snapped. 'Just open the lid, dip the stick in it and watch to see if the little window turns pink or blue, or whichever way it's supposed to go. If that sample's positive you'll be able to have your fingernails gilded, darling. Twenty-four carat.'

'I'd trade in gilded fucking fingernails for a pair of plastic gloves right now, I can tell you,' said Donna, resentfully.

'Buy some at the bloody chemist's then,' Claire told her. 'Honestly, Donna, if you want to work in PR you really are going to have to rid yourself of this squeamishness.'

'Whatever,' Donna snorted, swivelling in her chair to open the petty cash box.

Justin was twenty minutes late, in all, which was actually early by his standards. His lack of punctuality was the real reason behind his desire to break into Hollywood. He'd been fired from his soap for turning up late more often than Marilyn Monroe, and the rest of the cast were sick to the back teeth of him. Having been written out in a tear-jerking deathbed storyline, Justin Vercoe was then free to do what he did best – devoting himself to the business of 'Being a Celebrity'.

Say what you like about his acting ability, or lack of it, he more than compensated in the eye-candy department. At first glance he looked like the tall, dark, romance hero type, guaranteed to keep the primarily female audience happy. Up close he had a twinkle in his eye and a naughty-boy vulnerability that ensured that every granny in Britain wanted to fling their knitwear at him. Not to mention the sizeable gay audience, who all thought he harboured a Big Secret.

'Darling, what are you eating?' Claire laughed, air-kissing him on both cheeks.

He removed his lolly from sugar-reddened lips with a

pop that was frankly suggestive. 'Given up smoking,' he said. 'Gives me something to put in my mouth.'

'Well, I knew you were orally fixated, Justin,' she said, thinking of all the filthy things he had suggested when he tried to persuade her to break her self-imposed rule about not sleeping with clients.

He smiled and shook his head. 'Come on, don't mess around.'

'I'm not messing around with you, darling,' Claire said. He wanted to mess around, she decided, despite what he said. He might call her a tease and claim he wouldn't rise to the bait, but she noticed he had selected the lowest sofa in the room, directly facing her desk. It was helpful to place young male clients – especially boy-band members – on that sofa in order to see if they were telling the truth about their sexuality.

Claire always found it best policy to engineer any declosetures of such boys before they were neatly packaged as wank-fuel for teenage girls. Teenaged girls tended to react as badly to one of their lust monkeys coming out as they did when they got married. They locked themselves in their rooms, turned their old Barbies into voodoo dolls of the missus, cut up their posters, dashed their teenage dreams – and ultimately, worst of all, they stopped buying records.

It was best to deal with the comings out when they were unknowns. As a policy, it looked honest and progressive thinking, suggesting a commendable lack of prejudice. Claire found it made sense to also target the pink pound early whenever such a thing was possible. Adult gay men had a lot more disposable income than teenaged girls. This was the thinking behind Claire's positioning of the sofa. It was like a Pavlovian response – show them knicker and their eyes were inevitably drawn to it. If they didn't look, then it was time to deliver quality time, TLC and plenty of Diana Ross to bring them frisking out of the closet into the light of day.

Claire would usually have been only mildly amused by Justin's choice of seat, but she remembered she still didn't have any knickers on. She remained standing in front of her desk but she realised that if she sat up on her desk or sat down behind it then Justin's gaze would be drawn helplessly up her skirt and he'd get the shock of his life.

'I'm not into messing about, Claire,' Justin said.

'No. Of course not, darling. It's not like you to be twenty minutes late,' It was more like him to be two hours late. 'Something bothering you?'

'I think I need a detox,' said Justin.

Claire leaned back against her desk, arms folded, instinctively going to professional mode. As she moved to stand with her feet apart she was aware of the lips of her sex parting and the sensation of cooling wetness between them. She was vaguely annoyed by it. This was no time to be getting turned on. 'What's brought this on?' she asked him.

What indeed? Claire immediately blamed the scaffolder. Maybe he'd retrieved her knickers from the back of the scaffolding truck and was pulled up somewhere enjoying a good wank with her silky underwear wound around his dick. He probably had blue dots tattooed on his knuckles and callused fingers that snagged the skin pleasantly as he rubbed his cock. She felt her internal muscles contract at the thought.

'This morning's papers,' Justin said. 'I look like shit.'

He was looking a bit raddled. He strolled into the office with dark shadows under his eyes and a streak of premature grey was trying to reassert itself at the front of his dark-brown hair. His fake tan had subsided from violent celebrity orange to a shade that looked sunkissed; he smelled rather sweaty and his hair was stiff and dull from last night's hair gel. In Claire's opinion, it was a definite improvement.

'Yes, but how do you feel in yourself?' Claire asked, like a psychotherapist. She often felt like one.

'Like shit.'

'Righto,' said Claire. 'I know just the place. It's a New Age thing.' She was suddenly impatient to get him out of the way and scurry off to the toilets with her pocket-sized vibrator. 'They even have tepees and everything.' She leaned over the desk to pick up the brochure for the detox centre. 'The Priory is just so 1998 anyway.'

She reached for the brochure. It was made of New Age, organic, right-on recycled flimsy paper and slipped out of reach onto her chair. If she bent over to retrieve it she would be showing everything – that freshly waxed porno pout of smooth lips showing beneath the curves of her arse. She knew his eyes would be on the backs of her legs trying to steal a look up her skirt. He was a man. They couldn't help it.

'I want to give up the lot,' Justin was saying. 'I need to totally detox. My body's like a toxic-waste dump. Cigarettes, booze, drugs . . . sugar . . . I gotta give up sugar too . . . once I've finished this . . .'

Yes, Justin. Of course, Justin. Anything you so desire, Justin.

She was so sick of people making demands of her that she bent over the desk, partly to shut him up, partly because she wanted to.

'Red meat,' he continued. 'And . . . er . . . sex. Yeah. Sex.' His voice trailed off into a kind of idiot monotone. She felt her skirt hike higher over her buttocks and her stomach clenched at the thought of the view she must be presenting.

'What's up with sex?' she asked, innocently, grabbing the brochure. 'I thought it was good exercise.' She straightened, turned around and sat on her desk, not bothering to keep her legs crossed. It felt wet and silky between them and she could feel her pulse thrumming in her clit.

'It stops you from being centred,' Justin said, his face flushed.

'Really?' Claire asked, sarcastically. She had never felt more centred in her life – a soft, juicy centre that would inevitably draw him off the sofa, across the room and towards her. When he got there he would take out his stiff cock and thrust it inside her without questions or kisses and they'd do it hard, fast and dirty right there on the desk.

She slid so that her buttocks were on the very edge of the desk, her feet on the floor. Her skirt caught between the desk and her bum and moved so high on her thighs that she felt cool air move between them. Justin was staring, and breathing rather heavily, so she beckoned to him.

He shook his head. 'What happened to your no-client rule?'

'I have the right to remove it,' she said.

He got up from the sofa. His lollipop was tucked inside his cheek, so that it made one cheek bulge like Brando's, while the stick protruded from his mouth like a tough's toothpick as he swaggered towards her. His jeans looked pleasingly bulky.

He removed the lollipop from his mouth and grinned. She could smell the sweetness on his breath. 'It isn't fair, Claire,' he sing-songed, teasing. 'Changing the rules just when I'm giving up pussy.'

'You say that like it's a dirty habit,' she said, leaning in for a kiss.

He drew back. 'Nope,' he said, smiling. He trailed the lollipop over her thigh, leaving a sticky trail of red sugary stuff over the skin. 'I'm going to have to say no, Claire.'

She managed to collar him and drag him close enough

to whisper in his ear. 'I'm very, very wet,' she breathed, knowing that if a full-on Sharon Stone moment didn't get 'em, then porno dialogue always did the trick.

'I bet you are,' Justin said, knowingly.

She felt something bump against her clit – not the familiar touch of a finger, but something more solid and round. She looked down between their bodies to see if he had unzipped his jeans while they were entangled. He hadn't. It was that fucking lollipop. The sticky red end of it was being rolled back and forth over her clit. She gasped as it dipped lower and moaned as it entered her body.

'You're soaked,' murmured Justin.

Claire squirmed and clenched her muscles against the sweet inside her, eager for more sensation. 'For God's sake,' she said, 'just fuck me.'

He shook his head and removed the lollipop, then smiled at her frustration as he put it in his mouth and sucked up the taste of sugar and sex. 'I only wanted a taste,' he said, taking the brochure from the table and heading for the door. 'Thanks again.'

Claire jumped off the desk, fuming. 'You cheeky fucking wanker! How dare you?'

'You had it coming, Claire,' Justin said, looking disgustingly pleased with himself as he walked out of the door.

'You arsehole!' she shouted after him. Donna was not at her desk, but the man waiting in reception turned to stare at her. He wore a Day-Glo workman's vest and had tattooed arms.

'I thought I recognised that mouth,' he said, slyly, looking at Claire. Justin made his escape, still giggling. The wanker.

'Did you follow me?' Claire asked the scaffolder. 'You followed me back to my office?'

'Returning lost property.' He shrugged and stood up,

holding out her knickers. He had a filthy look on his face and smelled richly of sweat. 'You're all the same, aren't you?'

'What?' she snapped.

'You posh birds,' he said. 'You can give it out, but you can't take it back, can you?'

She reached out, snatched her knickers from his hand and grabbed him by the front of his belt. 'Oh, we'll see about that, mate,' she said, pulling him quickly through the double doors of her office and closing the door behind them.

He was a big man, but he was easily overpowered. His kisses were stubbly and tasted of cigarettes and beer. She hadn't asked his name – didn't care, didn't need names when his thick, rough fingers entered and stretched her without sophistication. 'You dirty bitch,' he muttered. 'You really fucking want it, don't you? You're fucking soaked.'

Claire ground her hips into his touch and moaned loudly. If he kept on rubbing just there she would come, no question, but she had other plans. 'Do you have a sweet tooth?' she asked, nipping his earlobe.

'Wha?'

'A sweet tooth. Do you have one?'

'Yeah, I suppose so,' he said, pulling and frowning in puzzlement. No doubt he was a nice Alpha male boy who liked his sex straightforward and without any of that 'kinky stuff' that the repressed middle classes indulged in. He looked like he was worried Claire was going to suggest something kinky.

'Down you go, then,' she said. She had to reach up to place her palm on the top of his scalp and guide him down onto his knees to where she wanted him, but he went down.

Revenge was most definitely sweet.

3

Santosh had never imagined she'd remain a friend of Claire Sawyer. Claire represented everything she'd learned to despise – plastic capitalism centred around the sale of things that didn't matter – handbags, fizzy drinks, designer labels and people with more ego than talent. But once you stripped away the handbags and gladrags, Claire was still Claire – the same outrageous fun-loving young woman Santosh had grown to love and despair of simultaneously. Claire had been the wild one, the one who counted the notches on her bedpost without the slightest flicker of shame; the one who had taught Santosh to drink for free all night by showing cleavage and batting eyelashes at men. It was impossible to be indifferent to Claire – you either loved her or hated her.

Covent Garden was still milling relentlessly at seven o'clock. The Eternal String Quartet was packing up their instruments and the street entertainers had long since gone off to the pubs or home for dinner. The self-consciously trendy evening crowd were moving in – soap actresses high-heeling it across the cobbles in Jimmy Choos and various celebrities mingling with the last few straggling tourists and tired students buying coffees.

Claire was in her element, moving along with her cheeky, high-heeled, bosomy gait, smiling and waving hello to famous faces who (astonishingly) smiled and waved back.

'You haven't changed in the slightest,' Claire said, as they picked their way through the tables of the indoor market. 'Except for getting thinner maybe. Bitch.'

Santosh laughed. 'I thought I'd gained a few pounds, actually.'

'In fucking Kabul? Darling – the food must be bloody shocking.' Claire had gained a few pounds, but she had never been able to keep it off for long. She claimed she had an addictive personality, which was why she could never get enough of any form of cheap gratification, be it cigarettes, chocolate cake or casual sex.

'It wasn't so bad,' Santosh said. 'Provided you like goat, of course.'

Claire cackled. 'Fucking hell. Goat? How did your film go, by the way?'

'Fine. Well, it should be. Providing the baggage handlers at Heathrow manage to find the bloody thing.'

'You're joking?' Claire turned sharply on her heel, knocking over a young man carrying a tray with a cup of coffee on it. He wore a battered parka and old boots and his hair was matted into those grungy, slightly pathetic white-boy dreadlocks. When he looked up from retrieving the remains of his coffee, Santosh saw that his face was young and unbearded. Just a boy.

'Whoops. Sorry.' Claire extracted a note from her purse and handed it to him.

He shook his head. 'It's cool,' he said, holding his hands up as if he were about to be shot.

'Least I can do,' Claire said, stuffing the note into his hand. 'Get yourself another coffee.'

The boy nodded. 'OK. Thanks.' His voice was well-bred and Santosh wondered what it was that had driven him from home and onto the streets, but she didn't get a chance to ask because he had gone and Claire had returned to expressing her outrage about the missing film.

'You really should sue them if it doesn't turn up, you know. It's a fucking disgrace, darling. Weeks of work down the shitter. I absolutely wouldn't stand for it. I know just the lawyer ... oh, and I really fancy a cappuccino, now that my shoes practically reek of the stuff ... honestly, I seem to have spent the entire day being smothered in food of one variety or another – although best to wait until I'm utterly shit-faced drunk before you go asking me about the lollipop.' She laughed her crackly smoker's laugh and paid for a couple of coffees.

Sometimes she was impossible to keep pace with; her mind firing on all cylinders at once, a barely contained ball of energy careening from one subject to another like a ping-pong ball in an earthquake simulator.

Claire must have already forgotten about the boy, because she frowned in puzzlement when he strolled up to the table and placed a handful of coins and a ten pound note on the tray. 'Excuse me,' he said, politely. 'You gave me twenty, so I brought you change.'

Claire stared at the money on the coffee tray, stared back up at the boy for a moment and smiled. 'It's all right,' she said. 'You can keep it.'

'No, but it's yours,' the boy said. 'I mean, I know this stuff's expensive in London, but a cappuccino isn't twenty quid. Yet.'

Claire looked over at Tosh, who was looking fairly neutrally at the kid – that combination of neutrality and potential compassion that Claire called her 'journalist face'. This was of no help whatsoever to Claire. She had no idea what to do. When you gave money to homeless people they weren't supposed to bring back your change. They were supposed to be bloody grateful. Claire knew she couldn't give to every beggar on the streets of London – if you did that you'd be taking out a bank loan within a week – but when she did buy a *Big Issue* or give someone a pound for a cup of coffee she expected at least some kind of karmic warm fuzzy glow for her trouble.

She decided to leave the poor boy with his dignity

intact and offered to buy a *Big Issue* – thirteen of the things, if that's what it took.

The boy looked thunderous. Santosh winced.

'Do I look like a fucking *Big Issue* seller?' he asked, angrily.

'Well, yes,' Claire admitted. The grotty parka, beaten-up boots and dreadlocks made him look fairly destitute. If he'd had a couple of facial piercings he might have looked as though he were making a fashion statement but he was unpierced and really rather unwashed.

'Am I carrying a bag full of *Big Issues*?' he demanded, sarcastically, spreading his arms to demonstrate the distinct lack of said publication on his person. 'Am I standing outside the tube station shouting "*Big Issue*"? I don't think I am, am I?'

'I'm sure she didn't mean to cause offence,' Santosh said, lamely.

'No, I didn't.' Claire nodded. 'Besides, there's nothing wrong with selling the *Big Issue*: it's a very good cause.'

The boy folded his arms and sighed. 'Oh, don't back-track. I know exactly what you meant – you and your bloody designer handbag. You meant that I look poor and you look rich, you snotty cow. What the hell gives you the right to go lording it over people in Covent Garden just because you've got twenty pound notes for small change and Prada stamped on your arse?'

Claire's mouth dropped open. Santosh was attempting to apologise but Claire kicked her in the ankle and added pain to the list of her problems as her three-hundred-pound strappy, insubstantial shoe collided with Santosh's well-worn Doc Marten. Tosh never made an effort to dress up unless she had a meeting with some important broadsheet editor.

Fuck apologies. Claire had just been called a snooty cow for doing someone a favour and she was not prepared to take that lying down.

'I bought you a cup of coffee,' she said. 'In good faith, I might add!'

'Oh, well, that counts for something, doesn't it?' the boy said. 'You'd best take your halo off to wherever the fuck you were going while it's still shining bright enough for all the other piss poor wannabes to admire, hadn't you?'

Claire rose from her seat, furious. 'Listen up, you soap-dodging tree hugger,' she snapped. 'I eat piss poor wannabes for fucking breakfast. I don't know who the bloody hell you think you are, lecturing me on personal morality –'

Santosh stood up and sighed. 'Claire, he was just bringing you change from a twenty.'

'Fuck off,' Claire said, impatiently. 'Really, darling, don't go all Kofi Annan on me now. This is Covent Garden, not bloody Kabul, and Swampy's evil twin here just called me a snotty cow, amongst other things.'

'Oh Christ,' muttered Tosh, rolling her eyes and leaving them to it.

'You *are* a snotty cow,' said the boy, his voice rising loud enough to attract stares. 'How dare you judge me on what I look like? For all you know, I might be prime minister one day – when you're old and ugly and weeing into a bag.'

'I'm thirty-three, you cheeky little cunt!' Claire shouted.

'Is that with or without Botox?' taunted the hippy.

That was way below the belt. Even Santosh was appalled. 'Um ... actually, that's quite rude,' she said. Claire wondered for a split second how on earth Santosh had managed to survive multiple war zones when she negotiated like a Prozac-abusing female version of Neville Chamberlain.

Claire scowled at the boy, just to prove that she could. 'You couldn't become prime minister,' she said. 'You couldn't become anything. You dress like a tramp, you smell faintly objectionable and you desperately need to moisturise.'

'Oh, and you're an expert, are you?' he asked. 'I suppose you know everything when it comes to how people should look in order to suit your shallow little view of the world, do you?'

'As a matter of fact, yes,' Claire said. A small crowd had now gathered to watch the altercation – the best real-life entertainment on offer since Sarah's reality show had ended its run. 'I *am* an expert,' Claire announced, playing to her audience. 'There is nothing I can't do when it comes to people and their public profiles. Even you, darling. You may look like a chimp that's been strategically shaved, but if I had you on my books I could put you on the covers of magazines. Parties, premieres, red carpet – the whole fucking shebang, darling.'

For a second she thought she saw the look in his eyes – the look she'd learned to watch out for. It was a look that all human beings were prone to: a tiny spark of greed in the eye; a flicker of hunger and frustration that they were merely ordinary. Everyone needed love and acceptance, but Claire had made her fortune by turning that need into raw greed, training her clients to want more – more love, more acceptance, more than fifteen minutes of fame.

'Come on, Claire,' said Santosh. 'I've just spent three months in a war zone.'

'So what are you doing hanging out with her?' asked the boy, directly addressing Santosh.

'We go way back,' said Santosh, loyally. 'Look, you're obviously intelligent so you must realise that we can't all have the same opinions and perspectives as one another. And it would be really boring if we did. So, you know ... I'm sure she's sorry.'

'No I'm not,' said Claire.

'Like I care,' said the boy, shrugging. 'I really don't give a shit what anyone thinks about me. I don't exist in that shallow little world.'

'Exist is the word,' Claire said with a sniff, removing her card from her handbag. 'If you ever get bored of mere existence and fancy doing a bit of living, darling, give me a call. Not could that you could afford my fees, but ...' As a final gesture of bravado she tossed the card and the change from the coffee back at him before heading off towards The Strand.

'I am absolutely sick of kids today,' Claire ranted, as she walked. 'Whiny little do-gooders bleating about saving the planet and dossing in fucking tepees. They don't know how much they owe people like me. If it weren't for us there would be none of the toys they play with as children, no pop groups to adore, no CDs and DVDs, no film stars, no perfumes – nothing to *want*.'

'They might not have wanted them in the first place,' said Santosh, over the noise of the traffic, black cabs and buses slowly crawling to their destinations through the gridlock. 'Advertising just invents things to want. Manufactured desire, they call it in media studies. Things you'd never dream of wanting unless someone pointed them out to you and told you that you might want them.'

'Exactly,' said Claire, pulling up her collar against the foul-smelling wind. 'And wouldn't it be boring if we were all completely content with nothing to look forward to? Didn't you want things when you were a child?'

Santosh shrugged. 'I suppose so. Never got them. I wanted a Crystal Barbie for Christmas one year but I got a book on astronomy and a new pocket calculator. I was only seven. Maybe that's why I rebelled.'

'You?' Claire laughed. 'You rebelled? You were always

the straight A student, always handed your essays in on time, always knew how much booze was too much booze...'

'I turned down a place at Oxford. In Indian families that makes you a rebel without a cause.'

Claire laughed. 'Good lord,' she said, heading into the open door of The Coal Hole. 'Why did you turn down a place at Oxford?'

Santosh stepped off the crowded, smelly, pigeon-stained streets into the crowded smoky pub. 'I loved London,' she said, over the hubbub of voices. 'One of those teenage love affairs that turned sour pretty bloody fast.' She exhaled and contemplated the crowd. 'Right. I'm assuming there's a bar in here somewhere?'

They made their way to the packed bar and drank steadily until it started to empty out, as the commuters abandoned their post-work drinks to take a less crowded train home and the self-consciously fashionable headed for dinner at eight, nightclubs at ten. Claire had never been able to share her friend's dislike for the city. Like most adopted Londoners, Claire complained loudly about the traffic, the fumes, the Underground, the crime, the homeless, even the pigeons, but had she been dumped down in some quiet, picturesque corner of Cornwall she knew she would die of boredom within a week.

She had grown up in one of the prettiest parts of the Cotswolds – a life for which she was temperamentally unsuited. She liked new people, new clothes, new places to go and new things to do. Weekends spent watching Dad shovelling horseshit onto his prize-winning roses hadn't exactly made her life feel worthwhile. Placidity and contentment seemed always out of reach and over-rated – something to do when you were too old to do anything interesting any longer.

Santosh was a native Londoner and had had time to become jaded. When Claire had first met her at university, Santosh was so exotic and exciting that Claire was determined they should become friends. Santosh had a flat, barrow-boy twang beneath her cultured accent and talked about exciting places with Monopoly board names as though they were mere thoroughfares rather than part of the personality and essence of Britain itself – Threadneedle Street, the Kings Road, Camden Market, Leicester Square, Tottenham Court Road and Covent Garden. Santosh had been to Delhi and Mumbai. She spoke Hindi as well as English and when drunk she would tell fabulous tales about churning oceans of milk, of the Goddess Lakshmi on a lotus blossom and then explain that they were absurd and the reason she was an atheist. She set great store by physics and took Hawking for her bedside bible. She was clever and rational and would offend Claire's very white, very middle-class parents by her very existence, so Claire had to be her friend, had to impress her at all costs.

Claire had gone so far in her attempts to impress that she supposed she had eventually become more interesting than Santosh herself, who these days insisted on recounting long anecdotes about her adventures in lost luggage at Heathrow. 'I tried appealing to the girl's sense of celebrity by telling her I was on TV.'

'Doesn't do any good,' said Claire. 'It's only *Guardian* readers of a certain sensibility who watch *Channel Four News.*'

'Don't I know it,' Santosh said gloomily. She peered into her beer for a moment, then asked, apropos of nothing, 'Who's Fred Hill, by the way?'

Claire stared at her. 'Uh, darling ... he's only, like, sex on toast.'

'Right,' Santosh nodded understandingly, obviously understanding nothing. 'What does he do? Or is he one of those people who are so fabulous they don't actually have to do anything to be fabulous?'

Claire pouted. 'Don't take the piss, Tosh. We can't all be worthy and highbrow. I would have thought you'd adored Fred anyway – just the kind of moody "rawk" star you always had a thing for.'

'Oh, he's a musician?'

'Yes. Why do you ask?'

'Saw him at the airport – I think. He was in there somewhere, somewhere amongst the entourage. The Prime Minister doesn't even have a retinue like that.'

'The Prime Minister doesn't have an arse like that,' said Claire, burping. 'If he did, he'd have a vast entourage to prevent people from attempting to grab it.'

'So it's not about the music, then?' asked Santosh. 'It's about the . . . arse?' She made a two-handed gesture that was so awkward that Claire nearly inhaled the olive in her dry martini.

'Of course it's about the arse, darling,' said Claire, wiping her eyes. 'The arse is fantastic. Usually clad in leather. Occasionally whips it out for music videos – which is delightful of him. The boy embodies the spirit of generosity itself with the way he shares his finely shaped and dimpled gift with the world.'

'His arse?'

'His arse!' Claire concurred, raising her glass to the rear of the year. 'Don't suppose you got a glimpse, did you?'

'I can't place his face, never mind his arse.' Santosh finished her beer and yawned. 'It is good to see you, though,' she said. 'I'm getting to the age where I'm starting to feel like a dirty old woman. Then I meet up with you and I realise I've got a long way to go.'

'I'm only a year older than you,' Claire said. 'Are you having another drink? You must have a Bellini.'

'A what?' Santosh blinked and adjusted her glasses. 'Isn't that a lesser-known Renaissance artist, or was he baroque?'

Claire sighed. 'Oh, whateverthefuck, darling, everyone's drinking them. Peach juice and champagne.'

'I don't *like* champagne though,' Santosh said awkwardly. Several people at the bar looked at her like she'd sworn in a church.

'It gives me heartburn,' she added, defiantly.

'You can't drink pints,' pleaded Claire. 'It's so ladette.'

Santosh shook her head. 'I drink pints because I like pints. What is this strange world you inhabit, Claire? Bellinis and ladettes?'

'The real world!' Claire said, defensively.

'Claire, this is la-la land compared to my world.'

'It's the same world. Just a slightly different version of reality. Has less ... goats.'

'Goats?' said Santosh, blankly.

'You said Kabul was crawling with the animals.'

Santosh sighed. 'Right. Goats. No, it's not about goats. You don't understand. It's about keeping it real.'

'Oh God, you're pissed, aren't you?' said Claire. Santosh would never have used that expression sober.

'Of course I'm pissed. You try getting a beer in Afghanistan.' Santosh swallowed a burp and tucked a stray strand of hair behind her ear. 'Look, if you'd seen what I'd seen you'd realise there are bigger things at stake than who's hot and who's not. You'd see what people really want – they want the water supply to run regularly, they want the electricity to be reliable, they want people to stop shooting each other so that they can get on with their lives, raise their sprogs, do their jobs – no matter how boring. They don't have any use for Bellinis or Prada bags or two-page glossy pictures of some dead-eyed bulimic advertising perfume. They have real priorities, Claire.'

'Darling ...' Claire shook her head. 'Get off your cross. You always launch into the anti-capitalism lectures the moment you get a drink inside you.'

'I do not!'

'You bloody do!'

'I've just come from a country where until a few years ago women were stoned to death for learning how to read. Forgive me if I think our hard-earned right to education is being prostituted on reading about shoes.'

Claire exhaled, frustrated. 'Dictating to women what they should read is just as bad as not teaching them to read in the first place.'

'I agree, absolutely. But we're blinded with shoes and cocktails and knickers and handbags and vibrators and we're just not seeing.' Santosh thumped the bar, fumbling for the next word. 'I don't know. We're just not seeing the ... I dunno.'

'Goats?'

Santosh sputtered her drink, laughing and coughing. 'Will you fuck off with the fucking goats?' she said. 'Jesus, I'm so pissed. We should probably agree to differ again, shouldn't we?'

'I think so, yes.'

'You know it's ridiculous, don't you?'

Claire lit another cigarette. 'Not really. I think I'm just endlessly amused by human gullibility. If someone told them wearing scuba gear and a tutu was the latest fashion, Bond Street would be alive with the sound of flippers pirouetting merrily in and out of Chanel boutiques. It's funny, honey. That's why we do it. It's a colossal piss-take.'

'Would you be willing to put that in writing?' asked Santosh. Despite the booze, she had a look in her eye – an acquisitive journalistic look, lit by the misguided fuel of revolutionary fantasies. Tosh had always been the one to drag Claire to the polling booth on election days, the one with the posters of Che Guevara pinned fangirl-style next to Black Sabbath on the bedroom wall. That was the fundamental difference between them, Claire decided.

Tosh wanted to change the world, while Claire just wanted to make it work to her advantage.

'And undermine my powerbase?' Claire said. 'Sod off, Kapoor. You're not getting a *Guardian* exclusive out of me, missy.'

'I was thinking of the *Independent*, actually,' Santosh said, hiccupping. 'And come on, you've got to be slightly sick of it, haven't you? I mean, the big names – the people who've actually worked to be where they are today – you have to be impressed by them. But the one-hit wonders, the fifteen-minuters, the famous for being famous? What do they actually do for you?'

'Nauseate and irritate me, mainly,' Claire admitted, sure she was going to regret the words the next morning when she sobered up.

'Yeah. So say you expose the process by which these demi-celebs are made – wearing the right clothes, going to the right parties, making all the right friends . . .'

Claire groaned and buried her nose in her Bellini. She always did this – underestimated Tosh. For all her bleeding heart bullshit, the damn woman was a ludicrously savvy journalist. Neil absolutely hated her and Santosh had often cheerfully assured him that the feeling was utterly mutual. 'You are *not*,' Claire said. 'No, no, *no*. I won't do it. I can see where your evil little mind is going.'

'Expose just one as a fraud,' Santosh continued, holding up a finger to illustrate her point. Her voice was slightly slurred and her eyes were sleepy and unfocused behind her glasses, but her brain had gone on hack-autopilot. 'And the whole house of cards comes tumbling down. You expose the process, it becomes demystified and we cleanse the red carpet of Z-listers forever!'

Claire blinked. 'You *are* drunk. What you're suggesting is nothing short of celebrity genocide. Anyway, it's been done to death. There are talent competitions all over the place, and no matter how many of the little bastards sing their hearts out, get stuffed through the celebrity meat grinder and come out reconstituted in the vague semblance of pop stars, there are still kids lining up around blocks to sign up for the next big contest.'

'OK, so maybe you can't get rid of the Z-listers,' said Santosh. 'But think of the publicity for you if I wrote the exposé.'

'I don't want to be the subject of an exposé,' said Claire. 'I sell illusions. I sell bullshit. The moment people realise it's a steaming pile of poo I'm going to be collecting my P45.'

'No you won't. There will still be an endless supply of stupid people who think being famous is glamorous. There are three constants in life – sex, death and morons.'

'Spoken like a true cynic, my darling,' Claire said, raising her glass.

'I mean it,' said Santosh, refusing to be sidetracked. 'Put your money where your mouth is. After your little performance in Covent Garden tonight, the likes of Neil Savage will eat you if you don't. You say you can turn a nobody into a star for no apparent reason. Go ahead and do it.'

Claire felt her stomach curdle at the thought of Neil Savage hearing about her contretemps with the hippy. The sod would hear about it. He always did. As well as his official set of reporters who were regularly packed off to all the right parties, she knew very well that he had a few undercover minions and the obligatory kiss-and-tell tarts who lurked around the tawdry edges of showbiz and dished the dirt for a fee. Claire's 'Do You Know Who I Am?' turn would not make front pages, but it would make her enough of a laughing stock to seriously damage her client list.

'You know what?' she said, suddenly beginning to feel

queasy-drunk and in need of something to eat. 'I could and I would – just to put one over on him. Christ, I remember that little shit when he had to kiss arse just to gain two square column inches in the *Sunday Sport*, and now look at him. Talk about absolute power corrupting absolutely.'

'He was hardly ever a saint,' said Santosh. 'Actually he was always a subliterate little creep.'

'Well, yes,' Claire sighed. 'Come on. Let's go back to mine. I've got a pasta craving and you can't get carbohydrates for love nor money outside your own four walls these days.'

Claire had feathered her nest quite substantially over the past ten years – enough to buy a small, fashionable flat in East Dulwich. It was new enough to appear impressive to Santosh, whose criteria for luxury was probably currently defined by the presence of roofs and lack of goats.

'It's not really that nice,' said Claire, uncharacteristically embarrassed into modesty. 'I got it cheap before the property market went stratospheric.'

'Lucky you.' Santosh dropped her bag and flopped on the couch, drunk beyond the limits of her usual good manners. 'You must be sitting on a fortune.'

'Only a few hundred thousand.'

'Oh, just a few.' Santosh rubbed her forehead. 'I'm still renting in bloody Tooting, surrounded by students – nightmare ... well, sort of. You can't argue with attractive twenty-year-old boys in close proximity, can you?'

'I can,' Claire said, grabbing her by the wrists and pulling her up off the couch. 'Come on. Food. Talk to me while I cook.'

Santosh followed unsteadily then sat down at the kitchen table with her head in her hands. 'You can't,' she said. 'Twenty-year-old boys. No way.'

'I can,' said Claire. 'I never sleep with men under twenty-five. I've seen so much delectable male flesh come in and out of my office that I am completely immune to pretty-boy charms. They may as well be blocks of wood as far as I'm concerned.'

'What have they got to recommend them over the age of twenty-five?' asked Santosh. 'More likely to commit or something?'

'If I wanted commitment I'd check into a mental hospital.' Claire dropped pasta into a pan of heating water.

'Well, they say marriage is an institution.'

'So is Broadmoor.'

'I may have to get one of these as a mirror,' said Santosh. She was staring into the shiny dark granite surface of the kitchen table. 'Hides a multitude of sins.'

'Darling, try the chrome surface thingy over the cooker hood – kind to eyebags *and* you have to tilt your head up to look at yourself. Everything falls backwards. It's like an instant facelift.'

Santosh lurched over to peer into the cooker hood. She pulled a face and leaned on the worksurface, arms folded and head drooping like a woman who had drunk enough to know that her centre of gravity should be much lower. 'Maybe for you,' she said, gloomily. 'You're shorter than me. Is there any booze?'

'Chardonnay, French beer, Belgian beer, Chablis and champers. Red wine's in the rack, spirits on the bureau in the lounge.'

'Are you sure? I wouldn't want you to run out.'

Claire made a rude gesture. 'Yet another one of the pleasures of life without men. I can have a fridge full of alcohol and there's nobody to accuse me of turning into Mrs Robinson.'

Santosh opened a small bottle of French beer and sniffed it suspiciously. 'You sound bitter, Clarice.'

'Me?' Claire turned down the pasta and poured herself more wine. 'God no. I love being single. When you've seen as many relationships crash and burn in public as I have then you learn to rely on yourself.'

'Yes, but you're looking at it from the perspective of drama queens who see a break-up as a way to gain even more pointless tabloid coverage. I'm talking about real people with actual private lives.'

'No no no no...' Claire shook her head so vehemently that she had to hold onto the fridge to keep her balance. 'Doesn't work for them either. The only difference is that nobody documents it. You see, once a woman gets a man in her life she ... she stagnates. Turns into a Stepford Wife. Devotes her time to trying to please him, or worse, trying to change him. Now that's the real fucker, darling, trying to change them. I've seen too many beautiful, brilliant, talented, charming women throwing them-selves away on abject incorrigible gobshites, and all because they dare to imagine that this clod of raw material they've got hold of can somehow be sculpted into the perfect Adonis.'

Claire burped and waved the pasta spoon in what she fondly and falsely imagined was an effective rhetorical gesture. 'Doesn't happen. Never happens,' she finished. 'Silk purse, sow's ear. Never works.'

'Then surely the solution to that would be to find a good man in the first place,' said Santosh. It didn't matter what persuasive bullshit Claire talked. Santosh had always been irritatingly capable of adding logic and sense to the equation. It was fortunate she was a jour-nalist. She would have died on her arse in PR.

'There are no good men,' Claire said. 'The only house-trained ones are gay or over seventy.'

'You can't mean that!'

'I can and I do. I'd turn gay but I just can't handle the idea of going down on a woman, which leads me to suppose I'm as straight as a steel rule.'

'Damn,' Santosh muttered. 'I thought you were going to try to seduce me.'

Claire laughed. 'Even if I were that way inclined, I wouldn't. Nothing like sex to wreck a beautiful friendship.'

'So I don't even get to cop a feel of your tits?' teased Santosh.

'No!'

Santosh laughed. 'You can take the girl out of Gloucestershire, but you can't take the Gloucestershire out of the girl. Sometimes I think half of your misanthropy is because secretly, deep down, you're a total Middle England prude, Claire.'

'Oh, I don't think so,' Claire said smugly. 'You would not be uttering those ill-chosen words if you'd been a fly on my office wall today.'

'Really?'

'Mm-hm. Some builder who imagined I'd cut him up at a roundabout. Came into my office bristling with road rage and left me a very happy woman indeed.'

Santosh gawped. 'You dirty cow!' she said, half-admiringly. 'Honestly?'

'Honestly,' said Claire, angelically.

'You just boned a total stranger?'

'Not exactly. Bodily fluids were exchanged but no "sexual relations" took place by way of the Clinton criteria.'

'There wasn't a cigar?' asked Santosh, frowning.

'No. No cigar.' Although there had been a lollipop, but fuck Justin and fuck his bloody lollipop. All mouth and no trousers.

Santosh exhaled. 'I can't beat that,' she said. 'Best I

can do is Daniel feeding the fish while dressed as a transvestite.'

Claire blinked, fearful that 'feeding the fish' was some kind of new code for a sexual act that she hadn't been brought up to speed on. 'Feeding the fish? And who's Daniel?'

'One of the students next door. I shouldn't, but when a fit twenty-year-old offers to feed my goldfish while I'm away...'

'Ah...'

'And does it in suspenders and high heels.' Santosh pulled a face. 'He's *twenty*.'

'And he wears women's underwear?'

'They were having a *Rocky Horror* party. He was Frank. The really galling thing is that he's got better legs than me.'

Claire prodded the pasta on the stove. 'Dear God. Students still have *Rocky Horror* parties like we used to do? Are they stuck in some kind of timewarp?'

'Well, it *is* just a jump to the left,' said Santosh, deadpan.

'And then a step to the right,' Claire sighed. 'Some things never change. I'm sure I've got my old French maid's outfit somewhere. How many times did we see that fucking show?'

'Twenty-seven,' replied Santosh, promptly. 'We've got nothing on the real hardcore fans. Trust me.'

The pasta had turned to mush and so had Claire's mood. She attempted to serve it up with herb butter but Santosh only picked, threw up in the sink, apologised and then decided to crash out on the couch.

Claire dropped the rest of the pasta in the bin and went to bed feeling less like a character from *Sex and the City* and more like a dirty old woman who couldn't handle her drink any more. Worst of all she had songs from the *Rocky Horror Show* running through her head –

a tedious reminder that life was no longer as much fun as it had been ten years ago, when running through the West End in a barely adequate bustier and frilly suspenders had felt like the height of naughtiness. You had to throw your knickers at builders for a thrill these days.

4

In London, rebellion was no longer the serious business it had once been. Once upon a time it had meant that somebody was mounting a challenge to the throne, protesting taxes or protesting absolute authority. Heads would roll. People would be locked up in the Tower. There would be assassinations, discreet dynastic murders, heads on pikestaffs and occasionally civil war.

That was the London James had read about at school, thousands of miles away in the blistering heat of Dubai. Some childish part of him had been surprised to find that the monarchy was secure in the hands of its elderly matriarch, that parliament was managerial rather than rambunctious, and that the peasants, although still pretty fucking phenomenally revolting, were happy enough decking themselves out in designer labels and entering talent contests.

He was further surprised to find his contemporaries were not engaged in out and out student rebellion. Tuition fees? Oh, Mummy and Daddy would cough up – they'd have to. Degrees? Paid to get a good one. Politics? No thanks.

He had been hoping to find a bunch of earnest kids determined to change the world and instead found people who made a big deal out of changing their hair. Even their capacity for outrage seemed dulled down. It was as if nobody remembered how to rebel against authority or feel even slightly discontent with their lot.

Bloody students.

Their complacency had only amplified James's carefully

cultivated teenage snottiness. He had started at home, matting his hair into dreadlocks and lurking in a pot-addled bedroom with the express desire to piss his parents off. He had been a late baby, something of an accident, and while in his better moments he thought they quite liked him, they allowed him to do pretty much what he wanted, which smacked of indifference.

Mum said she could cook, but didn't care to do it. Dad could exert discipline, but didn't think it was important since people had a habit of learning from the consequences of their actions and made it clear he expected his son to follow suit. When James had started smoking dope around the house they'd put it down to teenage experimentation and refused to go mental. When he'd said he wanted to go to England to study politics they'd been all 'That's nice, dear' and drawn up a budget of the costs of the air fare, tuition and lodging.

Desperate to meet some form of opposition, James had exploded. 'Anyone would think you wanted to get rid of me! Why didn't you just have a fucking abortion, Mum? Save yourself the trouble.'

'Don't be so silly,' Mum said. 'It's not an easy thing for a woman – to have an abortion. Besides, you're eighteen now. You're a grown man. It's about time you made your own way in the world.'

'You've been saying that since I hit puberty. Admit it. You're desperate to see the back of me.'

'Of course we're not, Jamie. But you always were a clingy little thing. You wouldn't even let go of my hand when I tried to take you to school.'

'Mother! I was five!'

'Big enough not to make a fuss,' she'd said, tapping away on her computer. When she wasn't playing mah jong with 'the girls' she wrote articles about home decorating. 'I don't know what's wrong with young people today. They're so terribly insecure.'

'Or totally neurotic because they've been sat in front of MTV and raised on Ritalin and Coca Cola by a bunch of selfish baby boomers.'

'Don't be over dramatic. I never gave you anything stronger than a Junior Disprin and you know I wouldn't have pop in the house because of your teeth. You haven't got a single filling in your head and that was partly my doing.'

'Great. So you know my dental records back to front?'

'Any mother would, darling.'

'Right. So when they find my rotting corpse in a ditch somewhere you'll be a perfect position to identify it, won't you?' He had stormed out of the room, slamming the screen door and dislodging something that had descended with a crash and causing his mother to plaintively exclaim; 'Oh, be careful, James!'

Turned out he'd destroyed a 1912 Favrile glass decanter from Tiffany's, and even then she was so resolutely phlegmatic of temperament that she was forced to admit it was an ugly thing and she'd only kept it around because it was an antique. In short, she failed to behave like a mother. She wouldn't criticise the way he dressed, she thought his taste in music 'jolly good fun', had never rebuked him for swearing and trusted him to do his homework with a composed show of good faith that was entirely maddening.

When James arrived in London to begin his degree, a few months shy of his nineteenth birthday, it was no wonder he was spoiling for a fight.

He didn't find one.

His personal tutor, one Dr Graham Mulholland, was understanding in the extreme. The acquaintances he made seemed excessively contented and didn't seem entirely sure why they were studying politics. Susanna thought she might like to be a journalist but hadn't taken up the offer of a degree in journalism because the politics course 'looked interesting, and anyway, the SU bar is way cheap'. Daniel had taken politics because all the psych courses were oversubscribed and Natalie had picked it because she thought it was a feminist statement.

'When men tell women politics is boring it's only because they want to keep them out of it,' she said, when they were sitting in the union café, known esoterically as G1 (Ground Floor One). 'It's a pathetic cop out when you think women chained themselves to railings.'

'Why aren't you doing women's studies, then?' asked Daniel, who was reading a book on Daoism and looking stoned. He was one of the surf set from Cornwall and had been largely acknowledged as desperately cool before the end of the first week, mostly on account of him being very good-looking, slightly caned and often not showing up to parties that others would have given their eye teeth to attend. This suggested he had other, even cooler things to do and made him an object of fascination.

'I don't need to do a course in being a woman,' said Natalie. 'I *am* a woman. It's a totally Mickey Mouse subject cooked up by women who'd do better taking the time getting some electrolysis.'

'Or shaving their armpits,' Sue added, nodding. She was a pretty brunette with a 1950s pin-up figure and was stuffing a *pain au chocolat* into her mouth with the strange mixture of contrition and starvation that all young women seemed to employ when eating anything that contained more calories than an undressed iceberg lettuce salad.

Daniel yawned. 'Dude ... you're expressing solidarity with Emmeline Pankhurst one minute and saying all feminists are mingers the next? What the fuck?'

'It's a matter of pride,' said Sue. (She actually said 'Itsh a marrer awf pride', having half a French pastry in her mouth at the time, as if trying to stuff it out of sight before someone accused her of actually enjoying herself. She couldn't have been more furtive if she were shooting up smack.)

'It is a matter of pride,' agreed Natalie. 'And I think it's incredibly rich for men to accuse women of vanity.'

'I didn't accuse you of vanity,' said Daniel. 'I accused you of contradicting yourself. When did I say women were vain?' He turned to James, appealing for back-up.

'You didn't,' said James.

'Well, actually it's not a contradiction,' Natalie persisted. 'We've moved on beyond feminists flour-bagging beauty contests. If you look at the feminist icons of history you might notice that a lot of them put the war-paint on regularly. Nefertiti, Cleopatra, Elizabeth the First . . .'

'Totally,' said Sue. 'A woman gets dressed up and the only reason it's seen as anti-feminist is because sexist males assume that it's for them. Just like men to make everything about themselves. They're so selfish.'

James wanted to point out that Nefertiti, Cleopatra and Elizabeth I – although a fairly disparate trio of women – had one thing in common. They were queens in societies where queens were expected to be magnificent and relied on dazzling the populace to maintain the mystique of royalty and, in some cases, keep their heads attached to their bodies. Neither would they have seen themselves as feminists in the modern sense.

He would have weighed in but Daniel had already retreated from the argument with a series of nods and grunts of accord designed to irritate the girls and James always found himself annoyingly tongue-tied in Natalie's presence.

She was so fucking beautiful. She was one of those pale, strawberry blondes with a dusting of light freckles. Everything about her was pale – pale hazel-green eyes, pale red-gold hair. The fine hairs on the backs of her thin, delicate wrists were so fair they were almost white. Where her neckline plunged her skin was lily-coloured, giving rise to strangulated fantasies about pure-white breasts and barely rose nipples.

She always wore a thin gold ring with a tiny diamond set into it on her middle finger – her eighteenth birthday present – and twisted it while she talked. She talked a lot, her voice overconfident and sometimes strident as she defended her corner.

James was only dimly aware that he was gazing stupidly at her. She often talked like this – in extreme terms about intense subjects close to her heart. Sometimes late at night when they'd drained the coffee pot to the dregs and their eyes were closing of their own accord she would shake, either with caffeine or passion, and her tired eyes would fill with tears as she described a novel or a piece of music that had moved her in some way. He would want to steady her trembling hands with his fingertips, lap the tears from her golden eyelashes, move his lips over sleep-flushed cheeks to her mouth. But he never did. He never dared.

The argument dried up. Daniel continued reading his book on Daoism. Natalie went through her lecture notes. Sue dropped pastry crumbs on her gossip magazine. Desperate for something to do, James asked Daniel if he could listen to his MP3 player for a bit and plugged the tiny headphones into his ears.

He watched people move around the room – unwitting participants in a music video. He knew the album, of course – *Random Playlist* by Shade. They'd been around as long as he could remember being aware of the charts but they were on a roll lately – punkier and noisier than their usual brand of all-American alienation angst. They'd acquired a new frontman after their last one, Wayne Klusky, had had a huge rock 'n' roll meltdown, called them all a pack of cunts and went storming off to record the greatest solo album ever written. So far this work of self-styled genius hadn't materialised, and Shade had acquired a British singer called Fred Hill, who was doing them no end of favours by being not only talented but sexy, charismatic and suitably witty at press calls. He had a lighter voice than Wayne Klusky's contrived death-metal rasp and, for a change, you could actually hear the lyrics.

'Mea culpa, mea culpa, mea maxima culpa,
The preacher says it's Latin but I know it's Greek to you.
When you're shouldering the pain
And you wanna nail the blame
Pick some other motherfucker,
Cause it's anyone but you.'

James smiled at the memory of the stink that the video to that single had caused. Church leaders had demanded that blasphemy laws be invoked and, when Fred Hill had been confronted about it, he had feigned surprise, laughed wildly and cried, 'Nobody expects the Spanish Inquisition!' – earning the love of nerds on both sides of the Atlantic.

He was even happier to retreat into selective deafness when Jeremy showed up. Jeremy (or rather Jez, as he preferred to be called) was dark, handsome in a boring sort of way and quite patently after Natalie. James knew she'd never go for him because he was a sexist twat, but it didn't make him any less annoying. He was a second year and a student union rep, but he made a sport of 'Fuck a Fresher Fortnight' and always seemed to be attached by the lips to a different skinny girl every time James saw him in the SU bar.

Jez plonked himself on the shabby plastic banquette and pulled the headphone out of James's left ear. 'Afternoon, Jimbo. And what are we listening to today?'

'Music,' said James. 'It's Daniel's.'

Jez grinned at Daniel. 'All right, Lama? Didn't see you there behind Marley's Ghost.'

It was Jez's policy to give people nicknames as stupid as his own, probably because he'd seen *Lock, Stock and Two Smoking Barrels* too many times and was desperate to demonstrate that he wasn't posh. James was Jimbo or Marley's Ghost (on account of his hairstyle) and Daniel was the Dalai Lama because of his interest in Eastern religions.

Jez tweaked one of James's dreads to demonstrate the hilarity of his joke. James suppressed the urge to elbow him in the throat.

'Jez!' Natalie said, plaintively.

'Working hard, ladies?' Jez asked, peeking at the MP3 player. 'Huh. *Random Playlist*. That was funny for about five minutes. My cousin was at Harrow with him. Said he was a complete twat.'

'Who? Fred Hill?' Sue looked up from her magazine. 'He never went to Harrow.'

'He fucking did. Too thick to get into Winchester.' Jez looked as though he was settling down to make himself comfortable. Fuck. 'Aren't they playing here next month?' he said, as though he didn't care that they were. 'I suppose I might go – just to point and laugh. Got a spare ticket if anyone's interested? Natalie?'

'You must be joking,' said Natalie. 'They're a bunch of Neanderthal misogynists.'

'Oh, come on. You wouldn't have to pay for anything. Including drinks.'

To James's disgust she looked as though that might sway her. Feminism, it seemed, was about taking as many men for a ride as possible and cadging free drinks along the way. Once they had a few drinks inside them, Sue and Natalie would carry on like a couple of Holly Golightlys – the book Holly and not the pre-sweetened movie Holly. Tarts with no hearts, taking advantage of men because they believed it was better to get in there first before men took advantage of them.

James wanted to shake her, remind her who she really was – the sensitive girl who cried on cue every time she heard the Elgar Cello Concerto, someone intelligent, someone with standards – not some slag who would simper and show her legs at the promise of free drinks.

He decided to go back to the Hall rather than visit the library. Anything to put distance between himself and Jez. He contemplated throwing himself under the next Northern Line tube before deciding that he was too depressed to even do the Anna Karenina thing and had no particular desire to depart this life before he'd had one last lonely wank.

The tube tunnel was foul-smelling and grimy. Mice scuttled across the platform. The wall beside the track where so many desperate and heartsick Londoners had ended it all was thick with billboard posters; a vague promise of glamour and excitement in a city where the poor and plain were ignored, anonymous, of no more consequence than the grubby, fast-skittering mice.

Film posters, album promotions, perfume advertisements. Angelina Jolie glittered in Dior gold. Fred Hill skulked in the shadow of a graffiti-ed underpass, kohl-rimmed eyes fierce and unnaturally bright in the shade. Supermodel Zoe Luscombe pouted at him from a cosmetic billboard – all lips and legs and baby oil. He knew these people by name but he had never met them. They wouldn't know him from Adam. He mattered less than the glossy paper their images were printed on. He knew it, and worse, Natalie obviously knew it.

James looked at the travel alarm clock on the desk and realised midnight had come and gone. It was three o'clock in the morning and today was officially his nineteenth birthday.

He stared again at the essay on his laptop. The cursor blinked interrogatively at him and seemed to pose the question, 'You do realise this whole essay is crap, don't you?' He'd realised before he started it. He hadn't done the bibliography or the reading and he would have to go back to the library to lift some appropriate quotes, type them in and then add the books to the appendix in order to look as though he'd read them from cover to cover. Academia – a worthy grounding in the noble art of bullshitting.

He heard unsteady footsteps in the hall outside – someone who had sneaked in past the night porter or who had been drinking in someone's room downstairs. He was surprised when that someone knocked on his door. Maybe that someone knew it was his birthday.

James opened the plywood door and Sue wobbled through it. She was dressed in some sort of French maid's outfit and carried a pair of high-heeled black shoes in one hand. Her hair was back-combed into a mad gothic mane around her smudgily made-up face. She looked totally drunk.

'Jaaaames!' she screeched, collapsing on his bed in a flurry of frilly petticoats and suspenders. 'You missed the party!'

'Wouldn't be much point,' said James. It had been a *Rocky Horror* party and James had never understood the fascination with *The Rocky Horror Show*. 'I had that essay to finish.'

Sue sat up, shook her head and gulped in a manner that made him worried that she was going to throw up on his bed. Her large breasts jostled inside the tight bodice of her dress and a nipple looked as though it was about to make a break for it and fall out any second. She was obviously even drunker than she looked. 'You should have come,' she said. 'Jus' buy the essay, or nick one off the internet. Got any booze?'

'No,' said James. 'I think you could stand a black coffee though.'

'Got any fags? I've smoked all mine.'

He handed her his tobacco pouch and filled the coffee filter from the tiny sink. He wished he had instant coffee. Anything to sober her up enough for him to push her down the hall with a clear conscience and dump her in her room. Right now he wouldn't have felt safe to leave her because she looked like a case of choked-on-vomit waiting to happen. He wished he could leave her, because he was exhausted and needed to sleep.

'You're not cross with me, are you?' she asked, in a babyish voice that made him want to answer yes – yes, I am, because you're pissed, I'm sober, I work, you don't and you wouldn't even be here if you hadn't run out of cigarettes.

But he looked back at her sitting on his bed and she looked merely dishevelled, pitiful, slightly stupid. He couldn't shout at her or throw her out, not when she was this drunk and uncomprehending. It would be like attacking a small child.

'I'm just tired, Sue,' he said. 'And it's my birthday today. And so far it's totally shit.'

'It's your birthday?' She jumped unsteadily up off the bed and wound her arms around him. 'Oh, you poor baby – why didn't you say?'

'I just did.'

'Come here, birthday boy,' she slurred, coquettishly.

He turned round, meaning to tell her there wasn't a chance in hell, but her lips immediately came down hard on his. Her tongue slid into his mouth and she tasted about eighty per cent proof. One of her boobs had fallen out of her dress and he could feel the warm, soft squash of it against his chest. He didn't mean to kiss her back but did so from reflex more than anything else. The rest of his body followed suit.

'Can't not have a pressie on your birthday, Jamie,' she said, drunkenly, pulling his hand to her exposed breast. It was softer than he had expected it to feel because no matter how hard Sue tried to dress like the skinny girls, she had a big Marilyn Monroe shape and her tits always stuck out in what looked to be a solid, unyielding shelf. It was weird to discover they were so squishy. When he touched her nipple it puckered and creased under his finger.

She was totally pissed. She'd let him do anything. She let him put his hands under the ruffled net mass of her petticoats and he grabbed her big, round bum, dizzy with the thought of how close his hands were to the main prize. He would have done more if the small voice still talking sense at the back of his mind hadn't managed to scream loud enough to grab his attention.

She was drunk. She was probably so drunk she wouldn't have any recollection of this tomorrow and she might have been saying yes now but she might have a whole different take on the situation when she sobered up. He had a scary vision of just how ugly this could get and quickly pulled away.

'No, come on,' he said. 'Sit down. I'll make you that coffee.'

Sue flopped back down on the bed. Her breasts hung loose from her bodice and her matted hair fell forwards as her head drooped. She looked so insensibly drunk that James was certain he'd made the right decision.

'Don't you like me?' she asked, raising her head with difficulty. One of her false lashes had come loose, giving her right eye a weird, spidery, off-centre look. He didn't like her. He resented that she was even there, that she had the power to lead him on and cry foul if she wasn't happy with her behaviour the next morning. He resented her for leading men around by their dicks – her and Natalie both. They'd spout feminist clichés until they were blue in the face but when they skipped out to the pubs and clubs, arm in arm, they wore the shortest skirts, the tightest tops and a ton of make-up. They trotted along on high-heeled feet, bottoms wiggling delectably, then danced hip to hip and face to face, touching and flirting with one another in a way that had nothing to do with lesbianism and everything to do with attracting even more male attention than they could handle with their lips and tits and arses.

It was monstrous that even drunk, bedraggled and looking like shit she should still wield such power just because she had a cunt between her thighs. It terrified him that she could make him hate her so much in that instant.

'Of course I like you,' he said, trying to pull her dress back up over her breasts. They fell out easily enough but trying to stuff them back into that corset was damn near impossible. 'I just don't think it's the right time for ... that.'

'There's nothing to worry about, Jamie,' she said, coyly, giggling. 'I'll be gentle with you.'

He stiffened, turned back to his coffee pot and watched it drip.

He had told Natalie he was a virgin. He had told her in confidence, late at night when she was being normal, being herself, sipping coffee and conversing. He should have known better. He should have known women talked, but the sting of her betrayal was like no pain or humiliation he had ever known before. His cheeks flamed and he wanted to scream at Sue to get out, but when he turned around she was lying sprawled on his bed, motionless.

The stupid cow had passed out cold.

He tried to wake her but she just groaned and grunted and swore and he was too reedy to shift a girl of her size.

He had to settle for moving her into a rough approximation of the recovery position and pulling a blanket over her. Then he just sat for a while, drinking his coffee and listening anxiously to her irregular snorty breathing.

A great start to his birthday.

She woke up at about five and staggered back to her room as if on auto-pilot. James finally crawled, exhausted, into his own bed, too tired to care if his sheets smelled of booze, sweat and stale perfume. Anything for a few hours' sleep before facing the rest of what already promised to be a totally fucking hideous day.

When he got up at about one he lurched downstairs and looked for post in his pigeonhole. There were the usual crap cards from aunties and a card from his parents with a cheque in it. The money was useful but compared to previous birthdays spent at the races or having tea in the precarious, vertiginous surroundings of the sky bar of the Burq Al Arab, a cheque in rainy London seemed obvious, perfunctory.

He decided to forget that it was his birthday. It was just a day and if you tried to wish it any less shittier than any other shit day, it seemed even more craptaculous. He took the train into the city and went to the library – business as usual. He made up his bullshit, fraudulent booklist and went for coffee in G1, but Natalie was in there. She was sitting on a banquette with Jez, snogging his face off.

Furious, James went elsewhere for his coffee. Pret a Manger was packed, the café in St Martin's was closed for maintenance. He kept walking, so hurt and angry and fucking lonely in this horrible, grey, stinking city that he couldn't think straight. He just wanted a cup of coffee so he headed for Covent Garden.

James had been spoiling for a fight ever since he had arrived in London. When he bumped into the blonde with the expensive shoes, he found one.

5

The tapes turned up in the Lost and Found at Heathrow, but Santosh was less happy about their retrieval than she would have expected to be. She had told Daniel that enough was enough and that he'd do better with someone his own age. Some simpering, whimpering eight-stone bimbette with a collection of sexy underwear and perfectly assembled CD racks.

Santosh had been grappling with the instructions on her flat-pack CD rack for over three hours – as part of her new initiative to sort out her life. She'd contemplated a haircut, because apparently that was what you were supposed to do, but she imagined her mother's hysterical reaction and decided she must organise her music collection, label her videocassettes and stop fucking Daniel.

He hadn't taken it well.

'I'm twenty and you're thirty-two. We could hardly *be* more sexually compatible!'

'It isn't about sex,' she had said, although it was. 'I have to travel a lot and when I'm away you're going to be thinking I'm sleeping with someone else and I'll think you're sleeping with someone else and we'll just end up throwing accusations at each other.'

'Um, how about we try trusting one another?' Everything was that simple when you were twenty.

'Trust is fine. In theory. But doubt always gets you in the end.'

So that was that. No more Daniel.

Perversely, the moment she told herself she couldn't have him, she craved him – like craving chocolate when you'd banished the stuff from your fridge because of a diet. He had been right about the sexual compatibility issue. They could hardly have done it better together. She was sure that was why women hit their sexual peak at thirty-five and men at just twenty. Older women were not only in a position to teach young men to make love, but were also old enough and wise enough to appreciate the beauty of young flesh.

Perhaps that had been the way of things back in the mists of time – the tribe matriarchs took the young men in hand and taught them. She wasn't sure who taught the young girls. Maybe they taught each other. Who knew? It just felt like a tremendous, malicious evolutionary joke. Women reached their sexual peak at 35. Way back when, when humans were still hunter gatherers, most of them probably hadn't even lived that long. You popped out babies at the expense of your teeth, bones and occasionally your life and didn't even make it to the age where you had the potential to come every time. Mother Nature was most definitely a bitch.

She had to stop feeling sorry for herself and stop thinking about Daniel – about Daniel's body, Daniel's hair and skin and smell. He'd always smelled so fresh, even in the mornings. It was as if dirt couldn't find a groove to get a foothold because his skin was so perfectly smooth, appetising as freshly pressed butter. His teeth were too young and too slippery-shiny to allow plaque to grip and he never seemed to have bad morning breath because of it. The Incredible Wipe Clean Boyfriend.

She worried about that too. She worried that once the skin around his eyes began to crease and when time and wear roughened the surface of his teeth then she would no longer want him. She worried that it was just his youth she found attractive. She worried that she was turning into a dirty old woman.

She had to be hard on herself. She had set the washing

machine in motion after stripping the sheets off her bed – trying to eradicate all trace of him and rinse away the smell of his tempting skin, trying to be practical, housewifely and grown-up. She had scrubbed traces of his bristles off the bathroom sink – the spiky, amber-coloured stubble that was so pleasant to feel on her face or scratching between her breasts when he nestled close in bed.

She would organise and reprioritise and try to be more like Claire, who never had these problems because she was capable of kicking men out of her bed with impunity and admirable lack of conscience and then returning swiftly to the important business of running the world.

Santosh was convinced she could do it herself. She could have a successful career and be as good a house-keeper as her mother and sisters. She felt pretty pleased with herself when she managed to stand the CD tower upright after giving it the required length of time for the wood glue to dry. Take that, flat-pack fucker. You messed with the wrong lady.

The phone rang just as she was standing back admiring her handiwork. It was Claire.

'Darling, you'll never believe what's happened...'

'I don't as it is,' Santosh said, tentatively pressing a palm on top of the tower to test its strength. 'What's up?'

'You want your exposé still? Because if you do, get down here right now – I can't tell you over the phone but, oh God, it's the funniest thing.'

With a spiteful inevitability, the side of the tower – one of the pieces she had laboriously glued and hammered into place – slowly sheared off and hit the carpet with a thump. 'OK,' she said, too sick of the thing to try putting it back together. 'I'm on my way.'

She hung up the phone and left the tower on the floor after giving it a hefty kick with her heaviest pair of boots. Determination had given way to anger. She knew how to say, 'Don't shoot! Journalist!' in six languages, which was more useful than having organised CDs. Who really cared if you kept your CDs on the floor or piled on your desk anyway? Who gave a toss if they were alphabetically arranged? Who on earth was that anal? What did it matter if she preferred sleeping with boys in their late teens and early twenties to men her own age?

She fumed all the way to Claire's office. If women just dropped all this 'older men are sexy too' bullshit and admitted it to themselves they would stop trying to be generous and be as honestly shallow as most men were. The only reason you ever saw a young, beautiful woman with an older man was because he was either rich, powerful, brilliant or funny. All of those were potent aphrodisiacs but surely they were no substitute for real lust?

There was only one type of man in the world that could supply that kind of lust for her and the trouble was they were all too fucking young. They had all the desirable physical attributes – smooth, soft skin, wiry muscles, clear, bright eyes, flat bellies, perfect arses and perky dicks – but at nineteen or twenty they had the disadvantage of being unformed, tentative, personalities still seeking a definitive identity. Older men could hold conversations, behave like the finished article instead of the raw clay – and that was fine, or would have been if she could get over her shallow preference for body beautifuls.

Claire's receptionist Donna was texting on her phone when Santosh entered the office. 'She's in there,' said Donna, pointing with a finger whose nail was an inch long and painted sky blue with a pink butterfly motif. 'Don't ask me what it's about. I think she's finally gone off her nut, personally.'

'OK,' Santosh said, warily, and entered the office.

Claire was perched on the edge of her desk. It stood on a sort of dais so that she was higher than her latest client/victim. There was a boy sat on the couch and it didn't take an instant for Santosh to recognise the dreadlocks and realise that it was the boy from Covent Garden.

'James,' said Claire, expansively. 'This is Santosh Kapoor. She's an extremely brilliant journalist and if you behave yourself and do as you're told she'll write up your transition from lumpy nonentity to media darling in a national newspaper.'

'Oi! Lumpy nonentity?'

'Whoa, wait,' said Santosh, holding up both hands. 'I didn't say I'd do that. Besides, I've got a documentary to edit.'

'What on?' asked James, sounding interested.

'Er . . . women. In Kabul. Post-Taliban.'

'Cool!' He looked at her with approval. Oh God. No. Behind his geeky round glasses his eyes were pale blue and attentive, appealing. His face, partially hidden by the mop of ratty dreads, was fairly handsome and firm-jawed. He must been about nineteen or twenty and his admiration of her could only lead to trouble. More trouble.

'Oh, for God's sake,' Claire groaned. 'James, you're going to have to stop having opinions if you want my help. You may have opinions when you are famous. Until then, kindly keep it bland.'

'You can't do this,' said Santosh. 'Claire, what about his parents?'

'They're in Dubai,' James said, shrugging.

'See?' Claire jiggled her foot impatiently. 'It's perfect. They don't want him, so we might as well have him.'

'Actually they do want me,' James protested. 'I just . . . I just prefer to make my own way in the world. That's all.'

'And so you shall,' said Claire, like a fairy godmother.

'By the time I've finished with you, you'll be the stuff of every woman's favourite wank fantasy. You will be adored by millions for no apparent reason.'

'Well yeah, but a reason would be good,' said James, in an upspeak tone that turned the sentence into a sarcastic question and reminded Santosh of Daniel. No. She just couldn't. It would only be a matter of time before she really *did* turn into Mrs Robinson.

'I'm sure one will turn up, darling,' Claire said, airily, with a wave of her hand. Her phone rang and Donna announced someone called Justin on the intercom. Claire went to take the call in reception – 'Client confidentiality, darling' – and left Santosh alone with James.

There was an awkward silence until James said, 'Would she mind if I smoke?'

'I don't think so,' said Santosh, glancing at the brimming ashtray on Claire's desk. James removed a roll-up from somewhere beneath the dreads over his left ear and lit up, apologising because he only had the one.

'No thanks, it's fine. I don't,' said Santosh, sitting at a safe distance on the couch.

He had that scrawniness of late adolescence, where the last big growth spurt that turned boy to man stretched some of them out like chewing gum. Most of him was lost in baggy pants, a loose sweater and an army surplus coat but it did nothing to disguise the thinness – rather, it accentuated it. The clothes looked like they were about to fall off him any second, as if just a tug at his waist would make the whole lot drop off and leave him white, naked and shivering in the middle of the office. In her present mood it felt as though he had dressed like that on purpose to taunt her, wrapped like one of her mother's packages of home-made sweets. They kept their wrappings on decently until you tugged gently at the right part of the thin silver ribbon and then the confection inside was revealed – creamy and silky to touch, taste and smell.

'What are you doing here?' she asked him, as directly as if it had been Daniel sitting there beside her. He was probably about the same age as Daniel. Maybe he was even at the same college. Maybe he even knew Daniel. She hoped not.

He looked at her and shrugged. 'Got bored of being nobody, I suppose,' he said, as if he wasn't quite sure why he was here either.

'Yes, but the other night ...'

He sniffed. 'Whatever. So she's a cow. I don't care. She says she can turn me into something else and I want her to do it.'

'Why?'

'Just sick of being shat on from a great height,' he said, lightly, bitterly.

'Yeah, but that happens regardless of who you are. That's just ... people. There's always going to be someone who lets you down and messes you around.' Like me, she thought. Poor, poor Daniel.

'You won't change my mind,' said James. 'It's made up. I checked out your friend on Google and she's the real thing, all right. So I just showed up and she laughed at me for a bit but then she said she might as well do it just to prove she can. She gets to test her professional reputation, I get to stop being a loser and everyone is happy, I suppose.'

He stared defiantly at her like the child he was. He had a funny-looking face, with a jaw that pushed forwards a little too far, a slight overbite and a nose that ski-sloped into a tilted tip and gave his whole profile a mischievous, simian quality. Santosh was uncomfortably reminded of Claire's boast to strategically shave a chimp and chuck it at the red carpet and resolved that she had to speak to Claire about this.

'One second,' she said, and went out into reception where Donna was typing with her precarious fingernails and Claire was finishing her phone call in usual Claire fashion.

'Justin, you're a fucking cunt and I have every reason to drop you like a hot prick, I mean, brick . . . no, I didn't say that. Now, get thee to a tepee, immediately. If I have to read any more headlines like this morning I will personally tie you to a fucking totem pole, OK? Right. Fuck off then.'

Claire hung up the phone and grinned at Santosh. 'Well, what do you think? Isn't it the most delicious challenge? He's so gorgeously *dingy*.'

'I don't know,' said Santosh, hesitantly. 'I'm not sure. He's very young.'

'You wanna see some of these boyband kids,' Donna said. 'Not much older than my Dwayne. Practically foetuses.'

Claire shook her head. 'He's over eighteen. He's old enough to vote and if he's old enough to make absurd decisions at the ballot box then he's old enough to make absurd decisions about his own life as well as everyone else's. He wants to be a celebrity, Tosh.'

'Yeah, but what are you going to do when you've finished with him?' asked Donna. 'Once he's been eye-balled by the world and his wife and all over the telly he's not going to be able to go back and have a normal life, is he?'

'Thank you!' said Santosh. 'Yes! That's just it. Celebrity is like . . . virginity. Or the losing of. You can't take it back or go back.'

'Oh, of course you can,' Claire snorted. 'You can fuck off and run a trout farm in the Outer bloody Hebrides or whatever.'

'I hate fish,' Donna said, and announced that she was going for a pee before sloping off.

'I'm really not sure,' Santosh pleaded. 'I mean, what do you want *me* to do for him? I don't know anything about who's hot and who's not or where to be seen or what to wear. I mean, if you want help avoiding land-mines, I'm your girl, but what am I supposed to do for him? What can I contribute aside from newspaper expo-sure – which, by the way, I don't have time to do ... and how old is he, anyway?'

'Er ... nineteen, I think,' Claire said.

Santosh leaned heavily on the desk and whacked her head against its surface once or twice, gently. 'Oh no. No no no.'

'What?'

She groaned. 'Claire, you do not understand. I have this thing ... with boys. About that age. You know Daniel?'

'Daniel? Daniel? Oh yes. Daniel. Cross-dressing next-door neighbour?'

'Yes. He's just twenty and I ... I'm already getting too fond of him.' Santosh raised her head. 'I can't. Not Daniel, not James, not any boy of that age. I can't help myself. They're like puppies, but ... sexy puppies.'

Claire beamed. 'But this is wonderful. Darling, I'm the type that *kicks* puppies. If you want to pet them then that couldn't be better. Strikes a nice balance and you can provide the acid test once we've shaved and deloused the creature.'

'Acid test?'

'Yes. Tell me if it's desirable or not. I've never had much use for males under thirty and absolutely no use for under twenty-fives. I'm not a very good judge of these things.'

'Neither am I,' protested Santosh. 'You don't get it, Claire. Boys of that age ... it's a thing with me. It's like I turn into a female version of Humbert Humbert.'

'Oh, don't be silly,' said Claire. 'Just try not to push me under speeding cars and go off on the lam with the subject material, all right, sweetie? Because you know he'll only run off with a sleazy playwright-manque and you'll end up shooting someone.'

'You're not going to let me say no, are you?'

'Of course not.'

The Justin Situation, as Claire persisted in calling it, was showing few signs of improvement. He had telephoned from somewhere in the arse end of Wiltshire to say that he was having a nervous breakdown.

'You're just bored,' Claire had told him. 'And I meant what I said about tying you to a totem pole. So don't even think about setting foot in this city until your head is on straight.'

'Coming from a woman who wants to tie herself to my totem pole,' Justin had muttered.

'Darling, you couldn't handle me. If you stuck your appendage in a woman with an iota of intelligence you'd likely spontaneously combust or castrate yourself or something.'

'Oh please.' She could hear the smirk on his face. 'I've already had a taste of what you've got to offer and I'm coming back for more. There's sexual tension there, don't deny it.'

'Yes, I make you sexual and you make me tense. Stay right where you are. I'm coming down and we'll discuss this sensibly. You come back to London now and you can bloody well find yourself a new agent.'

Claire felt like she needed to get out of the city for a few hours anyway. The constant ringing of the phones was starting to jangle her nerves in a way it didn't normally. There was definitely something to be said about not taking one's work home. James had been installed in the spare room of her flat for the past fortnight, under strict instructions to watch MTV and read gossip magazines until his hair grew back to a reasonable length. Getting rid of those vile dreadlocks hadn't been easy. He now resembled a startled sheep that had had a run in with a particularly overzealous sheep-shearer. His running commentary on the vapidity of the very things he was supposed to be absorbing was as annoying as it was pointless.

It would be good to get away and get far enough to from the city to actually press the pedal down and give the car a run for its money. And maybe, if she was very good, Justin would let her play cowboys and Indians in his tepee. She supposed he must have a little campfire in there and some fur rugs chucked about the place. He'd be gagging for it after a long, boring fortnight of being hugged by men named Tarquin and encouraged to weep at the beauty of the woods, and he responded so well when she fobbed him off and told him no. He was so used to women falling at his feet that he enjoyed chasing her. This time, she told herself, no fucking lollipops. If he teased she'd pin him down between her thighs and ride him until he howled. Big Chief Boogie Dust at her mercy on the floor.

She was just leaving the office when a man waiting in reception grabbed her by the elbow and demanded to speak to her.

'I'm sorry, I'm very busy,' she said, and headed out of the door. He followed.

'Ms Sawyer, I won't take up a moment of your time.'

'You've taken two already,' Claire said, heading for her car. He kept following.

'I really must have a word.'

'OK. I'll give you two for the price of one,' said Claire, opening the car door. 'The second one is "off" and I'm sure you can hazard a guess at the other.'

To her astonishment he opened the door on the other side of the car and sat down in the passenger seat. 'I'm not leaving until we talk,' he said.

'You're leaving before I call the police,' Claire told him,

impressed in spite of herself at the stranger's chutzpah. 'You might be a serial killer.'

'Do I look like a serial killer?' he asked.

She looked at him. He wore horn-rimmed glasses, had short dark hair with a few flecks of grey and was fairly pleasant-faced. He was, however, wearing a rather unfortunate checked shirt and socks with sandals. 'No,' she admitted. 'But you do dress like one.'

'I'm a doctor,' he said.

'So was Jack the Ripper, allegedly. Out.'

'Ms Sawyer, I'm a doctor of politics – PhD. I don't have any specific knowledge of anatomy. I could probably just about tell your pancreas from your earlobe but that's it.'

'So you're single then?'

He bit his lip, stifling a laugh, then grinned. Nice enough smile. 'That's quite funny,' he said.

'Are you going to get out of my car?' she asked, looking at her watch. She needed to get going in time to be back to beat the rush hour.

'I really do need to have a word.'

'Fine,' Claire started the engine. 'Don't try anything funny. I have a brown belt in judo and I'll tie you in fucking bows if you do. What's your name, anyway?'

'Graham,' he said. 'Nice to meet you . . .?' He paused and waited as if wanting to be let in on first-name terms. Somehow he did so in such an endearingly pathetic way that she found herself telling him her first-name, although he must have known it anyway. She had no idea why she'd allowed him in her car or put them on first-name terms. He was horribly dressed, would be distinctly unpresentable in any of her favourite restaurants and he would probably insist on talking about politics all the time. And his name was Graham. Graham!

His eyes were brown and the lashes were very dark – almost jet black. His smile engendered a strange mix of pity and amusement.

'So, Graham – are you going to tell me what this is all about?' asked Claire, giving herself a brisk mental shake-down. She lit up a cigarette. He had the temerity to cough and she glared at him.

'Sorry ... sorry,' he said. 'It's your car, of course. May I open a window?'

'You may open the door and hurl yourself out if you don't tell me what this is about. And yes. Open a window if it bothers you.'

'Thank you.' He opened the window a fraction. 'Well, what it is, I need to speak to you on a rather sensitive matter.'

'Fire away,' said Claire, opening her own window and shouting at an idiot blocking the traffic. 'Come on! Park, you wanker! You could get a fucking bus in that space! Sorry, you were saying?'

He looked appallingly diffident again. She wished he wouldn't do that. For some strange reason the look reminded her of her mother's favourite cat, Squishy – the look he'd give when chastised for some feline misde-meanour, and it brought with it the same odd desire to cuddle.

'Sorry,' she found herself saying. 'I'm not really known for my sensitivity. Carry on.'

He swallowed and his Adam's apple bobbed above the collar of his awful shirt. His throat was dark and stubbly and a tuft of chest hair peeked out of his shirt collar. 'Well ... it's like this. I'm missing one of my students. He hasn't been to his tutorials for two weeks now.'

'Take it up with the Dean,' said Claire. 'I left university years ago.'

'Oh really? Where?'

'London School of Economics. Bachelor's. And don't look at me like that.'

'Like what?' he asked, ingenuously and maybe a little flirtatiously.

'Like economics isn't a proper degree. Politics is just market forces with a dash of ideology, and less of the ideology these days.'

Graham smiled. 'James was always arguing that. He's the one who's missing, by the way. James Bowden. He said if I had any problems with his increasingly poor attendance I should contact you.'

'Did he really?' said Claire. 'The little shit. And yes, I have your student. He's taking part in an experiment.'

Graham looked wildly startled.

'Drag your mind out of the gutter,' Claire told him. 'It's nothing like that. I find him about as sexually appetising as tofu. Really not my type.'

'And what is your type?' he asked. He was definitely flirting. How bizarre.

'Sweaty,' said Claire, looking slyly at him in the rear-view mirror and enunciating the word carefully. 'Earthy. Hairy. Preferably anonymous.'

'So you often have strange men in your car?'

'Frequently, yes,' she said, crisply, trying not to look down at his crotch. 'And you're not strange enough.'

'You really should be more careful,' he said, with a subtle air of unexpected menace that made her forget the sandals, forget that his name was Graham and focus entirely on where his chest hair might have ended. She tapped her finger on the steering wheel in rhythm with the blink of the indicator light as she waited to turn off onto the motorway, slowing her thoughts with the steady tap, tap, tapping. It would be too easy to find a secluded lay-by surrounded by trees, crawl into the back-seat and do it right there, like teenagers desperately seeking privacy. She kept imagining fumbling up the front of his shirt, tearing open his fly – hairy belly and a thick red cock bristling with bushy, jet-black pubic hair. It would be quick and rough because of the titillating risk of getting caught and she knew she'd come hard and fast – excited by the insanity of it, rubbed raw with rough hair.

'I think I can handle myself,' she said.

'I'm sure you can.' The cuddly-cat demeanour was back in place. 'Where on earth are you going anyway?'

'Wiltshire. Just outside Amesbury.'

'Wiltshire?' He stared. 'I can't go to Wiltshire! How the hell am I going to get home?'

'Well, you should ask strange women if they plan on driving to Stonehenge before you get into cars with them, shouldn't you?' Claire told him. 'I'll drop you off at the next service station.'

'But what about James?'

'What about him?'

'You can't just abduct my students in order to experiment on them just because you feel like it. What form does this experiment take?'

'A socially relevant insight into the nature of celebrity culture,' Claire said, glibly, reeling off a phrase from Tosh. 'James wants to be famous and I'm going to make him famous.'

'Famous for what?' asked Graham.

'Absolutely nothing. That's the point.'

Graham frowned. 'Why?'

'Because I can.'

'That's unethical.'

'No it isn't. He's an adult. He's agreed to put himself in my hands. Nothing is being done to the boy that he hasn't consented to ... well, except for the haircut, maybe. Wasn't too happy about that, but I had legitimate concerns about headlice. I didn't want my flat crawling with the things.'

'He's in your flat?' asked Graham, sounding horrified.

'Of course. Why are you so concerned? You're not his father are you?'

'No.'

'You're not sleeping with him, are you?'

'No, I am bloody well not!' shouted Graham. 'How dare you! I'm not that way inclined and I do not sleep with my students. It violates all known teaching ethics – and the thing you're proposing to do with that boy is downright wrong. He's an extremely promising student and you're disrupting his education.'

Claire laughed and lit another cigarette. 'Bollocks to his education. There's no value in a decent education these days. The world's full of morons and you can't beat the fuckers, darling – they're too bloody ubiquitous – so you may as well scoop the grey matter out and enjoy the ride unimpaired.'

Graham shook his head incredulously. 'Who on earth are you? Mephistopheles in a Wonderbra?'

Claire stuck her boobs out. 'Correct on both counts,' she said, with a demonic grin as she pulled into the service station.

'You can't do this,' protested Graham. 'Look, I'll come to the point ... James's parents are extremely wealthy building contractors out in Dubai.'

Claire threw her head back and howled with laughter. 'Oh my God – so all that about the value of his precious education...'

'...was bollocks, yes.'

'You fucking shyster. I adore you!'

'His parents contribute significantly to the faculty. '

She wiped her eyes. 'Have you no morals?'

He looked pained. 'You've seen the state of university funding these days. We haven't been able to afford them since the late seventies.'

Claire handed him her card. 'We'll come to some arrangement. Call me.'

'It is a significant contribution,' he said, stepping out of the car.

'I'll see you all right. Don't you worry about that,' she promised. 'One way or the other.'

'The other?' he asked, peering through the car window.

'That's for me to know and you to find out, darling. Pleasure meeting you, but must dash.'

She hated to think she'd been rattled by the man. He was just wrong on so many counts. He probably thought of himself as an intellectual and Claire couldn't stand intellectuals. They had an annoying tendency to think too much. He wore frightful clothes and frightful shoes with such nonchalance that they looked as though they'd grown on him. The first thing she wanted to do was change him, and that was a no-no – because that way lay misery. That way lay the effort of making him presentable and the inevitable disappointment when the finished product wasn't perfect.

It was safer to run to Justin, who she knew was imperfect and ultimately disposable. She hadn't created him. She'd just found him and he'd come seeking representation as a means of getting into her pants, and the more she refused, the more he pushed.

She ended up being disappointed by his tepee. He didn't have one. The guests at the retreat stayed in turf-roofed, half-buried 'eco-lodges' that reminded Claire of hobbit burrows. There was a cosy little bunk, but no roaring fire and animal pelts.

'No messing,' she warned Justin. 'I'm only getting my own back for that dirty trick of yours with the lollipop. You had no right to leave me high and dry after all the filthy suggestions you've made over the past seven months.'

'High, maybe,' he said, looking infuriatingly smug as he pulled off his sweater. 'But you weren't dry.'

She wanted to tell him to shut up but she didn't want

to risk annoying him when she needed to get laid. She'd meant to screw him simply to demonstrate that she could if she wanted to, but that damn nutty professor had reminded her she had an itch that needed scratching.

It was probably indecorous to fantasise about a man while fucking an entirely different one, but Claire found herself drifting away if she allowed herself to remember that she was in bed with Justin Vercoe. She stared up at the curved wooden ceiling above the bunk and tried to concentrate on what he was doing between her thighs ('I give great head,' he'd said, before ducking down and slipping his tongue where it counted) but it didn't seem to do much for her. Justin had probably eaten so much executive pussy to get where he had that this was most likely his last-resort rehearsal technique.

Claire closed her eyes and tried to forget where she was. 'Shh...' she told Justin, whose theatrical grunts and moans of ecstasy were interfering with her concentration. 'I like it quiet.'

She knew he'd do it, because he always did as he was told. With him silent she could concentrate on the wet, delicious licking noises he was making between her legs and imagine herself back in her car.

Back in her car with Doctor Geek.

Do you often have strange men in your car? You should be more careful.

Coulda, shoulda, woulda, Doctor – and let's face it, careful is so bloody *boring*.

Skirt up, knickers off in a lay-by. He'd have to take off his glasses, fold his awkward long legs up to get down on the floor, get his face between her thighs ... get down and dirty down there, lapping and slurping, face squished in her crotch by the cramped surroundings, so crammed that her juices slid down his chin and loving it like the furtive pervert he was.

Struggling to bring his fingers up and stuff two,

maybe three, inside her, giving her something to clench her muscles against. Oh yeah – that was it. She could feel it coming on, contracting and rippling in slow waves as he ate her. Right there. Oh yes, oh yes.

'OH YES!' It was so good her hips came off the bed once, twice, three times. She shuddered and had to wriggle away when the sensations became too intense.

Jesus. Fucking hell. Her heart thundered. Her mouth was dry. That dirty, dirty bastard. It was always the quiet ones.

'Told you I gave great head,' said Justin, smugly.

She didn't have the heart to tell him.

6

When James asked why on earth he would need to go to a fashion show, Claire told him to think of it as a practical examination and to shut up. Santosh was less brusque, as usual.

'Think of it as a test of your knowledge. Like, which model is which designer's muse; who she's going out with. I think that's the kind of thing that's important, isn't it?'

He liked Santosh more than Claire, which wasn't difficult. He liked most people more than Claire. If her idea of a celebrity lifestyle was sitting on one's arse watching E! or MTV or running on the treadmill watching E! or MTV then she could stick it up her bum, because he was bored witless. He was almost looking forward to the fashion show that afternoon just to provide a change of scenery.

In Claire's absence, James rattled around the oversize flat like a piece of loose change in a large pocket. To amuse himself he sometimes nosed through her bookshelves in search of a diary or a secret stash of porn, or jumped on her bed like a little kid expressing defiance in the only way it knew how. It was out of boredom that he found his way to her bedside drawer, knowing that if he was going to find anything incriminating or pornographic it would be there.

She hadn't locked the drawer, so James pulled it open and hit paydirt. Inside was a jumble of batteries, a couple of dirty books and a large pink vibrator. He handled the thing gingerly by its base, aware that at some point it must have been inside her, because she definitely hadn't bought it for its aesthetic value. It was partly translucent and filled with what looked like pearl beads, and it had a sort of a prong thing that stuck up like two miniature fingers. It didn't look anything like a penis to him. He pressed a button and jumped at the noise it made. It buzzed loudly and the finger-things quivered in mid air. The shaft remained stationary. James's mind took a sudden logistical lurch and he realised where the finger-things would be if the shaft was inserted. Right. Clitoris.

Did she even have one? She must have. It was just hard to imagine her with anything but welded-on titanium knickers. She did have nice tits though. They usually stuck out in the cups of her bra, looking like they could overbalance her sway-backed, high-heeled posture altogether and topple her flat on her face, but he'd seen her in the morning before she'd got the armour-plated bra on. Her boobs dropped slightly under their own weight beneath her dressing gown and, if it was cold, as the mornings frequently were, her nipples were stiff and clearly visible under her clothes.

He'd caught glimpses when she leaned over the kitchen table to grab her morning coffee, but it didn't really register. Her relationship to him was as such that it was like looking at your mum's tits. He found it impossible to imagine her using the vibrator, even though the evidence was right there buzzing in his face. He pressed another button and the top end of the shaft began to squirm and wriggle in a way that made him giggle incredulously.

If there was a man on the planet who could do *that* with his dick then he'd make a fortune in a freak show. If Claire liked this then it was no wonder she was single. There was no human male who could measure up to Mr Plastic Fantastic's tricks.

He wished he could have stayed with Santosh, but

apparently her place was too small. He much preferred her to Claire. She was all angles where Claire was all curves, as if her lean, efficient body had no desire to waste skin on excessive ornamental flesh. Sometimes she would complain of being pushed for space and come round to do her yoga exercises on Claire's balcony.

'It's freezing out there,' James had said, thinking her mad for going outside barefoot in tracksuit bottoms and a tank top.

'Self denial,' she'd said, wryly. 'Does you good – or so I'm told.'

She was surprisingly muscular, but not in the way James was becoming muscular – buffed and toned at the gym in order to be more pleasing to the eye. Hers were the muscles developed by lumping heavy camera equipment over inhospitable terrain in search of the perfect story. It wasn't vanity that kept her fit, she insisted, in her self-effacing way. It was just a general disquiet that set in if she didn't feel as though her body was her ally.

'Can you get your feet behind your head?' James had asked, jokingly.

'Yeah,' she'd said, with a sigh and not a trace of humour. 'But I can't put a shelf up for toffee. Go figure.'

He liked to watch her exercise. She would stand in the cold, breath freezing and nipples pebbled under her top, arms impossibly twined, fingertips perfectly aligned, balancing on one bare foot with the icy concrete no doubt managing to sting through her yoga mat. When she bent over he'd seen that she had a tattoo of a snake eating its tail at the base of her spine. She said she thought it was a symbol from Norse mythology but couldn't be sure because not enough people had seen it to comment and it was probably significant to a whole bunch of other cultures too.

Whenever Claire caught him watching she would tell

him to stop staring so sharply that he wondered about the nature of their relationship. Santosh slept in Claire's bed if she stayed over, but that might have been due to James's continuing occupancy of the spare room. Besides, the bed was big enough to sleep three and Claire called everyone darling regardless of how long she'd known them for. He simply didn't know, although he thought it would be typical of his luck to be adopted by a couple of hardcore lesbians who wouldn't let him watch. Couldn't do without something like a dick though, he thought, smirking as he navigated the control panel and shut the vibrator off. He wondered if Natalie had one.

He doubted it. For all her hypocritical claptrap she probably still believed in white weddings and perfect handsome husbands whose cousins had been to Harrow. If James ever slipped a squirmy pink plastic monster like Claire's best friend up under her houndstooth skirt, Natalie would probably spontaneously combust. She'd clamp a hand over her mouth to keep from screaming as she came like never before – skirt round her waist, hair mussed out of place, hips slamming up and down in search of the perfect sensation. James rather relished the image.

He replaced the vibrator in the drawer, carefully closing it to replicate the slight angle at which it had hung open when he opened it, and smoothed down the bed where he'd sat before returning to the couch to watch MTV according to instructions.

He found he couldn't watch TV without thinking of the vibrator, as if it had poked its head into the prior Eden like a pink plastic serpent. It was impossible to watch the gyrations of some bubblegum pop princess without imagining her playing with herself. She had a pleasant, dumb, pretty little face, glossed lips gaping like those of a sex doll as she lip-synched the wails and whoa whoa whoas of her latest hit. She was just tits, teeth, hair and prefabricated purity – a wide-eyed slice of American pie fresh from a clapboard church somewhere in the Bible Belt, a fragile adolescent in her early twenties. He knew for a fact that she was three years older than he was and no more a teenager than her ten-year-old fans.

She was a total fake. He would be willing to bet she had an entire weapon's rack full of sex toys hidden behind the dolls and teddy bears that probably crowded her pink, lacy bed. She probably really craved black leather instead of blue gingham – kissed her daddy goodnight and went up to her bedroom to fantasise wildly about PVC boots that were strapped all the way up to the tops of her shiny tan thighs and corsets that pushed her breasts up so high the nipples popped out over the top.

Dirty little bitch. She had probably eaten out every one of her cheerleading colleagues in high school. Never mind a human pyramid. He imagined that those cookie-cutter freckle-nosed blondes could arrange themselves to form one huge simultaneous female orgasm, each one working on the next in a human chain of sticky fingers, moans, groans and toned bottoms bouncing under tiny pleated skirts.

He didn't think that this was the kind of thing he was supposed to be thinking about while watching these videos. After all, they marketed these girls to be cleaner and sweeter than Bambi, but James thought you'd have to be blind or a eunuch to miss the teasing, transgressive sexual message underneath the wholesome gloss of shiny white teeth, shiny blonde hair and jostling smooth-skinned boobs. Obviously the svengalis had thought about this and made a point of covertly capital-ising on it – a dirty trick but one that Claire would have bitched about and dissected in detail before admitting that you couldn't help but be impressed. He thought he was getting good at spotting fakes.

Just as Little Miss Purity was probably a secret lesbian SM queen, the multi-pierced baby rock goddess wearing nothing but a few strips of leather and her tattoos probably spoke to her mother on the phone daily and knew how to make an apple pie from scratch. The lady-lovin' Latino crooning to a swooning bevy of housewives was either gay or the bulge in his tight trousers was ninety per cent sock and ten per cent penis. The tattooed gangsta rapper flexing polished pecs all over the screen may well have been from the hood, but the hood in question was more likely Beverly Hills than South Central.

James flicked through the channels, feeling bored and horny. That in itself was nothing unusual. He'd seen the same videos time after time. They seemed to be on a permanent loop, interspersed with congratulatory celebrity profiles and the painful at-home reality shows of pop stars convinced that they were interesting enough to be the next Osbournes. When the boredom became too severe he'd end up abusing himself in the bathtub and thinking that this must be how you became a celebrity – by cultivating a nice empty mind and an overactive dick.

He peered at the screen with a jaded eye when he heard a dirty guitar riff he recognised as one of his mother's favourite songs – 'Twentieth Century Boy'. Great. Another insipid cover version of ancient crap.

But then he looked twice.

It was Fred Hill, prowling with an air of mischievous menace through an abandoned and half-demolished sky-scraper in New York. He was dressed in an outfit remi-niscent of a gothic circus ringmaster, swinging a cane like a pimp and flashing a predatory gold-toothed grin straight into the camera. His weird grey eyes were crazed with eyeliner and silver glitter, staring out from under the brim of his battered black top hat like the eyes of an alley cat peeking from beneath the lid of a trashcan.

This was new. This was interesting.

The scene cut between the skyscraper and a New York penthouse, where a woman was rolling out of a tangled, rumpled bed of white linen. She wore plain white knickers and a vest top and stalked through her apartment on fashion model long legs before the director saw fit to reveal her face via the bathroom mirror.

Right. It would have had to be her – Zoe Luscombe, Fred's supermodel girlfriend, the latest face of Dupois. She stuck her tongue out at her reflection, scruffed up her short blonde hair and rubbed bleary eyes.

The music was grinding now, pounding its way up to the first big hook. Fred was moving in time with it, like something being wound up to spring loose, approaching a girl who looked like she'd roamed into the abandoned building by mistake. She was as dark-haired and feminine as Zoe was fair and tomboyish – a tiny curvy girl with large lustrous brown eyes, olive skin and a silky sheet of jet-black hair falling past her shoulders. She was dressed in the outfit of an American Catholic schoolgirl – long socks, plaid skirt and school tie.

Fred crept up behind her. She whirled around and he was gone. She turned back and there he was, twirling his pimp stick and smirking at her. She sneered, held up one hand in a *Jerry Springer Show* gesture and walked away, flicking her long black hair. He followed, pleading and cajoling, until she consented to listen and he whispered something to her that made her huge eyes widen further and her hand fly up to cover her gaping lips.

The song thundered into the hook as Zoe Luscombe joyfully trashed her bathroom and bedroom and flung all her clothes out of the apartment window. Designer dresses, sequinned wraps and lacy lingerie fluttered down on to the streets of New York like confetti. A traffic cop caught a pair of her knickers – a tiny black thong with an arrow-pierced heart on the front. Zoe laughed at his perplexed expression, blew him a kiss with pouting lips and turned on her heel to face the interior of her apartment. The smile on her face softened into one far more dirty and knowing and she ran her tongue over her lower lip. The camera panned back and revealed that she was looking at a tailor's dummy with a full-length mirror next to it. The dummy was wearing a beautifully cut man's three-piece suit. Zoe was looking at that suit like it was already filled with the most gorgeous man on the planet.

James knew what was coming and squirmed in anticipation. Fred was dancing with the schoolgirl, who was shaking it on down to the band. She flung her arms above her head, swung her glossy hair and gyrated slender hips so that her skirt rode higher and flashed tan thighs. She turned her back to Fred and shimmied in front of him, peeringly slyly at him from the corners of her dark eyes.

'She is unbelievable,' James muttered to himself. She looked to be Spanish or Mexican or something Latin – all gleaming brown eyes and glossy black hair. She moved fluidly and elastically, her small, pert arse shaking the short plaid skirt this way and that.

Zoe was dressing up in her apartment – binding down what little breasts she had, stuffing rolled up handkerchiefs down her knickers to pad out the front of her trousers. The suit fitted her like a second skin, the way a good suit should. The waistcoat fitted her so sleekly that the line of her front invited the same desire to stroke as the bared belly of a submissive cat. When she slipped on the padded-shouldered jacket and buttoned it over the waistcoat she looked like a Wildean wet dream – an exquisite boy in beautiful clothes, with spiky gold hair that curled over her scalp like the petals of a chrysanthemum. She straightened her collar with studied masculine arrogance, brushed her lapels and stepped out of the apartment. The maid cleaning the hallway, a teenage soubrette in a pink uniform, stared lustfully at her as she walked down the hall. Zoe faced her as she stepped into the elevator and winked boldly. As the elevator doors closed, the maid fluttered, flushed and fanned herself with her feather duster.

'Shit,' moaned James, lighting a cigarette. He'd been hoping she was going to make out with the maid but Zoe was off and out, climbing into a limo outside the building.

Fred was completing his seduction of the schoolgirl. He handed her a Polaroid picture of Zoe in her full male drag and whispered in her ear once more. She nodded and offered her cheek for a kiss, but he cupped her chin, turned her face to his and devoured her. When she could breathe again she caught her breath in a long silent sigh, dark hair streaming back from her upturned face, Fred's hand creeping up under her skirt. She seemed to pull herself together then and slapped his hand away before walking away and out of the building.

This was completely new – like nothing Shade had ever done before. It was theatrical and playful and blatantly sexual, as opposed to their previous sixth-form moodiness. The band looked sidelined and Fred looked to be in his element, fondling young girls in a way that would no doubt scandalise armchair moralists on both sides of the Atlantic. James found himself loving it – adrenaline pumping from the punked-out grubby sound of the music, his eyes glued to the tan flash of the schoolgirl's legs as she strode down a New York street.

She turned as a limo passed her on the street, twirling on her sensible heel and staring at the vehicle as it stopped at a red light. She furtively checked the Polaroid she was holding and waited, legs apart, hand on hip – more like a hooker than a good Catholic girl. Maybe that was what she was supposed to be – part of a game between Fred and Zoe – a whore he'd dressed up to bait her. James leaned forwards on the couch, eagerly anticipating a bit of girl-on-girl action.

He wasn't disappointed. Zoe stuck her blonde chrysanthemum head out of the window of the limo. She made an incredibly convincing boy with her gangling height and chiselled face, but there was enough femininity in her enormous brown eyes and sumptuously large, curving lips to give her a sleek, androgynous look that perversely made her even more beautiful as a male.

She beckoned to the schoolgirl. The schoolgirl baulked for a moment before climbing into the limo (there would be letters to the newspapers about this and no mistake) and settled herself on the black leather seat opposite Zoe, crossing her long legs while she accepted a glass of champagne.

How much was she supposed to know? While she flirted and flashed her legs and flicked her hair was she supposed to think that Zoe was a man, never suspecting that instead of a dick hardening for her inside that suit there was a moistening, melting pussy? James bit his lip, thinking of the ways they might discover one another, fingers straying into pin-striped trousers and up skirts, touching on the punchline of the joke they were unwittingly playing on one another. It had to be soon, because they had stopped flirting and they were close to one another in the back of the limo. James forgot to breathe, his cigarette smouldering down to the butt in the ashtray, watching them move closer and closer. Were they really going to kiss?

'Oh ... my ... God ...'

The two women kissed. It was a deep wet kiss with

long slow swirls of tongue but it didn't look staged the way the attention-seeking kisses of college girls sometimes did.

But whatever was going on in the back of that limo, those girls were not messing around. They looked like they were into it, into each other, until the schoolgirl's hand reached for Zoe's crotch and was pushed away quickly while Zoe adopted the diversionary tactic of unbuttoning the schoolgirl's blouse. The Polaroid tumbled to the floor and Zoe spotted it, picked it up and frowned. The schoolgirl laughed, shrugged and continued to unbutton her blouse. Zoe shouted something at her, waving the Polaroid and reached angrily for the girl's hair.

In the tussle it came away in her hand – the whole head of hair. Underneath it was a short spiky black crop. The girl's blouse had come wide open and she was lying back panting on the seat of the limo, her padded bra revealing the extent of her deception. She couldn't be! That would mean that *Fred Hill had kissed a boy*, and that was never going to happen in this universe. She just couldn't be.

But she was. She took off the bra and instead of breasts was a lightly muscled boy's chest, flat and smooth with tan nipples. Zoe stared with something between lust and shock before pulling the handkerchief out of her pants like a magician producing a silk cloth from his sleeve and the whole deception unravelled. She smiled, softened, and produced a camera-phone from her pocket, waved it suggestively and then pounced on the boy in the schoolgirl's outfit as the music ended.

'That is the coolest video ever,' James found himself saying aloud, in Beavis and Butthead tones.

But there was more. One more shot. Fred was still in the abandoned building, quiet now that the band had stopped playing. He removed his hat and ran a hand through his messy black hair, loosening his collar in a way so as to suggest that he was now off duty – show's over, guys. Someone had just left the camera running. His phone beeped and he opened it up, looked at what was coming through and stared at the image the viewer was only allowed to guess at. It was kind of obvious what the revelation was – Fred realised he'd kissed a boy, stitched up at his own gender-bending game.

His fingers stole unconsciously to his lips and into his mouth, and he looked up as if seeing the camera on his face for the first time. His pale, hueless eyes gleamed and he smiled slightly around the fingertip caught between his teeth – as if he knew what he'd done and he'd liked it, loved it. The image faded to black.

James stared at the screen for a few more minutes, not processing the bland R&B video that followed. Fred Hill had kissed a boy – the big rock star, wet dream of millions of teenage girls. He'd kissed a boy and not been threatened by it. That seemed like the bravest, coolest thing James had ever seen in his life and it continued to jangle his nerves and his balls even when Claire came in in her customary fug of cigarette smoke, demanding to know if he was ready to go to the show.

James tried to follow instructions. He tried to walk with the false confidence Claire had tried to instil in him and look as though he belonged at a fashion show but he didn't see why he should mingle with a bunch of squawking soap opera actresses.

'Sooner or later you're going to need a famous girl-friend,' Claire insisted.

'Girlfriend?' James asked, avoiding the actresses and following Claire to their seats on the other side of the catwalk.

'Just for the cameras, darling.'

'Good. I was just about to tell you I wouldn't fuck any of them.'

She stared balefully at him. 'Why are you so horrible?'

James bared his newly fixed teeth in a humourless grin. 'Monkey see, monkey do.'

Claire shook her head. 'You can't afford to be picky. And lose the attitude before you lose your favourite organs.'

The lights went down and the room went black for an age before spotlights began to dance up and down the darkened catwalk and a voice boomed from a PA: '*Madames et messieurs, je me presente ... la collection de Jacques Dupois.*'

'Are we in fucking Paris?' whispered James, already feeling nauseous at the pretension of it.

'Shut up and try not to wank,' hissed Claire, kicking him hard in the ankle.

'Fine. Whatever.'

Wanking was the last thing on his mind when the drum beat started, slow and accompanied by a single whiny Arabian flute. He didn't know what the designer was going for with the theme of his collection – Moroccan or Arabian or something eclectically exotic that bore no relation to the East that James knew. The drum pounded steadily and the spotlight lit a single crouched dancer who must have shuffled onto the stage in the dark. The androgynous figure was barefoot and appeared to be wearing nothing more than a layer of gold and blue bodypaint applied to look like a mosaic.

When the head snapped up in a sharp, stylised movement designed to accompany a crashing beat of the drum, he saw that it was a woman, her small, narrow face painted gold and her golden-green eyes ferocious with thick rings of black kohl. She uncurled from her pose so sharply that James had difficulty training his eyes on her breasts and crotch to ascertain whether or not she was wearing anything at all, but as she began to pirouette with the effortless ease of a professional dancer he saw something like a thin belt of gold threads flaring out at her waist above a tightly moulded pair of gold pants. Something Greek, maybe. He would have consulted his brochure but it was too dark and the fucking thing had been printed in French anyway, so he had no idea what constituted the inspiration for this display.

The dancer whirled around before snapping to a standstill, one foot slightly ahead of the other, back arched, small breasts thrown out and straining under a tight wrap of gold fabric. As she threw her arms up above her head she was suddenly surrounded by other dancers, dressed the same, whirling onto the stage with flaming torches in hand. The dancer stretched out her arms and caught a torch from two of her comrades, then she tipped back her head and swallowed the flames one by one. James thought he heard the audience gasp for a moment before they remembered they were not supposed to be easily impressed and gave forth with scattered applause.

She breathed fire back at them.

She was fantastic. What kind of woman would teach herself to play with fire like that? He thought she must be some kind of hardcore adrenaline junkie, the kind of girl who liked her thrills larger than life and twice as crazy. He was sorry when she left the stage. The models were nothing compared to her – skinny women with legs like flamingos and faces like outrageously painted china dolls, fleshless bodies artistically draped in clothes that no sane person would dream of wearing in public.

The audience were applauding a preposterous gown composed entirely of looped gold threads that barely covered the malnourished body of the model and James wondered why, then he looked again and realised that they weren't applauding the dress. They were applauding the model. It was Zoe Luscombe.

She was almost unrecognisable under an elaborate bejewelled headdress of turquoises and gold wire, but when she turned and faced them it was unquestionably her, with the huge brown eyes, high forehead and with her trademark pout painted a bizarre burgundy red.

'Is that . . .?'

'Yep,' said Claire. 'My God. What is she wearing?'

'I thought haute couture was meant to look stupid,' whispered James, as Zoe Luscombe stalked backstage whence she'd came. 'I can't believe it though. It's really her. I was watching her on TV a few hours ago.'

Claire shook her head and pushed a blonde bang out of her eyes. 'James, when I said celebrity girlfriend I did mean for you to be slightly realistic, you know.'

'Oh, I know that,' said James. 'Anyway, she's going out with Fred Hill.'

Claire bestowed a dazzling smile on him in the near darkness and, to his intense horror, James found himself basking in the glow of her approval. It was probably because it was so hard-earned and rare, he told himself.

'I can't get you an audience with Zoe,' said Claire. 'But it is nearly time to duck backstage.'

'I thought we were watching the show?'

She leaned close and whispered in his ear. 'Darling, it's not really about the show,' she said, conspiratorially, her voice gravelly as she breathed smoky breath on his face. For the first time he thought he could like her and enjoy being her partner in this scam she perpetuated on a daily basis. She flourished two small laminated cards under his nose. 'It's all about the backstage passes.'

James adjusted his glasses and leaned in. 'Free handbags?'

'And shoes,' Claire said, promptly. 'Don't ever forget

the shoes. I *must* have those strappy gold sandals with the turquoises.'

'I'm at the mercy of your Imelda Marcos instincts.'

'You'd better believe it, baby,' said Claire, shifting in her seat and eyeing the exit.

They were just about to leave when there was another gasp from the audience, this time not as well suppressed as the last one. James looked back at the catwalk to see if the fire-eating girl had come back, but had to look twice to ascertain if he really was seeing what he was seeing.

Zoe Luscombe had just walked down the catwalk. She was wearing a pair of bejewelled, knee-length, high-heeled boots, an absurd gilded Afro wig and nothing else.

There wasn't much to look at because her breasts were starvation-sized and her pubic hair had been shaved to a thin strip of short brown fuzz, but it was the fact that it was Zoe Luscombe – one of the most highly paid models on the planet, girlfriend of rock stars, five times cover girl of *Vogue* – and she was totally naked.

'Oh my God,' he said, slowly.

She strode down the catwalk as though she was oblivious to her nudity – strode, stopped, turned and posed with legs apart so that the tantalising sliver of pink flesh between her legs would make the inside of the more daring magazines for the next fortnight and all over the internet before the sun had set that night.

The audience didn't know what to do. Some applauded, some heckled and booed and some preserved a tight-lipped silence. Claire let rip with her loudest, witchiest smoky cackle. 'Talk about the emperor's new clothes!' she laughed, grabbing James by the hand and dashing for the backstage exit. 'Or pussy in boots!'

Both phrases would be all over the tabloids the next

morning, along with typical red top headlines like LUSCIOUS LUSCOMBE BARES ALL!, complete with photographs of Zoe's nether regions discreetly covered with a star or the face of a cat. Tits were fair game, particularly famous tits, but genitals were still off limits. James didn't think he had ever laughed so hard in his life. As vile as Claire could be, he had to admire her turn of phrase, especially when her wit wasn't aimed at him.

Backstage was uproar. The place reeked of stale cigarette smoke and flat champagne. There were models everywhere in various stages of undress, elbowing their way past in the cramped spaces between clothes rails. Make-up artists were applying glitter to partially bared breasts, dressers kneeling and pinning frantically, melted ice buckets everywhere containing bouquets of hothouse flowers, hairdressers fitting wigs and hairpieces. In the midst of it all, Jacques Dupois was busy having an enormous nervous breakdown.

James didn't speak French but like all adolescent boys he had seen *Betty Blue* enough times to know words like '*putaine*' and '*salope*'. The designer was being held down by two of his assistants as Zoe wriggled into a dressing gown and shouted over him in a didactic, sing-song voice.

'I did tell you how I felt about the fur, didn't I? You should have listened to me. I have fucking principles, you silly little man! '

'Ohhhh, it was an animal rights thing?' said Claire, butting in quite unabashedly. 'You see, I think it would have been better if you put the logo of the organisation across your arse or something, preferably in blood. Don't need to shed any – just find a good butcher.'

Zoe Luscombe had been in the process of lighting a cigarette with an almost post-coital air when Claire launched into a monologue. While Claire spoke Zoe's expression changed from one of angry incredulity and, by the time she had finished, Zoe was looking at her with something akin to admiration.

'Who the fuck are you?' asked Zoe.

'Claire Sawyer. CSPR. My card,' Claire rattled out and handed her the card. Zoe took it as if hypnotised before being hustled into her next costume change. 'Marvellous taco show all the same,' Claire added, out of earshot.

'Stay away from that bitch!' screamed Jacques Dupois, launching himself at Claire. 'She will contaminate you, poison you. My God, how that cunt hates me, *cherie* – I book her because she is big business, but she is fucking poison. She is arsenic, she is cyanide.'

Claire consoled him in French that was not only surprisingly fluent but, even more surprisingly, quite sexy. In English she just sounded like a chain-smoking harpy, but French sat smokily on her tongue. 'Champagne! *Depeche toi*!' she snapped at the assistants, before going returning to Jacques in English. 'Have a drink, darling. Have some champagne. You *deserve* it. You've done so very, very well.'

'I have no time!' Jacques ushered several more models on stage with panicked gestures and Claire quickly turned to James.

Her eyes were shining. 'I don't know how and I don't know why, but you're good luck,' she said, excitedly. 'Go and mingle – have fun. I'm on a roll.'

'Mingle?' asked James.

'Yes. Yes. Mingle, darling. Mingle. Find a drink, find a joint, don't talk about politics whatever you do and keep out of the models' way. Look, you're nineteen years old, you're adrift in a sea of tits and arse and there's bound to be some good drugs around here somewhere. These models don't live on food, you know. Go on. You'll love it.'

'But . . .'

'All right . . .' said Claire, one eye still on Dupois. 'Few simple instructions, OK? If there's any smack around here, don't touch it. Avoid the ecstasy because it's all cut with ketamine these days and I'm buggered if I'm dragging you out of here spun out and seeing aliens, all right? And try not to fuck anyone famous ... yet. OK? Darling, I *must* speak to Jacques. If I can bag him then Zoe will be a pushover.'

James sighed, shrugged and headed off in search of a drink. Tits and arse? What tits and arse? The models were so emaciated that tits and arse were in short supply and they were all so tall that as he made his way through them he felt like he was navigating his way through a forest of giraffes.

Behind a mass of clothes rails was a trestle table laden with bottles of champagne, which he assumed was a makeshift bar. A slim black girl wearing jeans and a sweatshirt was stuffing bottles into a rucksack. She stared defiantly at him when he looked at her.

'What?' she said, in a cockney accent. 'It's free, innit? So I'm not nicking it or nothing.'

She had tightly braided hair that glittered with some kind of gold spray and her narrow, wedge-shaped face looked shiny, as though it had recently been scrubbed bare of make-up. She'd missed some of her eyeliner, which smudgily accentuated her golden-green eyes.

'It's you!' James said, recognising her.

'Uh ... yeah.' She discreetly tucked the rucksack under the table and frowned, biting the inside of her cheek as she looked at him, puzzled.

'You're the fire-eater,' James explained. 'I really ... I liked you. I mean, I liked your ... thing. You know?'

Her face gave way to a slow smile, which broadened and broadened until she couldn't seem to hold back any more and started to laugh. Her laugh was loud, unrestrained and kind of demented-sounding, but she stopped quickly when she saw the consternation on his face.

'Sorry – I wasn't laughing at you, mate. It was just funny. You liked my thing.' She bent down to pick up the rucksack. 'I've got more than one, actually.'

'Yeah. I noticed.'

She looked up at him, her smile mischievous. 'So it was about thingies?' she asked. 'Because if you want to lay all that crap on me about respecting me as an artist then you can find someone else to have a spliff with.'

'They're very nice ... thingies,' he said, laughing as if he was stoned already. 'Not that the fire-eating thing wasn't amazing or anything, but yeah – thumbs up on the thingies. It's all good.'

She grinned and swigged from an open bottle of champagne. 'Want a smoke?'

'Sure. As long as you've got a light.'

She giggled. 'Oh, you're funny,' she said, laconically. 'What's a place like this doing in boy like you?' She beckoned him through a fire-door and they sneaked out back into the cold.

'I'm sort of working for a PR firm,' he said. 'Sort of. I suppose you could say I am kind of an assistant or something.'

'Boy Friday?' she asked, lighting up a joint. 'That sounds like a right fuckin' laugh. Not. You should see what they're paying *me*.'

'Bad?' asked James, sympathetically.

'Pants,' she said, blowing out smoke and handing him the joint. 'Total pants. Less than the price of one of Jacques's fancy handbags, so I thought I'd help myself to the Dom Perignon. It's only fair, innit? Who'd pay a fucking grand for a handbag?'

'A thousand quid?' James whistled. He struggled to

smoke the joint she'd given him. The stuff was strong and rough on the back of the throat.

'It's mad, innit?' the girl said, hugging herself in the cold. She was very pretty in an unconventional, gamine way. Had she been eight inches taller she might have been up there on the catwalk with the models but she was tiny, thin and, from what he'd seen of her on stage, all muscle. She had a watchful, wedge-shaped face made all the more catlike by her flat nose and the dip in the middle of her upper lip. With her green eyes and café-au-lait skin she looked as though she might have been part Caucasian, but he thought it would be rude to ask when he'd only just met her.

'You're smoking that like a girl,' she said, nodding at the joint in his hand. 'Gimme that. Want a blow-back?'

She took it from him and reversed it, cupping her tongue and hollowing her mouth as she put the burning end inside.

'You might burn my face off,' James said, making her laugh so that she had to take the joint out of her mouth to keep from scorching her tongue.

'I won't,' she said. 'Trust me. And don't make me fuckin' laugh, you bastard.'

She put the joint back in her mouth and leaned towards him. He sucked the smoke from her lips slowly – more easily now that the edge was taken off by the cooler air from her lungs. She smelled sweaty, smoky and boozy, with an oily make-up scent probably left over from the paint clinging to her hair and eyes. It was like kissing without touching lips, sharing breath. The drug crept smoothly into his bloodstream, loosening and relaxing his mind. Drugged with a not-quite kiss.

'Better?' she said, taking the joint from her mouth.

'Oh God – yeah,' he said, staring stupidly at her. He realised he didn't even know her name, so he asked.

'Phoenix,' she said.

'Phoenix?'

He must have sounded more incredulous than he meant to, because she looked defensively at him. 'My mum likes unusual names,' she said. 'Anyway – it's handy. Every time she has a go at me for playing with fire I tell her it's her own fault.'

7

'Baby, please – I'm dying here. I need a cocktail, a line, a fuck. Just anything like civilisation.'

'Stop right there,' Claire said, pacing her office. She'd been marching back and forth with the phone clamped to her ear for half an hour and her hair was sticking to her temples, her ear sweaty from the heat of the phone. 'I am neither an infant nor a moron, so don't imagine you can get round me by calling me baby. Just because I shagged you once in a tepee doesn't mean you have any influence over me whatsoever.'

'I can't handle this any more,' Justin pleaded. 'I'm appealing to you as a client.'

Assuming you were remotely appealing in the first place, Claire thought, lighting up a cigarette. He'd been OK, but nowhere near the sex god he imagined himself to be. She would have liked to have been fairer on him, admitting that her mind was on someone else while she was fucking him, but Justin's behaviour and over-inflated sexual confidence didn't make her inclined to be generous.

'I can't even open my mouth without having the talking stick. You know about talking sticks? If you don't have the stick you can't talk. It's like some form of New Age fascism.'

'Push the stick up your arse,' Claire advised. 'Then if anyone's got the nerve to extract it they'll know where it's been and they won't want to touch it, so you can talk to your heart's content. You might even get off on it.'

'PMS much?'

'It's just a suggestion, darling,' snapped Claire, realising she probably *was* premenstrual. 'Give yourself a pain in the arse like the one you give me. You know the deal. You detox or find a new representative. I've spelled this out time and time again and I've even driven down to Stone fucking Henge and sat on your dick to ram the point home, so do me a favour and shut the fuck up.'

She hung up with an almost sexual frisson of satisfaction. She should never have slept with Justin. She should have known that a whiny leech like him would be seeking every advantage he could gain from whatever relationship he imagined them to be having. Besides, he'd been pretty straightforward in the sleeping bag. The only way she had been able to get off at all was by thinking of Graham Mulholland, which was frankly bizarre. Maybe she had a subconscious sandal fetish or something. She couldn't even imagine him naked without the sandals entering the picture; Dr Mulholland walking around in nothing but socks, sandals and spectacles, smoking a pipe like some nudist refugee of the Summer of Love.

To distract herself she leafed through some photographs of James, who was shaping up nicely, very nicely indeed. She'd had a photographer in to get him accustomed to the camera and, although the kid was never going to be an Adonis, he had something, all right. His body looked a lot more sculpted with his shirt off and, when caught in the right light and pose, he had a little-boy-lost vulnerability that was kind of Rufus Wainwright.

She had elected to not tell Dr Mulholland because James would have gone all Tom Paine and delivered some emancipation proclamation about his human right not to be sold. Besides, she wasn't keen for anyone to know she even knew about Mulholland, never mind allowing anyone to know that the damn man had this annoying habit of crawling into her sexual fantasies and making a beast of himself.

The intercom buzzed and Donna spoke. 'Claire, got a Dr Mulholland on line one. No. Char, just *give* him the bloody sweets if he's playing up.'

'Sorry? What?'

'Oh, sorry – I was talking to my sister on my mobile. Dwayne's off nursery with earache and she's taking him to the doctor's.'

Claire lit another cigarette. Why the hell did all mothers assume that everyone found their fucking rugrats as interesting as they did? 'Donna, just take *me* to the doctor on line one, OK?'

Donna put her through.

'Doctor Mulholland – think of the devil.' She hadn't meant to sound provocative but she was choking slightly on an ill-advised gulp of cigarette smoke and she had been thinking about Graham Mulholland a lot lately. Either way, her voice sounded seductive to her own ears and a blatant advertisement to the sandal-abusing geek on the other end of the line that she'd been imagining him doing filthy, filthy things.

'Ah ... hello, Claire,' He said her name as if trying it out for size. 'You were thinking about me?'

'Yes.'

'That's very flattering – I hope, anyway.'

She laughed and he chuckled, sounded more relaxed.

'Do you often think about strange men when you're in the office?' he asked, playfully.

'Only when I'm alone.'

She hoped he would rise to the bait. She liked that slightly sinister vibe she had picked up from him the first time they met, but it had come and gone in a flash.

'Are you alone?' he asked.

'I'm alone,' Claire said, settling back in her chair. 'What can I do for you?'

'I wanted to thank you personally for the generous endowment.'

Claire tried to scrub her mind of the word associations that leapt to the fore. Personally. Generous. Endowment. They were grubby enough on their own but stuck together they assumed a dimension of double-entendre that wouldn't be out of place in a bad porn film.

'That's sweet of you,' she said. 'Sounds like a line from a movie I once saw.'

'Really? Which one was that?'

'*Stationery Cupboard Sluts II.*'

She could hear him trying not to laugh. 'No, I don't think I've ever seen that one.'

'I wouldn't bother if I were you.'

'Didn't live up to the promise of the original *Stationery Cupboard Sluts* then?'

'You know how it is with sequels. I think the slut in question was then asked to describe her underwear or something. No motivation. Very contrived.'

'Oh dear,' said Graham. 'There goes my next line then. I suppose I'll just have to ask you to have dinner with me, won't I?'

Claire sighed, disappointed. 'I'm booked solid for the next three weeks and whenever I do have an evening to myself I just end up flopping comatose in front of the television.'

'That's a pity.'

'I know,' she said, glancing through the slats of the blind into reception. Donna was still talking frenetically into her mobile, obviously briefing her sister on the best way to deal with an ailing sugar-crazed three-year-old who had the attention span of a goldfish with ADHD at the best of times. She'd be a while.

Claire drummed her fingers on the desk for a moment, listening to Graham breathing on the other end of the line. 'Of course,' she said, slowly. 'It's a long shot, but I could just save us time and energy by describing my underwear right now.'

Her heart thumped. She had nothing to lose if he freaked out, but her pulse was suddenly thudding in her ears nonetheless.

'I've never really understood the fascination, to be honest,' said Graham, quite coolly. 'Just flashy bits of lace that hamper a man's progress to the interesting parts of a woman.'

'If you were a real man you'd say that the most interesting part of a woman was her brain,' Claire countered, irritable at his rebuff.

'If I was a liar I'd say that the most interesting part of a woman was her brain. Men only say that to women in order to get somewhere else. What about lunch, if you're never free for dinner?'

'You're determined to feed me, aren't you?'

'That's generally the way one goes about things, isn't it?'

'What things?'

'Meeting women and all that.'

'We've met.'

'So we have. So what would you like to do?'

His voice was quiet and neutral again – the voice with the undertone of menace that kept permeating her dirtiest thoughts, issuing instructions. She wanted to tell him what she'd like to do. She wanted to tell him that she'd have been perfectly prepared to fuck him in the back of her car or that she imagined walking into his no doubt dingy little faculty office and taking her clothes off in front of him. She wanted to tell him how she imagined him stealing into her bedroom at night, crawling under the covers and telling her to kneel, bend over, spread her legs wider, but she couldn't. In the face of his chauvinistic candour she found herself, for the first time in her life, unable to confide her lusts to a near stranger.

'I can't tell you that,' she said.

'I thought you liked to tell strange men what you were thinking, Claire.'

She loved that flat, psychiatrist's tone of his. It didn't wheedle or plead like Justin's. She had become so expert in cutting through bullshit and hidden agendas over the years that it had become an exciting game to be played, but this infuriating man wasn't playing his part properly. The way he spoke to her was direct, polite, occasionally pushing her comfort zones out of nowhere so that it was slightly chilling and perversely exciting.

'I show, not tell,' said Claire. 'There's a difference.'

'Well, everything is easier with visual aids, isn't it?'

'I'll show you mine if you show me yours.'

'That's not going to be easy if you're never free, is it?'

'What a nuisance.'

'Yes.'

He left her hanging on that one word, leaving her waiting, impatient, determined to cut to the chase and tell him straight that she wanted him. She could have done it if he was there, demonstrated by guiding his hand to her breasts and letting nature take its course, but to *tell* him felt impossible. Every phrase that jumped into her head, all the 'Look, I really like you's and 'Maybe we should's sounded embarrassingly adolescent before they were even out of her mouth.

'Why did you call me?' asked Claire, irritated that she couldn't speak her mind for once. Her tongue – a well-sharpened and clever organ – had been at her beck and call since childhood and she couldn't understand for the life of her why the bloody thing had crapped out on her all of a sudden. 'Wasn't your endowment big enough?'

'It's sufficient. Enough to tide us over for the academic year.' No more endowment jokes. She had obviously pissed him off. 'I called you because I wanted to see you again.'

'I'm sorry,' said Claire, and meant it. 'I'm so used to people wanting things – and you did want money.'

He sighed down the phone. 'Well, that's true. But it's all very well for you to talk about money sitting there as part of a multi-million-pound industry built on ether. Try teaching sometime. We're supposed to turn out the best and the brightest, cram some sense into the stupid and build the glorious future of Blair's Brave New Britain – all on a shoestring budget. If you've ever got an hour to spare you should sit in on a lecture sometime. See what I'm up against.'

'I might just do that,' she said, figuring out what to wear and where to sit. Short skirt, front row seat. That should do the trick.

'Really? Slumming it with the intellectuals?'

'Yes. Really. Email me and let me know when and where.'

'All right. Make sure you're up to par on your constitutional history. Wouldn't want you to feel left out.'

Cheeky bastard. She hung up resenting the inference that she was some kind of moron. She hadn't got as far as she had in life by being stupid. You could be an intellectual in Jimmy Choos. Dr Scholl's weren't a requirement for MENSA entry as far as Claire knew, although she had to admit that unfortunate footwear probably helped. Look at Tosh – her overachieving parents had put their baby girl down for the entry test the moment she'd been big enough to scramble up on a stack of encyclopaedias to reach the chess table, and yet with all that equilibrium at her disposal Tosh still managed to walk like a duck with a hernia every time she put on a pair of high heels.

Claire called her. 'Darling, are you busy?'

'Er ... I'm trying to put together the voiceover for this bloody documentary.' She sounded frustrated. Claire could picture her clearly – glasses on the end of her nose, perched on a beanbag in her coffin-sized catastrophe of a flat, attempting to juggle the tools of her trade; a notebook and pen, a cup of that vile sickly Indian tea she loved and the remote control of a recordable DVD player that was state of the art but still had to be stood on an orange box because Tosh hadn't the energy or logistical capacity to assemble the IKEA TV stand.

'Oh, sorry. I won't interrupt you.'

'Interrupt away. Please. If I don't have a break I'm going to go postal on the editor. I don't get it. Normally this stuff just flows but I must have given the video editor too much leeway because I'm stuck with all these loving shots of the scenery. Don't get me wrong – Afghanistan is a beautiful country but I wasn't intending to make a fucking travelogue ... sorry, don't mean to go on. What's up?'

'James's tutor called me.'

'Ah. OK. They tend to do that when their students are off cavorting with exotic dancers.'

'Exotic dancers?'

'Calls herself Phoenix. James keeps talking about her.'

'Where in hell did she come from?'

'That Dupois show, I think. They were here earlier. I think James was taking her to the Tate Modern.'

'Jesus,' said Claire. 'That poor girl. She's probably trying to get laid and he's showing her modern art.'

'Maybe he's trying to be a gentleman.'

'Like I said, that poor girl. Anyway, his tutor wasn't calling to complain that his student was giving strippers guided tours of Bisected Cattle of Olde London Towne. He called to ask me out to dinner.'

'And?'

'I said no.'

'So?'

Claire took a deep breath. 'But I agreed to sit in on one of his lectures. I haven't got the first clue about constitutional history and I haven't got the faintest idea what to wear.'

'Constitutional history?'

'I know. Which shoes do you wear for that?'

'Oh God,' said Tosh. 'Please tell me you're not going.'

'I'm going.'

'You can't. Daniel might be there.'

'And? What use would I have for Daniel? He's far too young for me.'

'I know. He's far too young for *me*.'

'Look, if I run into your Daniel I won't say a word.'

'He's not mine. And don't you dare.'

'You shouldn't beat yourself up over him,' said Claire.

'I'm not. I just ... I sort of miss him.'

'Then tell him.'

'I can't. *I* broke up with *him*.'

Claire sighed. 'You're ridiculous sometimes – although you're going to have to do better than that to beat me. I'm chasing after a man in sandals.'

'You found Jesus?'

'No, idiot. James's bloody tutor. Graham. I mean, Graham, what sort of a name is that? He wears socks and sandals. And checked shirts. And I can't get the fucking man out of my head.'

'What's he like?' asked Santosh, as if socks and sandals weren't even an issue.

'He's ... he's sort of alternately Hugh Grant cuddly and James Spader pervy.'

'You've sold me on the James Spader bit already. Mmm. *Sex, lies, and videotape*. I must have a thing for sexually dysfunctional drifter voyeurs. Especially if they look like James Spader.'

'He doesn't. He has dark hair. And brown eyes.'

Santosh laughed. 'You noticed his *eyes*?'

'They're very brown. French chocolate.'

'Claire, you are boned already.'

'Shut up! I know! Sandals!'

Claire laughed and looked through the slats again. She double-taked, looked again and realised that this was no time to be making social calls to a friend. Zoe Luscombe was stood in front of Donna's desk, talking to her.

'Oh my God.' Claire hurriedly tried to tidy her desk with her free hand. 'Break's over, darling. Something just came up. Something huge. I'll call you later.'

'Have fun.'

Claire smoothed down her skirt, smoothed down her hair and went out into reception praying she wasn't too late to grab Zoe before Donna decided to regale her with an anecdote on the benefits of pull-ups as opposed to regular disposable nappies. 'Zoe,' she cooed, holding out a hand. 'What an unexpected pleasure. Did you get the flowers?'

'She got flowers. Who sent them is anyone's fucking guess,' said a man's voice from somewhere behind Claire. 'We're up to our fucking eyeballs in flowers.'

She turned around. Fred Hill was sitting in one of the orange plastic armchairs next to her office door. He was reading the *Evening Standard*, slouched in the chair, ankle on knee. When Claire turned to look at him he smiled his trademark toothy lunatic grin, said, 'All right?' and resumed chewing his gum.

'Hi,' said Claire and quickly returned her attention to Zoe, who was leaning against the reception desk, all legs, lips and bored brown eyes. 'How are you?'

'I was wondering if you'd got a minute,' said Zoe. 'I don't have an appointment.'

She seemed to have come off her pedestal. Her haughty manner had vanished and with the slight burr in her voice that the couturiers of Paris, London and New York had never managed to eradicate, Claire thought she could glimpse the pre-fame Zoe – the gangly girl from Dorset with the lips that would have sent Thomas Hardy into strangulated fantasies.

'Of course, of course . . .' Claire chivvied them both into her office. 'Coffee?'

'Champagne,' said Fred Hill, dumping himself down on the sofa.

'Please,' corrected Zoe, as if he were her child.

He pouted well-shaped lips and made a sarcastic kissing gesture in his girlfriend's direction. He played his bad-boy role well. He was obviously being deliberately cantankerous but, with his grey eyes smudged with fucked, messy eyeliner, his mop of bed-rumpled black hair and cockney accent, he pulled it off in a way that a less attractive man couldn't. His obdurate brattiness came across as sexy and obnoxious, rather than simply irritating.

'Donna – champagne, please,' Claire said, determined not to appear rattled by the entry of two real stars into her office. If anything came of this, Justin Vercoe could go jump in a lake. 'Well, what can I do for you, Zoe? Please, have a seat. Make yourself at home.'

Zoe didn't sit down. She lit up a cigarette, obviously deciding she'd look better standing up. She wore very little make-up and her natural hair – a short, blonde crop – was combed flat to her perfectly shaped skull. Claire thought it was part of Zoe's power-play – to come in without her make-up and prove she was more than paint and powder. Even in trainers she towered over Claire.

'Jacques isn't happy,' said Zoe. 'Actually he's totally pissed off. He said I made a mockery of his collection and my chances of getting another contract with him are zero.'

'His collection was shit,' said Fred, opening the newspaper. 'Nobody would ever wear any of that stuff.'

'I saw the articles,' Claire said, accepting a tray of

drinks from Donna, who slunk back out into reception. 'What Zoe did blew the lid on the whole fallacy of haute couture – clothes that look extraordinary but could never in a million years be worn in public.'

Fred glanced up at Zoe. 'Seriously, love?' he asked. 'Or did you just do it for cheap thrills?'

Zoe stared incredulously at him and took a glass of champagne. 'No, Fred. I didn't. I did it because I think the fur industry is disgusting, OK?'

'Even so, the Emperor's New Clothes thing was a masterstroke,' said Claire, raising her glass.

'It wasn't,' Zoe said. 'It shot me in the foot. I should have done the blood thing, like you suggested. Now everyone's blahing on and on about haute couture being an expensive heap of nothing and none of the top designers want to work with me anymore.'

'They hate it when a woman has a mind of her own, darling,' Claire sympathised. 'It's male chauvinist piggery with a pretty label.'

'It is.'

'So to counter the male chauvinist piggery you get your cunt out at a fashion show?' asked Fred.

'I'm sorry,' said Zoe. 'He insisted on coming.'

'I'm her reference,' Fred said, jerking a thumb at Zoe. 'She's here to get on your client list, all right?'

Zoe rolled her eyes. 'Well, there you have it. I need a new agent. I need a totally new direction.'

'How exciting,' said Claire. 'What kind of direction?'

Zoe stalked around the office, punctuating her speech with gestures. Claire wondered if the rumours about eating disorders were just that. The woman never seemed to sit still long enough to gain weight and the only thing that had touched her lips was an economical sip of Taittinger and several Marlboro butts.

'I am sick to the back teeth of this preconception that models are stupid.'

'Sing it, sister.'

'Fuck off, Fred.' Zoe swept past a ficus plant by the window. Her legs were so long they hardly seemed real. 'I never wanted to be a ruddy model in the first place. You know what I was doing when I was spotted?' She took a beat, took a drag of her cigarette. 'I was a dark-room assistant for a fashion photographer. I was going to do that, get my degree at Exeter and then go into photography full time. Then along came this bitch from an agency and told me I had what it took, and that it would be fun, and just for a few years and that was ten years ago. I mean, honestly – how old do you think I am?'

'Twenty-four, five?' Claire lied.

'I'm twenty-nine. And I know I'm no Kate Moss. She doesn't have a nose like mine in her genes. I'll be beaky as you like by the time I'm thirty-five and I don't want to have surgery and end up looking like a kabuki theatre player who's spent six weeks in a burns unit. I want to get back to doing what I love.'

'What a wonderful idea,' said Claire. 'I'd feel privileged to be on board.'

Zoe prowled past Claire's desk and peered at the papers as if she owned the place. 'Really?' she said, glancing up with huge eyes, exquisite lips slightly parted. Claire couldn't imagine her ever losing her looks, but it was a big enough coup to go along with Zoe's story about the family nose eventually asserting itself.

'Yes. I'd love to.'

'I've been directing,' said Zoe, flicking through documents and dropping ash all over them because she could. 'Fred will tell you. Directed your last video, didn't I, babe?'

'Directed, starred in and scripted,' muttered Fred. 'Anyone would think she had an ego.'

'You're a wanker. Everyone's talking about it.'

'"Twentieth Century Boy"?' asked Claire. 'Oh yes. They

most certainly are. Most controversial video since those two Russian fake lesbians.'

'Scandalous,' said Fred, nonchalantly. 'They're calling Zoe's vid "I Can't Believe It's Not Pussy". Carlito was pretty convincing, I thought.'

'Carlito?'

'The schoolgirl tranny.'

'Incredibly convincing,' agreed Claire. 'You mean you didn't cut with a body double?'

'Nope. He was all man,' said Zoe, with a look on her face that suggested that she knew. Fred was thankfully immersed in the newspaper. She peered down at the papers.

'Oh, who's this?'

She had found the pictures of James, looking sulky in black and white with his shirt off; in the next hiding behind his black-frame glasses and smoking a cigarette with a moody emo kid air; in the next screaming straight at the camera in a parody of *The Scream* that they'd had no trouble getting out of him at the end of the shoot.

'He's a client of mine,' said Claire. 'Aspiring musician, actor ... you know. Having difficulty placing him. He's rather odd looking, don't you think?'

'I like that about him. Interesting face.' She flung the emo-kid photo across to Fred. 'Interesting but ordinary. We could do something with him.'

Fred gave the photo a cursory glance and belched. 'Whatever you say, love.'

'He's sort of a pet project of mine,' said Claire, worried that James wouldn't behave himself. 'He's an untested commodity, I'm afraid.'

'I like untested commodities,' Zoe said, flashing a five-thousand-pound-an-hour smile. 'Do you want to make a deal or not, Ms Sawyer?'

8

Phoenix had said from the start that she wasn't into relationships.

'It don't work. Trust me. I'm sort of interesting for the first couple of weeks and then they get arsey and ask me when I'm going to give it all up and be a nice little wifeypoos.'

'Why can't you be a fire-breathing wife and mother?' asked James. They were flopped on Claire's couch smoking yet more of Phoenix's potent weed.

She rolled her eyes and sighed. 'Look, I might as well be honest with you, 'cause that's me. What you see is what you get. The fashion show was just a lucky break. I couldn't get into any of the fancy dance schools because we never had the money and, funnily enough, all the fuckin' scholarships went to the pretty rich white girls and not the funny lookin' black girl from Peckham.'

'I don't think you're funny looking at all. You're really pretty.'

It had taken one stern look from Phoenix to let James know she didn't care for flattery, regardless of how sincere. She relit the spliff and continued. 'I'm not very clever, even if I do talk a lot, and I'm not rich and I'm not white and I'm not pretty and I'm not saying cry me a river or making any apologies for what I do, but blokes *do* get funny about me stripping.'

'I don't see why,' James said, trying to look liberal and tolerant. 'You're an amazing dancer.'

She grinned. 'You should see me with a fuckin' pole,

darlin'. But that's the thing, right? I've had so many blokes give it the Roxanne thing . . .'

'Cyrano?'

'What?'

'It's a film . . . I think. Cyrano and Roxanne?'

'I mean the song,' said Phoenix, passing the joint. 'You know? "Roooo-xanne – you don't have to put on the red light . . ."'

Her voice was huge. When she sang the name Roxanne the sound was so powerful James was sure the glass shelves on the other side of the room rattled. It was incredible to think of that enormous voice coming from her slight dancer's body, but she acted like nothing was up and carried on talking.

'And it's always, like, "Baby, you don't have to do that any more. I'll take care of you – blah blah fuckin' blah." So I give it up and the red bills are piling up on the mat and I'm like, "When are you gonna get a job, then?" and he doesn't. So I go out and try and make a living and he beats the fuckin' shit out of me for being a whore.'

'Someone beat you?' asked James, horrified, handing her back the joint.

'Cunt didn't do it twice, pardon my French,' Phoenix said, with a matter-of-factness that was astonishing. 'I'm not having that. Seen enough of that with my mum and her ex. "Oh, he's sorry, he loves me" – yeah, fuckin' right, he is. Until he gets pissed and does it again. Bloke lays a hand on me again like that he'd better know he'll never see me again. And you know what pissed me off most? He called me a whore. I am not a whore. I ain't never done it for money and I never will. They can look at the goodies until their eyes roll out and sizzle on their steaming knackers but . . . what? Don't laugh!'

James apologised. 'I'm sorry. I can't help it. You've just . . . you've got a turn of phrase and I am so stoned.'

She smiled and blew out smoke. 'Yeah. I'm getting there myself. And don't look at me like that.'

'Like what?'

'You know what,' she said, peeping up from under her eyelashes. 'If anything happens, it's just a bit of fun, all right?'

'Totally,' agreed James, although he was keen to find someone to put Claire off this whole 'celebrity girlfriend' idea of hers.

'We need to do something,' said Phoenix, reaching for her tobacco tin with an air of determination.

'Like what?'

'Something stupid. Let's go out. Let's go to a museum or something.'

'Again?' asked James, sitting up on his elbows. 'I thought you'd always lived in London?'

She shook her head, rolling another joint with astonishing dexterity. 'Nah. I have. That's why I've never seen any of the museums. You don't when you live here. You need to hook up with a tourist to see the sights.'

'OK. There's the National . . . in Trafalgar Square.'

'Pictures? I need to be more wrecked for pictures. Here, have you got any music?'

She managed to surprise him again. She went through Claire's CDs, discarding all the plastic pop and the dance music, settling on a classical compilation. She liked Prokofiev, Beethoven, Bach and George Gershwin. ('Mum says me dad was a composer, from Zimbabwe. It's in my blood or something. Poor bastard got deported. Probably dead by now.') She shivered at Holst's *Jupiter*, saying it made her feel both sad and proud to be British, did the Charleston to *Rhapsody in Blue* and listened with rapt attention while they listened to Beethoven's Ninth and James told her about *A Clockwork Orange*.

'That's it,' she said. 'We've got to go out. This fuckin' city won't know what's hit it.'

They headed to Trafalgar Square. On the way there she asked him how the *Ode to Joy* went and he told her in his badly mangled schoolboy German, which couldn't have been that bad because the first thing she did was climb astride a stone lion and belt out: '*Freude, Schönen Gotterfunken, Tochter aus Elysium*' in her huge, tuneful voice. Several tourists took her picture.

'I'm high on life,' she said, grinning sharkishly at the tourists as she helped James up onto the lion behind her. 'I love the smell of nutters in the morning. You should have been here when they had the protests on, you know. It was fuckin' magic. They had this muezzin singing the call to prayer and the place was packed. It was a total trip. Have you ever sat on a lion before?'

'Can't say I have. We're quite high up, aren't we?'

'Not as high as Nelson up there. Say hello to Nelson, Jimmy.'

'Hello, Nelson Jimmy,' he said, making her laugh.

Phoenix shivered. Under her long red coat she wore a short pleated skirt and high-heeled pink suede boots. Her thighs were bare and goosebumped. 'Well, that's something new,' she announced. 'I've never straddled a lion or sung in German before. I am *so* off my tits.'

'Aren't you cold?'

'Freezing. Let's go in the gallery. It's your turn to do something mental.'

'My turn?' asked James, climbing off the back of the lion and helping her down. She stepped down with careful mincing steps and giggled coyly at the way he handed her down.

'Ooo, aren't you the gent?' she said. 'And yeah. It's your turn. I sat on a lion and sang bleedin' Beethoven – now let's see what you're made of. I dare you.'

'To do what?' asked James, as they hurried up the steps of the National Gallery, running from the cold. 'Phoenix, don't ask me to get my cock out or anything because I won't. I'm not getting arrested. Not in this state.'

She laughed. 'It's all right. I'm not going to do anything nasty to you. Come on.'

It was warm and quiet inside the gallery, the atmosphere so sedate that it was hard to believe the cold, polluted hubbub of Trafalgar Square was only just outside. The floors, like those of a church, amplified every footfall so that you felt obliged not to speak too loudly. Even Phoenix stopped talking and moved as quietly as she could on her spiked heels as she peered up at paintings by Holbein and Titian. Her demure demeanour made James worry what she was going to do next.

There were three people in the room besides them – an elderly gentleman and two women, whose Jaeger neck-scarves, bluish hair and padded bodywarmers marked them out as belonging to the Land Rover-owning classes. One of them looked askance at Phoenix's red PVC rainslicker and pink boots, then returned to her perusal of the guidebook.

'Shall we move on, Cynthia?' she asked the other woman, as she turned away from a Holbein. 'I never cared for medieval art anyway.'

James bit back a laugh at this, just as Phoenix seemed to materialise at his shoulder like a cartoon devil. 'I've got it,' she whispered. 'I dare you to say something rude. Shout something – then say you've got that syndrome. The one that makes you swear.'

'No.'

'It's that or get your cock out.'

'No!' James glanced around the hushed room. 'All right. No cock, OK?'

'Say cock,' suggested Phoenix, gleefully shifting her weight from heel to heel in her excitement. 'Or pissflaps. Or minge.'

James covered his mouth with his hand and choked

down a potentially noisy snort of laughter. He knew it was incredibly stupid and childish, but he was also stoned and there was something irresistibly seductive about swearing in an art gallery. It was the same kind of pleasure that there was to be had talking too loudly in a library or farting in church.

He watched the two ladies head into the next room and had a terrible idea. Well, if they looked funny at Phoenix, as if someone like her had no right to be in an art gallery but were ignorant enough themselves to think Holbein medieval, then they deserved to be the butt of a joke.

'I'm not going to shout minge,' James told Phoenix.

'Well, get ready to whip it out then.'

'No.' He grabbed her arm. 'Listen, you've got to keep a straight face, all right? Completely deadpan – otherwise it won't be as funny.'

'What do I have to do?'

'Nothing. Just stand next to me and don't laugh.'

'OK.'

They sidled along, looking at the paintings, then into the next room where the two ladies were peering up at a blowsy Peter Lely nude.

'Certainly a difference in the use of light and shadow,' said the one called Cynthia.

James manoeuvred himself alongside them before looking up at the painting. If he remembered his history then Peter Lely had mostly been commissioned to immortalise the opulent charms of Charles II's numerous mistresses. The subject of the painting looked like she'd given Lely an almighty hard-on, judging by the way she was sprawled out with her lips slightly apart and her sloe eyes gazing directly out of the picture. She had rounded, wide-spaced breasts and an arse and thighs a man could get lost in and need a map to find his way out from.

The only other naked woman James had seen recently had been Zoe Luscombe and the difference between Zoe's rangy, almost-breastless body and this rounded, white whipped-cream confection of a female with the dimples on her knees and bum couldn't have been more marked. Strange how the standards of beauty changed.

Phoenix, he thought, was a law unto herself – so exotic with her tropical-bird-coloured clothes and the cornrowed nobbles of her short black hair that she would have been interesting in any era. When she stood still and quiet she was just a small, skinny girl with beautiful eyes, but when she danced she was anyone she wanted to be. She was Madonna, Josephine Baker, Anna Pavlova, an ancient Egyptian temple dancer, a shaman's spirit guide, an African queen, an acrobat, a juggler, Salome peeling off her seven veils, one by tantalising one.

It pissed James off that the women had looked at her as if she was nothing more than a common tart. He knew what it was to be looked at and judged, and now that his hair was a respectable length, rather than the fierce buzzcut he'd needed to lose the dreads, he found people didn't look at him so much. He had been annoyed to realise that, in spite of his protests to Claire, he didn't give a toss about what people thought about him; in dressing like a tramp he *had* cared. A negative reaction was a reaction, which was better than nothing. He was somewhere in between right now – not stomping around in clothes that showed his anger like a badge of rank, but still lacking the glittery finish of celebrity. When he looked in the mirror in the mornings, he was confronted by someone who looked like what he was – a nice young man.

He couldn't stand it, but for his present purposes it was perfect.

'Is that a chiaroscuro effect, Florence?' asked the woman named Cynthia.

James's heart thumped as he opened his mouth to speak. 'Um ... minge, actually – I think,' he said, hesitantly, politely. Such a nice, helpful young man.

Phoenix made a strange involuntary noise in the back of her throat and he could hear the scuff of her heels as her body jolted slightly, like someone who had accidentally received a small electric shock from a nylon carpet.

Cynthia adjusted spectacles attached round her neck with a fine gold chain, consulted the guidebook and looked back up at the painting. 'That blurring effect? Minge, you say?'

Phoenix fled with a clatter of pink suede heels and an eruptive peacock-shriek of laughter.

'Yes,' James said, exhilarated at the success of his joke. 'Late seventeenth-century minge. Excuse me ...' He raced out after Phoenix, laughing insanely.

He found her outside the gallery, crying with laughter. Most of the girls he had known before would have rolled their eyes and told him not be so immature but Phoenix was of a different breed altogether. She was laughing so hard that she had to hold herself up with her bum pressed against the wall. Her half-crumpled pose made her slim legs look even more precarious.

'Oh fuck,' she moaned, wiping smudgy mascara from under one eye. 'Oh. My. God. Fuckin' genius.' She shrieked with laughter again and wrapped her arms dizzily around James's neck. He was high on his own bravado and tried to lift her, and her feet left the ground for long enough for him to realise how strong her arms were. Her body felt hard and fleshless, astonishing in its tensile strength, given her size.

'Good enough for you?' he teased.

'In-sane. I can't believe that woman said minge!'

'Obviously knew as much about minge as she did about the English Renaissance. Stupid people want to watch themselves when we're off on one.'

Phoenix grinned. 'Damn right. Jesus, I nearly pissed myself. I should have gone before we legged it. Nothing like the cold to make you piss like a horse, is there?' She peered up at the grey sky and hugged herself. 'Oh great. Fuckin' snow.'

A few flakes were beginning to fall and James stared at it in wonder. 'Snow?'

'Snow,' said Phoenix, shrugging as though this were completely unremarkable. 'What? You've never seen snow before?'

'No,' James said, breathlessly. 'Never. Only on television and Christmas cards.' It looked like tiny white feathers and he remembered learning at school that no two snowflakes were alike. It seemed miraculous. There were a few flakes in Phoenix's hair and the miniature ice crystals were slowly melting to glittering drops on her head. She looked amused, surprised and even more strangely beautiful.

'Seriously?' she asked.

'Seriously.' He realised he was looking at her with way more intensity than was entirely proper.

'Well, there you go,' she said, her smile almost shy. 'Something else that's new. Come on. Places to go. Stuff to do. You owe me a dare.'

They determined their next location by Phoenix closing her eyes and sticking her chewing gum to a giant wall-mounted map of the London Underground in Charing Cross Station. It landed roughly near Monument, so they backtracked to Embankment and got on the Circle Line. The Tube wasn't yet commuter-crammed but there were enough tourists and Christmas shoppers around to force them to strap-hang. Phoenix swayed on her ridiculous boots so that her hips moved towards James's in a way that emboldened him and made him remember sucking smoke from her lips. She was still smiling over his joke in the gallery and held his gaze while their hips bumped.

She really was very pretty. Her short, broad nose and gold-flecked eyes gave her the look of a watchful cat in repose but when she grinned she resembled a naughty, playful monkey, an impression enhanced by the long-fingered dexterity of her small hands. She was standing so close their noses were almost touching and he didn't know if he dared kiss her until she broke the deadlock and kissed him.

The train rocked them awkwardly against each other and neither of them took their free hands off their money, because you just didn't on a crowded Tube. Her lips were cold and the tip of her nose icy, but she was stoned enough to laugh off the botch they'd made of it and buried her face in his coat to let him know that she'd meant it.

'Just for fun,' she reminded him, with a brief, feline flash of seriousness as the train came to a halt.

'Nothing wrong with fun, right?' said James, slipping his hand under the side of her coat. The curve of her bottom was slight and delectable and all the more exciting for knowing that she wore only brief red knickers (he had seen them when she climbed up onto the lion in Trafalgar Square) beneath her short skirt.

'Nope. Nothing wrong with fun. Fun, fun and sightseeing.' She darted off up the escalator, through the turn-stiles and towards the monument – a tall column topped with a gilded flame.

'Pudding Lane,' she babbled, like a tour guide on speed. She seemed skittish suddenly. 'This is where the fire started. "In sixteen hundred and sixty-six, London burned like lots of sticks." Or something. Only thing I remember from school. Come on. We can go up to the top.'

There was a long, coiling, Hitchcock flight of stairs inside the monument and Phoenix shot up them with such speed that James panted and gasped to meet her even halfway. She had stopped to catch her breath and she was flushed from the climb.

'Long way up,' she said, her voice rasping and echoing around the circular tower. 'You have to excuse me. It's this monument. It's like a big willy stickin' up and it's given me a bit of a funny turn.'

'What?' James wheezed, laughing.

'I'm joking, idiot,' said Phoenix, looking purposefully at him. 'Kiss me again.'

She stood on the step above and despite the stairs being none too wide, it was better than before. He could touch her, although he had no idea where it was OK to put his hands. He kept one palm braced against the curved wall, nervous of falling, but he could cup her chin with his free hand and feel the motion of her jaw and throat as they kissed. She had her back to the wall and pulled him tight against her, adding to his sense of vertigo and excitement. She'd been joking about the monument, of course, but he realised incredulously that it had been lust making her jumpy, because she'd been fine before they kissed for the first time and she was making soft, appreciative noises when he kissed her this time.

Every sound echoed round the staircase, so that his ears were full of the liquid sounds and muffled moans of kissing. Phoenix's coat was open so he slipped a hand inside and touched her waist again. She shifted enough to give him access to her arse and this time his hand was able to reach the hem of her tiny skirt and negotiate beneath it. Her skin was smooth and cool, her thong underwear just a wisp between her buttocks so that her bum may as well have been bared to his touch.

His hips seemed to move magnetically towards hers.

If he had no idea where to put his hands, his dick seemed to know very well where it wanted to go.

'So you do like me?' she whispered.

'Yes. Oh yes. Very much.' He wished he could tell her just how much, but his brain wouldn't work in words when it came to her. There were always scraps of her floating in his head – the flash of a brown inner thigh when she sat down, the way she walked in high heels, all arse and ankle, the way her sweater clung to her ribcage and breasts or the exposed strip of skin at her waist. Just images without words, all of which combined to create an impression of aesthetic joy and mouthwatering desire.

There were footsteps approaching and voices talking in a rapid foreign language. 'Oh well,' said Phoenix, ruefully. 'Onwards and upwards I suppose, Jimmy. You still owe me a dare.'

Puffing, they reached the top and looked out on a spectacular view of the city. The snow had slowed to a fine dusting barely visible on the breeze and the sky was beginning to darken. Lights were beginning to come out, glimmering in the glass towers of the financial district, floodlight bathing the baroque dome of St Paul's. Phoenix's breath hung like smoke in the air.

'Higher than it looks, innit?' she said.

James could hear the people behind them approaching up the stairs. 'About that dare . . .' he said.

'OK. What?'

He peered down at the pavement below. People were beginning to trickle out of the bottoms of the office blocks. 'Get your tits out for the bankers,' he said.

Phoenix rolled her eyes. 'Call that a dare?' she said. She stuck two fingers in her mouth, gave a piercing whistle and yelled from the top of the monument. 'OI! BANKERS!'

Then she rolled up her jumper, under which she wore

no bra, and flashed her audience. Her breasts were small, firm and pointed, brown nipples hard in the cold air. She bounced them under their own light weight to the sound of catcalls from below and laughed as she rolled her sweater down. 'You should have known that was a piece of piss for me,' she said.

'Maybe I just wanted to see your boobs.'

'Well, now you have.'

'They're fucking gorgeous.'

Phoenix preened. 'Ta very much. They're all mine. One hundred per cent organic.'

'And free range too, apparently.'

'Underwiring gives you cancer,' said Phoenix, defensively. 'I don't know about you, but I'm gagging for a drink.'

The commuters were coming out of the office blocks and vanishing back underground like worker ants returning to their nests. James and Phoenix negotiated the crowds and got cheerfully lost in the backstreets of the City. He had never realised that the financial district could be interesting to anyone but the money people, but the area around St Paul's was full of hidden treasures. There were tiny churches where you least expected to find them, some so old that they must have miraculously survived the fire that had reduced the old cathedral to rubble. He was delighted when they found a pub of a type he hadn't thought existed any more. The windows were frosted glass, the walls panelled in dark, old oak and the upholstery as tired and threadbare-looking as the elderly shabby but genteel landlord.

The landlord addressed them formally as sir and madam and smiled indulgently when Phoenix cooed excitedly over the liqueurs like a kid in a sweetshop. 'Crème de cassis? No way. I'm telling you, nowhere stocks this stuff these days – not in the pubs down

Peckham. It's all fizzy stuff in bottles. I mean, where's the skill in that? Ripping the tops off bottles?'

She had vodka with grenadine, because she said pomegranates were her favourite fruit. She dared James to drink a pint of real ale and he rapidly realised why she had made a dare of it. As the pub filled up with loud-voiced, too-posh stockbrokers, James felt his stomach twist and turn at the heavy lukewarm brew that was nothing like his twenty-first-century notion of beer.

He bolted for the toilets and vomited, angry with himself for wrecking an otherwise perfect day. He was sipping water from the ancient-looking but well-scrubbed sink when Phoenix came looking for him.

'Are you all right?'

'Better now. You do know you're in the gents', don't you?'

'I don't mind if you don't,' she said, rummaging in her handbag. 'Here. Have a mint.'

He crunched a Polo mint and felt better.

'You probably shouldn't be in here.'

'I shouldn't be out there,' said Phoenix. 'Some bloke called Gervaise was trying to buy me a tequila. Or twelve. Oldest trick in the book, innit? Keep buying a girl drinks until she's pissed enough to take her knickers off?'

'I'll take your word for it.'

She shrugged. 'Yeah, well ... Gervaise can save his money. Or his daddy's fuckin' money.' With that she reached under her skirt and slid her tiny red knickers down over her brown thighs and long pink boots.

'What are you doing?' asked James. If she went back out there and sat on one of the barstools then everyone would see straight up her skirt. 'You can't go out there like that!'

'I'm not,' she said, stuffing her knickers in her coat pocket and wrapping her arms around his neck. 'I'm staying in here. Don't like suits – especially when they've got the horn. Clammy little bastards.'

She kissed him once more, thankfully not caring that he'd been sick. He was dizzy with drugs, booze and the possibility that anything might happen. He could hardly believe that he was here, kissing a girl who wasn't wearing any underwear and sticking her small, chilly hands under his clothes.

She leaned back against the partition wall of the stall, standing with her feet apart to keep herself upright. James thought of her exposed pussy opening just beneath the hem of her skirt and realised that if she so much as touched him he would come, messily and far too fast.

He breathed deeply as she pulled him towards her, against her, sandwiching herself between him and the partition. She guided his hands to her breasts and he squeezed them gently, delighted at their softness and the keen way her nipples perked and stiffened beneath his fingers. She rocked her hips against him and he felt powerless not to do the same. His dick seemed to demand that he move, as if by rocking against her he could erode the layers of jeans and boxers between them.

'You like that, don't you?' she whispered. 'Come on.' She reached down for his fly to free his cock and as he looked down to help her with the button, he saw that her skirt had ridden up. He could see a strip of black hair and pink, pink flesh between. It was nothing like seeing Zoe Luscombe striding around in the buff. This was Phoenix, who might let him touch, taste, even fuck.

'Oh God . . . ' he moaned, his head spinning as his dick sprung out into her hand. 'Wait . . . I have to tell you something.'

'You never done this before, have you?' she said, smiling knowingly.

'Oh fuck. Is it that obvious?'

She shook her head and laughed under her breath, her lips close to his. 'Doesn't matter. I don't mind if you don't. Gotta start somewhere, Jimmy.'

'I might be crap,' he said. 'I'll be awful. It's your fault. You're so fucking lovely.'

'Don't be silly,' she said. 'It's easy. Just takes practice.' She reached behind her back under her coat and unhooked her skirt, tossing it across the closed lid of the toilet. Apart from her boots she was naked from the waist down and James had never seen anything so sexy before in his life. Her bare hips and thighs – the wisp of dark hair between them and the knowledge that she was offering it to him – it was enough to drive him mad with lust.

'Dare you,' she said, leaning back against the wall and handing him a foil-wrapped condom. 'Go on. Put it in. Just to say you have.'

'Someone could come in,' he protested. He didn't know why he said that. He had to have gone insane. A beautiful girl was offering him the chance to lose his virginity at last and he was quibbling. It had to be something to do with him being so fucking terrified.

'Nobody has yet,' she said, taking the condom back from him and unwrapping it herself. 'Come on. I want you to fuck me. I dare you to fuck me, Jimmy.'

'You're insane,' he gasped, struggling to keep calm while she rolled the rubber onto him. Her hands were far too skilful to be safe and he prayed he wasn't about to lose his virginity to Durex. That probably would have necessitated suicide because he knew he'd never get over the shame.

'It's easy,' she whispered, pulling him close and guiding his fingers to her sex. Oh God. Hot. Wet. This was really happening. 'Feel? Find the hole?'

'Oh my God.' His fingers barely had to push and she opened up to him. He felt inside where it was even wetter, warmer – a slender passage that actually quivered and clenched when she moved – a sentient thing that wanted *him*. She made a soft sound of pleasure when he tentatively wiggled his fingers inside her and he felt inspired. 'How do I make you come?' he asked. He wanted to see that more than anything in the world. He wanted to hear her moan his name, tell him he was the best, the greatest, and she was coming for him.

'Oi. Patience, Grasshopper,' she giggled. 'One step at a time.'

She shifted her hips, pushed away his fingers and guided him with her own hand. He didn't want to look down because the sight of his cock approaching her and entering her was too much and he was sure it would make him come, but some part of him needed to see this. A mental record of a rite of passage.

He pushed in just as Phoenix froze. Her eyes were wide for a moment before she buried her face in his shoulder and clung tight to him. He was anxious about what he'd done wrong before his senses unscrambled enough to identify the cause of her alarm.

They had company in the gents' toilet. Fuck. Fuck and thrice fuck. He couldn't even say 'I told you so' for fear of opening his mouth because he had no idea what kind of strangulated noise would come out.

There sounded like there were at least two of them out there. City boys like Dad's executive twats. Oh Christ – and here he was with his jeans around his ankles and his cock in Phoenix, whose cunt felt like an exquisite instrument of torture designed to wring some sound from him that would give them away.

They were stuck there, frozen and forced to be silent until the twats left.

'Yah. Totally. I couldn't fucking *believe* Paul!'

'I know! "Oh, it's my responsibility as team leader, Sir

Charles." We should have him fitted with a fucking crucifix for the boardroom!'

James hardly dared to breathe. His hips wanted to move and thrust, but if he moved so much as a millimetre inside her he knew that he'd be unable to stop himself making a sound. And she was not helping. Her tongue traced the edge of his ear and she wouldn't keep her hips still.

'He's such an arse. And still manages to blame everyone else for his time management.'

Go, James thought. Fuck off and make some money or something. Just fuck off.

Phoenix was rocking her hips slowly, almost immeasurably. Every tiny movement made James's heart beat louder and faster and his dick throb inside her. He was poised there, unable to move and struggling to concentrate on anything but the way it felt to be inside her. She made a barely audible mewing sound in his ear and something inside her clenched lightly around him, making him jolt and shudder.

The City boys continued their character assassination of the bloke named Paul, talking in their loud, braying voices. James's world narrowed to a concentrated need to come. Phoenix probably had no trouble standing up against the wall on her strong dancer's legs, but James's knees were beginning to ache. She moved her hips in small, tiny circles, driving him mad with the desire to thrust and move inside her.

The creak of the door opening signalled the departure of the City boys and he couldn't hold back any longer. His hips jerked up towards and into her so that she gasped and steadied herself against him. When he moved his cock back and forth inside her it was like sparks bursting in his brain and balls, tremors of sensation that threatened to turn into earthquakes when he moved faster.

She murmured encouragement but it was too late. He counted up to six thrusts and he lost it, coming hard and fast and so loud that she laughed and put her hand over his mouth. His knees trembled and he could feel wet heat bathing the tip of his cock where he had filled the condom. 'Oh God,' he moaned, sliding to his knees and slipping out of her as he did so. 'Fucking hell.'

Phoenix looked disgustingly pleased with herself. She grinned down at him, her legs still apart. He was at eye level with her pussy – wet and freshly fucked – and he knew that as soon as he could get it up again he was determined to do it all over again.

'Ball's in your court, Jimmy,' she said. 'You're going to have to top that for a dare.'

9

Phoenix lived in Camberwell ('Slightly posher than Peckham. Moving up in the world, ain't I?') in a chaotic flat on a noisy estate. The first thing she did when they got through the door was apologise for the mess, because it looked like a bomb had gone off in a costume shop. She had a makeshift barre rigged up in the hall and several huge inflatable exercise balls bounced about the place. The sofa and armchairs were also inflatable and the armchair James attempted to sit in, being as it appeared to be the one least covered in items of PVC underwear, turned out to be occupied by a small black cat with very green eyes. It purred when he stroked it but leaped off his lap and ran to the kitchen when it heard Phoenix opening the fridge.

She said the cat was named Othercat, because he'd just decided to move in with her and her old tabby and made himself so much at home that it had been a case of referring to Tabs and the Other Cat, so the name stuck.

She complained of the cold and said she usually liked a nice hot bath before bed, and James had said he was happy enough watching TV before realising he was being invited to join her. She was tiny enough for it to be only a slightly uncomfortable squeeze in the tub and he sat soaping her back with her firm little bum pressed up between his open legs, tormenting the erection that seemed to have become more or less permanent in her presence.

Whatever economies Phoenix had made on her inflatable three-piece suite were obvious when they went to bed. Her bed was a huge sleigh bed that barely fitted in the pokey bedroom, and when James tumbled into it alongside her, he realised it had to be even more expensive than it looked because it was wonderfully comfortable.

'Need my beauty sleep,' said Phoenix, switching on a set of twinkling fairy lights over the head of the bed. A set of pink, fur-lined handcuffs dangled from the top of the bedframe. 'That and I'm the laziest girl in town. Come here, you.'

They did it again – more slowly this time and with James realising he was going to need a lot more practice. When he pushed inside her the sensation was delicious, but not as amazing as the realisation of what he was doing. With every thrust some jubilant part of his brain was reminding him that he was having sex – he was finally doing it – and the excitement of it made every nerve in his body ignite, made his flesh rebel completely and his balls spill their load once more.

He wished he knew more. She was four years older than him and had led a far less sheltered life but she didn't seem to hold that against him. She said she liked his body, pulling the covers off him and working her way over his skin, bared in the fairy-light glitter of her bed. She kissed where his tan line ended and teased that the pissing London rain had washed the sun right off his skin the moment he'd stepped off the plane from Dubai. She kissed his nipples, under his arms, his belly button, and then he realised with glorious trepidation where she was going next. When she took his cock in her mouth he was sure there was nothing else on earth that felt so amazing and he was desperate for it to go on forever. He ran his fingers over the tight braids that covered her scalp, touched the fine skin behind each small ear, concentrating on the texture of her hair and the shape of her skull under his hands to distract himself somewhat from the wet heat of her suckling mouth. Maybe this is why they call it giving head, he thought, and then she did something with her tongue, flicking at the sensitive tip of his cock while she sucked, and he came with a jolt of sensation so sharp it was close to pain.

She let him peer between her legs and directed his fingers where to go, but although he managed to elicit some moans from her, she was obviously as tired as he was and, by the time the sun was coming up, they were drowsing in one another's arms while trying to keep up a conversation about Dubai. Phoenix wanted to know everything about it, so he told her about the souks and the beach and the races and water-taxis and the time he'd had afternoon tea at the top of the Burq al Arab. She listened as eagerly as she could when he talked about the gold souk but her eyes were closing involuntarily and so were his.

He got about two hours' sleep before Claire called and demanded to know where the hell he was because she had plans for him and she felt bloody awful and he could at least have given her a more accurate time for coming home than 'sometime tomorrow'. Phoenix, of course, was working at night and could catch up on her sleep, so James kissed her goodbye, left her sleeping and let himself out to catch the train back to East Dulwich with the barely dawning realisation that he was no longer a virgin.

Claire was nursing a hangover. 'I was going to send out a fucking search party,' she complained. 'I thought you'd run off to the Antarctic like Frankenstein's bloody monster or something.'

'Frankenstein? Nice. I make you feel like Frankenstein?'

Claire shook her head. 'Sorry – no. Champagne hangovers. They always make me perfectly odious. Frankenfurter, maybe. Better shoes and lingerie, less Promethean angst.' She swallowed a burp and sang quietly to herself while refilling the kettle 'In just seven days ... da dum dum dum, I can make you a man...'

James snaffled a piece of her toast and munched happily on it, smug in the knowledge that he was already a man.

'Fantastic news, anyway,' Claire said, noticing James's appropriation of her toast and putting another slice in the toaster. 'Zoe Luscombe showed up at my office yesterday.'

'You're joking!'

'I'm not. And with the bloody awful boyfriend in tow. Nice arse, terrible attitude.'

James raised his eyebrows. 'I thought that was the point of Fred Hill – nice arse, bad attitude. What was he like?'

'A cunt,' said Claire, lighting a fag. She peered shrewdly at James through the smoke. 'But I did manage to get a concert ticket or four.'

James's mouth dropped open. 'Oh my God. Please?'

'Relax, darling – you can go and see the show,' Claire said. 'Providing you do something for me first.'

'What?' asked James, suddenly dubious. Claire had that crocodile smile which meant he probably wasn't going to like what she told him next.

'It's Zoe,' said Claire, sitting down gingerly, as though her hangover was getting the better of her. 'You know she's rather ... difficult, don't you? Well, she's agreed to sign up with me and I know she's a pain in the bum, but oh my God, darling, she's gold dust. '

'Claire!' James prompted.

'OK, OK. You're sort of part of the deal, all right?'

'Me? What do you mean, I'm part of the deal?'

'Zoe saw your photographs,' explained Claire, slumping green-faced over the kitchen table. 'She liked them. She liked the look of you. She wants to photograph you.'

'She's a supermodel. Why does she want to photograph me?'

'She wants to be a photographer again,' said Claire, rubbing her forehead. 'Something about her nose. Don't ask me ... God, those two can put it away. Please, James? Play nice and she might cast you in her next video or introduce you to a nice Argentinian transvestite or something.'

'Why would I want to be introduced to an Argentinian transvestite?' asked James, pouring himself a glass of orange juice. 'I'm sort of seeing someone, in case you hadn't noticed.'

'It's the "sort of" that convinces me it's not worth noticing,' said Claire, dismissively.

James ground his teeth. 'I might be in love.'

'Darling, you're nineteen. Trust me. It goes away.'

Irritated, he went to roll a cigarette. Claire quickly pushed her pack of filter-tips across the table at him. She had determined early that she wasn't prepared to have her project sucking on rollies like a vagrant. James ignored the cigarettes and rolled his own – a small gesture of defiance, but they were the small gestures that kept him going on a daily basis.

'Haven't you ever been in love?' he asked.

'Probably,' she said, shrugging. 'But after so many margaritas anything is possible. Right now I am deeply, passionately, head over heels in love with the idea of representing Zoe Luscombe, so the least you can do is help me out after everything I've done for you.'

'Hey, I didn't *ask* for all of this,' said James, waving a hand around the kitchen to indicate the flat, the clothes, the fashion shows, the stylists. 'I just thought you'd find me a job with the *NME* or something.'

Claire rose unsteadily from the kitchen table and pulled her dressing gown tight around her. 'If the next thing you're about to say is that you didn't ask to be born then our relationship will have shifted so far into maternal territory that I will have to seek psychiatric advice.'

'Yeah, well, some days it feels like you *are* my mum.'

'James, if you don't do this I will be worse than two mothers to you. Now, please – get dressed and remember what I told you about not acting too starstruck. I've organised this meeting with Zoe and I've got a horribly busy day ahead. And you've got to meet Darren at two.'

'Who's Darren?' James called after her, as she hurried out of the kitchen.

'The stylist,' Claire shouted back, her voice amplified by the tiling of the bathroom. 'If you will insist on wearing army surplus, we've got to get it styled right . . . oh, Jesus, how much did I drink last night?'

James found his clothes were already chosen for him, so he indulged in a quick flurry of text messaging with Phoenix before getting dressed. She was working that night, he wasn't free in the day, so their chances of seeing one another were practically zero for the next twenty-four hours. That or she was so disappointed by his pathetic sexual performance that she'd decided she didn't want to do it ever again. He wished he had someone to talk to about these things. There were mine-fields everywhere – like how often did you call a girl you'd slept with before she thought you were turning into a stalker? Or before she thought you were too serious when she had her mind set on having fun?

He got dressed in the clothes he was given – a tight black shirt and trousers. Maybe Claire was trying to tell him to lose weight again after he'd spent all that time guzzling protein and working out to gain some muscle. Fuck it. He didn't know any more. He wasn't even excited at the prospect of meeting Zoe Luscombe.

'She likes you,' Claire insisted, in the cab to Holland Park. 'And you like her, don't you?'

'I don't know her.'

'You've pretty much seen up her snatch. Counts for more than a handshake, doesn't it?'

'If that's a qualification for knowing someone then I must be on intimate terms with about half a dozen porn stars,' said James. 'I'd hate to be a gynaecologist. Their social lives must be chaos.'

'Oh, shush. You'll have a whale of time, I'm sure.'

James was so surprised by Zoe's place that he was forced to re-evaluate what he had expected and realised that, in spite of knowing the whole video was fictitious, he had expected her to live in a New York-style penthouse. Where she was going to find a New York penthouse in London he didn't know, but he didn't expect what he found.

The door of the Holland Park mansion was opened by a girl with blue spiked hair and piercings in every available bit of facial cartilage. There were paparazzi lurking nearby and she gave them the finger and called them parasitic arseholes before letting James and Claire in.

'Sorry,' she said. 'Don't know what they fuckin' expect. Like Zoe's going to go out there and give 'em another fuckin' minge shot or something.'

The hall looked sparse and shabby. It was grand enough in scale but had the neglected look of somewhere that had been partly decorated, then subjected to more parties than paint. There were anarchy signs sprayed on the walls and the chandelier hung off-centre, half of its crystal drops missing. Two large boisterous Dalmatian dogs bounded in and barked, jumped and licked. The blue-haired girl tried to restrain them and Claire, a dyed in the wool cat-person, smiled with ill-concealed distaste as she fended off one of the dogs.

'They want walking,' said the girl, and got down on all fours to speak to the dogs directly. 'Don't you, babies?

Yes, you do, yes, you do ... kissies for Auntie Vicky? Kissies! Ye-ess...' The dogs licked her face enthusiastically and Claire winced visibly.

Zoe Luscombe came down the stairs. She was dressed in a black silk kimono dressing gown decorated with painted chrysanthemums and looked like she'd just rolled out of bed. 'Oh, hi ... you're here,' she said, yawning. 'Excuse the state of me. Fred and I had a row last night and he tends to go overboard with the making-up part.'

'Best part of rowing,' said Claire, trying to look simpatico in a girly sort of way that James found frankly nauseating.

Zoe looked like she doubted it. 'So you must be James?' she said, sticking out a hand. 'Nice to meet you. Come on through. Vicky, can you do some coffee or something?'

'It's instant,' said Vicky, not rising from the floor where she was busy playing with the dogs.

'Tea?'

'Milk's off. There's champagne.'

'Right. Champagne then.'

'Lovely,' said Claire, with a sickly smile that looked as though she never wanted to see another glass of champagne as long as she lived. 'Hair of the dog,' she muttered, discreetly dusting Dalmatian hair from her skirt.

The impression of expensive squalor was carried through into Zoe's living room, where the dogs had clearly made their presence felt by chewing lumps out of the white leather couches. The floor was covered in magazines and photographs, the cracked glass coffee table powdered with white stuff that wasn't Johnson's Baby Powder. James had never imagined the rich and famous would ever live like this. It was like someone had taken the interior of a squat and stuffed it inside a Holland Park mansion. Spray painted on the wall above the fireplace was the legend, 'Only Dull Women Have

Immaculate Houses' which made it abundantly clear that Zoe Luscombe thought herself at least the most interesting woman in London, if not the world.

'I'd say excuse the mess but I'm not bothered if you aren't,' said Zoe, slumping down on a half-chewed sofa. She didn't appear to have much on under the kimono. Even without her make-up and with her hair on end she didn't look real, because her face was still the face that peered haughtily out of full-page glossy perfume advertisements.

'Oh, no. Not at all,' Claire said, smiling indulgently at the graffiti-ed wall. She took her seat gingerly, making James want to laugh when he thought of her immaculate chrome and beechwood home. 'How are you?'

'OK.' Zoe shrugged and turned to James. 'I liked your photos.'

'They weren't mine,' said James, heart in mouth. 'I mean, I didn't do them.'

Zoe looked witheringly at him. 'Actually you did. The photographer is only as good as his or her inspiration.'

'OK,' James said, nervously.

The blue-haired girl called Vicky handed out champagne in gold-stemmed glasses and enquired if she ought to walk the dogs. Zoe said yes and she and Claire started blahing on about collections and contracts and designers. James had no idea why Zoe had wanted to meet him, as she seemed to have no interest in the contents of his head whatsoever. He sat and smoked, drank his champagne and tried to look interested for a while until his eyes fell naturally on the contents of the messy floor.

There were fashion magazines and newspapers, but his eye happened on a computer-printed sheet that showed flesh. A lot of flesh. Buttocks with legs wound round them in a way that didn't look posed for the cameras. He wanted to pick it up and take a closer look, but he thought that would seem rude, so he peered down at the rest of the pictures.

There was one with hands on an obviously male torso, another with a dark-haired boy suckling the nipple of a breast – presumably Zoe's. Then another with two male figures entwined on a bed looking as though someone had just peeped in a doorway and snapped them unawares. Jesus. He hoped he wasn't going to be expected to do this for the camera.

'Excuse me,' he said, timidly. 'Um ... where's the bathroom?'

Zoe looked as though she was unsure she even possessed a bathroom in this shambles for a moment. 'Upstairs,' she said. 'You don't want to go near the downstairs one. Trust me. Up the stairs, turn right, third door on your left.'

'Thanks,' said James, getting to his feet. The champagne rushed to his head. He wasn't used to drinking so much, never mind first thing in the morning. He didn't really need the bathroom. He just wanted five minutes to call someone sane – Phoenix or Tosh – someone who didn't behave as if this insanity was perfectly normal.

He walked unsteadily up the grand staircase and up to the landing. The place was just as bare and tatty up here as it was downstairs. As he struggled to remember the directions to the bathroom, he heard the unmistakable pants and groans of a sex act in progress somewhere in one of the bedrooms and, while he thought he should just ignore it and carry on, his curiosity seemed determined to get the better of him.

It wasn't as if pornos gave you a realistic indication of how things were done and so, he reasoned, it was OK to look because hopefully Phoenix would reap the benefits of his insight. Or maybe not. He couldn't hear anything remotely feminine about the voices. There were grunts and gasps and the occasional 'oh, baby' but the sounds were distinctly male – the sounds of a man humping his way to climax. James's curiosity intensified and he felt that same needling sensation of pleasurable shock he'd felt at the punchline of Shade's latest video when he realised that Fred had kissed a boy.

When he moved further towards the sound he stopped dead in his tracks and realised that the bedroom door was wide open and the two people going for it in the sleazy black satin bed wouldn't have noticed he was there anyway, because they were so hard at it. There was a boy kneeling upright on the bed, his back to the door and his bottom pounding fiercely against the upturned rump of his lover as he rammed it home. The other man knelt face down, moaning into a crumpled fur bedspread, his hips somehow soft and limp between the white-knuckled grip of the boy's hands. It was as if he'd just abandoned himself to what was being done to him; had lost control of his own body so much that he couldn't do anything but go with the boy's aggressive thrusts.

James forgot how to move, how to breathe. He couldn't do anything but stare and wonder at the bizarre way this was turning him on. He liked girls. He liked Phoenix. He liked fucking Phoenix. But when he tried to think of her, warm under his hand, her moist, tender flesh giving way to his probing fingers, the thought only served to excite him even more.

The boy was making the most amazing sounds – soft panting noises and guttural stutters of breath. He opened his mouth wide and gasped sharply, throwing back his head before his face contorted with pleasure and his thrusts turned to quick, strained stabs of his slender hips. He cried out softly and fell forwards onto his lover's back.

James still couldn't seem to get his feet to move, even though this would really be a good time to make his exit, while the two men in the bed fumbled their way around one another to clean up and get comfortable. Instead, he found himself standing there like a moron until the boy surfaced from the tangle of limbs and bedcovers to clock him standing in the doorway.

'Don't you knock?' demanded the boy, in a strong American accent. He had short black hair and enormous brown eyes. There was something strangely familiar about him.

'The door was open,' James said, appalled. 'Sorry.'

The other person in the bed was laughing – madly and maniacally. The tangle of bodies somehow rearranged itself and from it emerged Fred Hill, laughing it off and quite obviously off his head. 'What you worried about?' he asked the boy. 'You've got nothing to be ashamed of, have you?' He looked directly at James – all tousled black hair and brilliant monochrome eyes, exactly the way he looked on TV, only naked. 'He's fucking gorgeous, don't you think?'

'Uh . . . I suppose so. Yes,' said James.

'Well, don't just stand there,' said Fred, pulling the covers up to a respectable distance. 'No standing on ceremony here, dear. It's fuckin' Liberty Hall. Want some coke?'

James wondered how best to make a run for it. 'No. Thanks,' he said. 'I just had champagne and I'm sort of gassy already.'

'Oh. My. God,' said the American boy, with a look of barely contained hilarity on his face. 'You're like something out of Salt Lake City. Who the fuck are you, anyway?'

'Play nice, Carlito,' said Fred. 'This is Zoe's new . . . thing.'

'Thing?' asked James, acerbically.

'No no no . . .' Fred Hill shook his mop of dark hair. 'Not like that. You want a joint, Thing? What's your name, anyway?'

James decided that as much as he disliked being called Thing, he wanted to know what kind of weed the A-list was smoking. He realised too late that when Fred said coke he hadn't meant cola. 'James.'

'James,' echoed Fred, removing a joint from a carved soapstone casket beside the bed. 'Take a seat, James, Jamie, Jimmy, Jim. Which is it?'

'Um ... Jimmy,' said James, preferring Phoenix's diminutive of choice. There wasn't a chair, so he sat down on the end of the bed.

'Right, about the Thing thing,' said Fred. 'Don't mean to be rude, but don't get your knickers in a twist over Zoe, all right? She's going to be a photographer this week but last week she was going to be an eco-warrior and before that a fuckin' Buddhist nun. She has these ... things.'

Carlito nodded. 'Yeah. It's like a sustained kind of self-inflicted insanity that takes her mind off how stone-cold batshit she *really* is.'

'Well, I'm not staking a career on it,' said James, his mind reeling at the thought that he was accepting a joint from Fred Hill. 'I'm not even a model.'

'Aw, baby, you could be!' said Carlito, teasing.

'Oh, you say that to all the boys, you slag,' said Fred. 'You know Carlito, right?' he asked James.

'No, I don't think so.' James passed the joint to Carlito by way of introduction.

'Bitch, please.' Carlito laughed and rolled his eyes. 'I've been Queen of NYC for the past two years.' He took a long toke and blew out smoke slowly, not even allowing Fred Hill to steal his thunder. 'They fucking hate me,' he added, confidentially. 'It's like, "Oh, I'm sorry – you don't get to look hot in a dress because you occasionally eat pussy." It's so prejudiced against bisexuals.'

'And Catholic girls,' sniggered Fred. '"Catholic girls, with a tiny little moustache ..."'

The penny dropped. The schoolgirl from the video. 'Oh my God!' said James. 'Sorry. I didn't recognise you without ... well ... without your clothes on.'

Carlito laughed and passed the joint back to Fred. 'You like?'

'I was totally convinced,' said James, sincerely. 'You had me fooled all along.'

Carlito lay back on the bed and grinned. 'Yay me.'

'He's a proper little fuckin' pervert,' said Fred. 'I love it. But you already knew that, right?'

'Er ... yeah,' James said, sheepishly.

'Not to worry.' Fred yawned. 'It's not like Zoe puts on much by way of hospitality. She's off on Planet Zoe most days. Probably didn't even order the fucking milk, did she?'

'Last I heard the milk was off,' James admitted. This had shaded into the realms of complete surrealism now. He had just walked in on a rock star being fucked by a transvestite – beg pardon, Queen of NYC – they'd invited him in for a smoke and now Fred Hill was asking him if he knew whether a supermodel had remembered to order the milk.

'See? Typical. She has a go at me for being rude and then goes and does it herself. What's she doing for you besides photographing your gorgeous mush?'

'Nothing, as far as I know,' said James. 'Not that she's like, obliged to, or anything. I'm not anybody.'

'You *are* somebody,' said Fred, pointing with the smouldering joint. 'From now on you're Jimmy. Arise, Sir Jimmy, the Voyeuristic.' He grinned his trademark toothy lunatic grin and handed James the joint.

James laughed, trying to disguise how exhilarated he really felt.

'You should celebrate,' said Fred. 'Go and raise hell with Carlito. He's not seen much of the London nightlife.'

'I've seen your ass. What else is there?'

'A lot more, darling,' said Fred, stuffing the joint in Carlito's mouth. 'A *lot* more. Go on. Get trashed on my account – and on my behalf. I've got to go and smile pretty at some bloody fashion awards thing for her madge and her now-infamous vadge. You want to go out with Carlito, don't you, Jimmy?'

'I'd love to,' said James. 'But I've sort of got a girlfriend.'

'Is she cute?'

'She's gorgeous.'

'Bring her along,' said Carlito, with a pearly-toothed smile. 'If I don't wind up fucking the both of you into a state of sexual nirvana you are officially allowed to tell me I'm losing my touch, OK?'

10

If there was one thing Claire loved it was dressing up. She had begun a lifelong love affair with the wardrobe as soon as she was loud enough to express her displeasure with whatever her mother tried to dress her in. If threatened with knitwear and trousers when she wanted to wear her favourite dress then it was more or less a given that little Claire would raise hell unless she left the house in red velvet, blue bows, pink ruffles or whatever constituted her four-year-old concept of couture.

Claire wrote her Christmas cards in front of *My Fair Lady* and peered up now and again to sigh happily or sip the Bailey's she insisted on to get her through the boring job of writing to Cheltenham aunties she hadn't seen for years. James was out shopping with a stylist and Claire had her flat to herself for a few hours. Nice enough, but with *My Fair Lady* as the afternoon matinee on BBC2 life was pure bliss.

She loved Audrey Hepburn, especially as Eliza Doolittle or Holly Golightly. She loved *Breakfast At Tiffany's*, but *My Fair Lady* remained Claire's firm favourite. She never tired of seeing Hepburn's transformation from bedraggled flower girl to the belle of the Embassy Ball. It was always the scene at Ascot that grabbed her – when Hepburn appeared looking sewn into that exquisite fin de siècle black and white dress, lithe as a reed and smiling sweetly the way she had been trained to smile, drifting through gaping crowds with her elegant brown-eyed head tipping her huge cartwheel hat. You always imagined Eliza couldn't get any more beautiful in successive scenes, but Hepburn didn't disappoint on the night of the ball when she came gliding down the stairs in empire-line satin and voile, doe-eyed and dripping with diamonds.

These were Claire's guilty pleasures. Santosh always had a long argument ready prepared about how the endings of both *Breakfast at Tiffany's* and *My Fair Lady* were travesties of the texts they were based on, so both women stuck to *The Rocky Horror Picture Show* and avoided Audrey Hepburn. Santosh didn't believe in fairy tales and as a child she would enhance her reputation as a good girl by claiming she had to study while her siblings went with their father to the cinema. In truth, it was because Tosh said she'd puke if she had to witness one more Bollywood happy ending. Claire found it funny that people had always taken her for the cynical one when Tosh seemed to have been born cynical.

'Claire, it's such crap. Those films were never for girls like me. Girls like me don't get swept off their feet. They get medical degrees and make their parents' proud. Just once I'd like to see a film where a geek like me *doesn't* have to take off her glasses and let down her hair to get the guy.'

Claire supposed she could see where Tosh was coming from, but the world was full of Cinderellas who wanted to go to the ball and flower girls who wanted to be duchesses – and why shouldn't they? If Claire herself was too blonde, too blue-eyed and too buxom to be Hepburn, then she'd be the fairy godmother, the one who said, 'You *shall* go to the ball.' There was no point believing you couldn't transform yourself. You could. You just had to want to, which Tosh patently didn't. Dressing the part was everything. The only difficulty was determining which part you were dressing to play.

She was not sure which role would best suit her when

it came to dressing for Graham Mulholland. So the man said he didn't care for lingerie. He had to be lying. All men liked lingerie. The whole point of sexy underwear was to look sexy and Claire was somewhat annoyed that he'd dismissed her entire Agent Provocateur collection without so much as seeing it. What did the damn man want? Huge grey-white underpants and a withered well-washed bra with its underwiring escaping painfully into one's armpit?

'He's some sort of sodding hippy,' Claire muttered aloud to herself, as she licked the last envelope shut and washed away the taste of envelope-tongue with the dregs of her Bailey's. She headed for the shower humming 'On The Street Where You Live' and with her mind set on the business of proving Dr Mulholland wrong.

Claire was not a woman to sit through lectures on constitutional history unless there was a good reason for doing so and, besides, she thought it would be gauche to dress down for a lecture purely because the lecturer thought socks and sandals were appropriate footwear. She selected her sartorial arsenal from the skin outwards – cream lace push-up bra, matching knickers and sheer shimmery lace-top stockings attached to a strategically visible suspender belt. Over that she elected for the tight angora sweater with the low neckline that could just about blind Neil Savage with cleavage long enough for Claire to pull the wool over his eyes as she pulled the wool over her tits, so to speak, and a new camel suede skirt that looked decent enough when she was standing up but verged on the pornographic when she sat down.

That would teach him.

She found it rather funny that she was attending James's erstwhile university lectures while James did the Bond Street boutiques – like one of those role-swap movies.

When she arrived at the college, fortified by several Bailey's and dressed if not to kill, then at least to maim, the sense of déjà vu was overpowering. Campuses seemed to look alike, painted that same shade of pale institutional green and smelling of book dust and stress. The halls swarmed with students – a twenty-something microcosm of society determined to wear their identities on their army-surplus sleeves. She wobbled slightly on her three-inch patent heels as two girls whooshed past in baseball boots, chains dangling from the back of their baggy skater jeans. Their faces were bare of make-up and they flipped their sleek hair in teenage disdain.

Oh, they liked themselves well enough now, but they'd be singing from a different hymn sheet once they reached their thirties and highlights became a diversionary tactic to fade out the grey hairs, and make-up was something you wore in order to avoid frightening small children. When they got there Claire would be waiting for them, packaging the beauties onto the red carpet, giving those girls someone to despise, someone to envy, someone whose life and face and figure was worth coveting.

Fortified by that thought, Claire studied the directions to the lecture room and made her way upstairs. There were a few students outside the door, huddled in a group beside a bulletin board – a brunette in a ludicrously short skirt, a redhead wearing a Burberry scarf and a good-looking chestnut-haired boy in a Green Day sweatshirt.

'Excuse me,' Claire asked. 'Is this the room for Doctor Mulholland's constitutional history lecture?'

The redhead looked her up and down. The brunette mugged in an 'Oh God, how should I know? I'm such a lovable shambles!' sort of way and the boy was left to do the actual talking.

'Yeah, it is,' he said. 'Are you new?'

'Mature student?' the redhead asked sweetly. Bitch.

'I'm just sitting in,' Claire said, smiling through her teeth. 'Research.'

'Into what?' the boy asked, ingenuously. His eyes were a perfect clear cat's-eye blue and his light-chestnut hair flopped engagingly over his forehead.

'Constitutional history,' said Claire.

'Seriously?'

'No.'

'Why are you here if you're not taking it seriously, then?' asked the redhead.

'Darling, when you get to my age you have to broaden your horizons any which way you can,' Claire said, waspishly.

The girl peered down her nose and went into the lecture room with her friend, leaving Claire with the boy. 'Sorry about Nat,' he said. 'She's just ... y'know ... got issues.'

'Gathered that.'

'We're not all horrible. Honest,' said the boy. 'If you're free, after ... we could go for a cup of coffee or something?'

The redhead stuck her head round the door. 'Daniel, are you coming or not?'

Oh my God. Claire bit her lip. 'I'd love to,' she said. 'But I have to dash off straight after.'

'OK. Maybe another time, then.' Daniel went into the lecture room.

Claire bolted a safe distance down the hall and called Tosh's number.

'Tosh – I'm at the college.'

'Uh-huh?'

'I think I just met Daniel.'

Tosh cleared her throat and then sighed. 'Claire...' she said, in a warning tone.

'Light-auburn hair, blue eyes, likes Green Day?'

'That sounds like him. Please. Don't say anything, OK? This is awkward enough as it is.'

'Tosh, he's gorgeous. Are you mad?'

'He's twenty.'

'He's a grown-up!'

'Back off, Claire. Seriously. I told him to find someone his own age for his own bloody good.'

'Well, the girl he was with was a vinegar tits hellbitch from the planet PMS. Scrawny little Burberry-clad number with a bad attitude. I don't know if he was *with* her but I know he could do better.'

'Claire! You didn't mention me, did you?'

'Of course not!'

'Keep it that way. It's over. He's far too young.'

'Your loss,' said Claire. 'But I think you're missing out.'

'Don't. OK?'

'OK.'

Claire was not convinced it was time to give up. Her fairy godmother instincts were on overdrive – probably something to do with too much Audrey Hepburn. She went into the lecture room and took her seat near the front. The room was inclined so that her legs would be at eye-level with the lectern. Good.

Daniel smiled at her as she sat down. Maybe he'd start passing notes. That would be fun. Passing notes under Dr Mulholland's nose so that he called her to account for disrupting his class and told her to see him in his office afterwards.

He came in, carrying books and notes. He wore a pale, checked shirt and those eternal hideous sandals. He looked surprised and pleased when he spotted her in the audience and she crossed her legs strategically and flourished a notebook and pen to demonstrate that she was taking this seriously. His baleful look back at her confirmed that he didn't believe her for a second.

'Right, OK. Settle down. I'd advise taking notes, as

much of what you hear in this lecture will be going towards your exams after Christmas. I won't prepare notes for you because you should have got over that before entering sixth form, but I will –' he paused, to add with a kind of sadistic relish that Claire enjoyed '– be handing out a comprehensive booklist.'

There were predictable groans from the class. Claire sat back, inching her demure camel skirt higher and deciding that this would be a whole lot more fun than she had expected. Graham looked different on his own turf – in control, clever, even somewhat sexy. He had his sleeves rolled up and his forearms, braced against the lectern, were muscular and hairy.

The lengths you had to go to to meet men these days. If it wasn't throwing your knickers at scaffolders then it was sitting through lectures on constitutional history.

'In order to gain a full understanding of the current political system at work in the British Isles we must first ask ourselves a number of questions. Firstly, which bodies and institutions are at work in the system today and what are their origins in history? Secondly, how do these systems work and why have they been put in place to work thus?'

Claire suppressed a yawn by the time he got to whatever thirdly was. She could have stayed home and watched the rest of the film, maybe had a few more drinks. Maybe a bath and a few more drinks in the bath, and then maybe a spot of self-abuse with the shower massager attachment. She sighed and rested her elbow on the desk, making her pen descend to the floor with a clatter.

The class were too absorbed in taking notes to notice. Claire leaned sideways out of her chair to pick it up. She had to stick out a foot to steady herself and realised as she did so that the movement had spread her legs wide apart. She straightened and saw Graham looking straight up her skirt. He pushed his glasses back up onto the bridge of his nose and gave her a look so resolutely prim that she felt heat flood to her face in a sensation she hadn't felt in years. She was blushing – which was downright peculiar because as far as she knew she didn't *have* any shame.

'I dropped my pen,' she mouthed, flustered and amazed to discover she rather liked being flustered.

Dr Mulholland sighed. 'Ms Sawyer, please pay attention. This is for your own good.'

The class looked at her. Claire was sure she'd turned crimson. Worse, the flush on her face felt like it went all the way down, peaking her nipples under her sweater. When she sat up, trying to look attentive, her tits seemed to stick out a mile and her nipples poked interrogatively towards Mulholland. She brought her knees tight together, her heels closing beneath the desk with an audible click.

His words seemed to slot into her dirty fantasies like the missing piece of a jigsaw: 'This is for your own good. Kneel down. Open your mouth, Sawyer. This is for your own good. Bend over. Spread your cheeks – it's for your own good.'

She'd be teacher's pet if that's what it took. She thought she should have brought him an apple like a little girl trying to curry favour – a juicy red apple polished to a high sheen against her sweater, rubbed between her breasts until it gleamed enough to be delivered to his desk. She kept her eyes fixed on him for the remainder of the lecture, not listening to a word he said and unable to hear anyway, over her mind's constant mantra of 'look at me, look at me'. Whenever his gaze did happen to fall on her, it was like a shock, a blessing, a brief glimpse of hope that her final marble had not rolled out of reach.

She meant to follow him when the lecture was over but Daniel was hot on her heels.

'How did you find it? All right?' he asked.

'Fine,' Claire lied. She'd lost Mulholland more or less around about the start of the Civil War. She was losing him now, watching his retreating back disappear down the hall. 'Is his office just down there?'

'Um, yeah,' Daniel said, struggling against her distraction. 'Look, we're going for a coffee – me and Nat and Sue. You're welcome to come.'

He really did like older women, this one. 'I'm sorry,' Claire said. 'I really have to get on. I'll tell you what – why don't I catch you some other time?' She fished in her handbag for a diversionary tactic and her hand happened on the Shade tickets given to her by Fred, on Zoe's insistence. 'Are you going to the Shade gig?'

Daniel rolled his eyes. 'Like I can afford it!' he said. 'I already put money aside for the Isle of Wight Festival this year – totally cleaned out.'

'Never mind,' said Claire, sympathetically. 'You *shall* go to the ball. See you there.' She pushed the ticket into his hand and headed off down the hall. Daniel followed, hurrying to keep up with her pace.

'You can't . . .' he gasped, delighted. 'I mean, seriously? You're giving me a free ticket?'

'Yes,' Claire said, wishing he'd give up and bugger off. She had no intention of going to that gig. The very thought of it gave her a headache. 'That's the next time I'll be standing still long enough for you to talk to me. Have fun.'

He stopped walking, at last. 'Thank you!' he called after her. 'Thanks so much!'

'All in a day's work,' Claire muttered, making her escape. Jesus, he was persistent, like a puppy determined to hump your leg no matter you whacked it on the nose with a newspaper. One of the many reasons she was a cat person.

She walked down the hall, peering at the names on the doors as she went. Dr Michael Porter, Prof. Morag McKuen ... nope, nope, no. Dr Graham Mulholland. Here he was. She hesitated before knocking, relishing the pleasant lurch of nostalgia. It was like being sent to the headmistress for being caught smoking or turning the hem of her schoolskirt too high. Too bad they'd abolished corporal punishment. If he'd had a cane she'd have dropped her drawers and let him whack her on the arse.

'Yep. I'm definitely sick,' she told herself, under her breath, and rapped her knuckles sharply against the door.

'Come in.'

He was sat at his desk in a small office the size of two broom cupboards bolted together. This didn't surprise her, since the faculty was buried in the ugly modern part of the sprawling college campus, away from the plush Victorian façade cultivated by institutes of higher learning. The educated elite had got bigger since the centuries when most London colleges were founded and the campuses had had to expand to accommodate them so that listed buildings swelled with cheap, rapidly growing carbuncles of brick or concrete. No wonder academics like Mulholland cultivated an air of asceticism – the better to pretend they were happy in these butt-ugly rabbit warrens of classrooms.

'Can I help you?' he asked, not looking up from the papers he was marking.

'I'd have brought you an apple if I knew you were going to be this charming,' said Claire. 'Nice lecture.'

He looked balefully back at her over the tops of his horn-rims. 'You didn't listen to a word of it.'

'It was very boring,' Claire said, closing the door

behind her and plastering herself against the back of it so that he couldn't throw her out. 'I should have taken you up on your dinner invitation instead.'

'And what on earth would we talk about?' he asked, acidly. He seemed genuinely offended.

'*Stationery Cupboard Sluts II*?' Claire suggested. 'I'm sure you're a fan. In secret.'

He didn't show any signs of thawing. Shit. He shook his head and transferred another paper to his inbox with irritated, impatient gestures. 'Ms Sawyer, it's perfectly clear to me that you have no interest in pretending to be anything but vapid.'

Claire's mouth fell open. 'Excuse me?'

He turned to face her at long last, arms folded and legs crossed. 'Well, you're not interested in my work, you're dressed in that extraordinary fashion . . .'

'You were the one who said you weren't interested in my brain!' she said. 'Make up your mind, why don't you?'

'I said I wasn't interested in your underwear,' he said. 'Although I've seen more of it in the past hour than I'd care to. I could see right up your skirt.'

'That was the idea.'

'I thought I told you I found all that nonsense boring,' he said, irritably.

'I don't,' she said. 'And don't treat me like one of your fucking students.'

He uncrossed his legs and cracked a smile at last. 'To all effects and purposes, you *are* one of my students. So you will mind your language in my office. Is that clear?'

There was a glint in his eye and she wished she knew him well enough to be in a better position to decipher it. 'Yes,' she said, then added, 'sir.'

He held her gaze for only a moment, but it was long enough for her to gauge that he would like to play teacher and student. Long enough for her brain to flood with memories of dirty daydreams in which he directed her to do obscene things in his prim, neutral voice.

He turned back to his papers. 'I don't want to see any more stocking tops, Ms Sawyer,' he said. 'Put your underclothes on the desk before you leave, please.'

'What?'

He looked up at her and sighed as if she were an idiot nineteen year old. 'I'm confiscating them. Put them on the desk, please.'

'I'm wearing them,' said Claire.

'Well, take them off, girl!' he snapped, rolling his eyes with impatience.

'You expect me to walk out of your office naked?'

'Don't tempt me,' he said, mildly. 'No. Take off your underwear and put it on the desk, please.'

'Fine,' she said. Since she couldn't tell him how she felt and he seemed determined not to make it easy for her, she thought she'd fall back on the tried and tested Sharon Stone method. Worked on scaffolders, after all. She reached under her skirt and pulled down her knickers. Mulholland didn't look up from his papers as she slid them down over her feet and bent to retrieve them. They were embarrassingly damp and smelled distinctly of lust and she stood there, bare-arsed, holding them for a moment, wondering what he meant to do with them.

'On the desk,' he said, pointing to the desk in an offhand manner.

She put them on the desk. If part of her had hoped he would do something entirely perverted like sniff or fondle her knickers, then that part was rapidly disappointed. He paid no attention, which was annoying, but she had yet to take off her stockings and that would give him an unavoidable floor show.

Claire put one foot up on the spare chair pushed against the wall, angling herself to show as much leg as possible and hitched her skirt up to unclip the first stocking. He carried on marking the papers. With a sigh of frustration she inelegantly divested herself of her stockings and suspender belt and dumped them on his desk. 'There,' she said. 'Happy now?'

'And the rest.'

'The rest?'

'You're wearing a bra, aren't you?' he said, glancing up only to wave a pen in the general direction of her breasts.

'I happen to need that.'

'The rest of it, Ms Sawyer.'

She reached behind and unfastened her bra, then awkwardly pulled the straps down under her sleeves and dropped it on the desk. Her lingerie sat there incongruously amongst the books and papers in front of him. Her sweater chafed at her nipples and, when she shifted her weight to slip her feet back into her shoes, she was acutely aware of her suede skirt brushing against her bare buttocks. She had never felt quite so naked in all her life.

'Will that do?' she asked.

He prodded the bundle of underwear with a pen, as if it wasn't La Perla. 'I think we should have words, don't you?' he said. 'Take a seat.'

'Do I have a choice? You're holding my underwear hostage.' She sat down anyway, careful to keep her legs together. The last time she'd flashed a man like that she'd ended up being sexually harassed by confectionery, and she had no desire to repeat the experience.

'I'm sure you could manage without it in a pinch,' he said.

'You'd think differently if you were filling a D cup. Why are you doing this?'

'Why are you going along with it?'

'I asked first,' Claire said, smoothing down her skirt. It

was too short. She regretted it now because she was sure he was enjoying her discomfort.

'All right,' he said. 'Since you ask. Why wouldn't you have dinner with me?'

'I'm very busy!' Claire said, puzzled as to where this decorous question had come from when she was sitting in his office with her backside almost entirely bared to the uncomfortable bristly upholstery of the spare chair.

'And that's the truth, is it?' he asked, looking schoolteacher-ishly at her over his glasses. He opened the window behind him and picked up her knickers between finger and thumb. 'The God's honest truth?'

'Yes! Why wouldn't it be?'

'We have ways of making you talk, Ms Sawyer,' he said, and reached out of the window so that he was dangling her pants over the quad below. 'The truth, now.'

'There's nothing to tell,' she said. 'And even if there was, I've lost underwear in far more interesting situations than this, believe me.'

'I believe you,' he said, and let go of her knickers. Instinctively, Claire leapt out of the chair to grab them but they fluttered off in into the dark, snowy evening. In reaching for them, she found herself bent over his lap with her fingers on the window ledge, her bum in the air and her skirt hiked obscenely high. She realised that extricating herself with any dignity was going to be impossible so she dropped back down into her chair with a graceless thump.

'And this is because I wouldn't have dinner with you, is it?' she asked, angrily. 'You defenestrate my fucking drawers?'

'Defenestrate.' He smiled. 'Big word for a woman pretending to be the sum of her cup size.'

'You're a cunt. I'm leaving. Goodbye.' She snatched up her coat and bag.

He started to laugh – a schoolboy giggle that transformed his solemn face into a picture of mischief and took years off him. 'Without your knickers? There'll be some happy men on the Tube tonight, I'm sure.'

Claire flung her bag back to the floor and glared at him. 'Yeah, well, there might be a chance that at least one of them would *do* something. Do you even have a penis?'

'Yes, thank you. Have you considered the possibility that you might not be my type?'

'Your type?' Claire said, fuming.

'Yes. You have a type, don't you, Claire?' He stood up and bunched the rest of her underwear in his fist. His tone could have etched glass. 'You know,' he said. 'The type that doesn't wear sandals, checked shirts, isn't called Graham – wouldn't embarrass you in public? Your secretary obviously made a bit of a cock-up with the telephone.'

He moved towards the window and Claire's contrition vanished as fast as it had appeared. 'Don't you fucking dare!' she yelled, lunging for her bra and stockings as he let go of them. He tried to grab her and her anger and her reflexes took over. Before the good doctor knew it, he was staggering across the other side of the office with a stunned expression on his face and crashing into a bookshelf before being knocked flat on his arse. Judo was generally designed to be practised in a larger room and the bookshelves began to topple.

Dr Mulholland quickly scooted on his back across the floor just as one bookcase collapsed across the narrow room and struck the one on the opposite wall with sufficient force to bring it crashing down against the other.

'Brown belt, did you say?' he asked, with impressive aplomb considering she had just trashed his office.

'I did, yes,' said Claire, standing over him. 'Sorry.'

'Not at all,' he said. 'I'm rather enjoying the view, actually.'

She helped him up, relieved that he appeared to be finding it funny. 'You're a wanker,' she said, self-consciously smoothing down her skirt.

'And you should be locked up,' he said. 'Are you always this violent?'

'Only when I'm sublimating.'

'Sublimating?' He was close enough to kiss or slap.

'Yes. It's when you say and do something because you mean something or want to do something completely different.'

'I know what sublimating means,' he said, taking off his glasses, folding them and putting them on the desk behind her, so that she was hemmed in against the desk. 'And you should stop it at once.'

'I should, should I?' Claire said, leaning back against the desk, presenting her boobs to their best advantage. Her sweater chafed her nipples and they poked lewdly against the soft wool.

'I think it would be a good idea,' he said, putting his hand on her waist. 'If this is what you can do to one small faculty office in the course of your sublimation then it's possible you could reduce London to a smoking ruin.'

'I like a challenge.'

'Well, you'll have to wait,' he said, tartly, and kissed her.

11

James had dumped the shopping bags in the hall with little or no intention of wearing any of the clean-cut clothes that Darren the Stylist (a Botoxed twit with a trendy haircut and a habit of nodding and saying 'yeah, yeah, cool' until you wanted to stab him) had picked out for him. He had no idea what one wore when hanging out with Fred Hill's transvestite bit on the side, but he had a feeling that tasteful white shirts that made him look like someone from a boyband were not going to go down well.

Claire was out. James was marooned alone in the midst of the first real style crisis of his life when Carlito showed up for their 'date'.

Carlito had pulled out all the stops, dragged up like Uma Thurman in *Pulp Fiction*. He wore flared black suede hipsters and a matching longline jacket, but under that there was some kind of sequinned bustier thing that with the right padding and careful lacing had given him the suggestion of a perfect little cleavage. His hair was quite obviously not his own, because James had seen his cropped hair only that morning, but the black wig he wore was so good that the bobbed bangs of it swung across his cheekbones like real hair.

'Will I do?' he asked, twirling on three-inch heels.

James gawped. 'You look ... er ... you look like a girl.'

Carlito raised perfectly plucked eyebrows. 'Honey, that's pretty much the whole concept of drag,' he said, extracting a cigarette from his purse and tapping a foot while he waited impatiently for a light.

'I didn't mean that,' said James. 'I mean, you don't look like a drag queen. You look like a woman.'

'Thank you very much,' said Carlito, grinning and showing what looked like a couple of hundred perfect American teeth. 'You're not wearing *that*, are you? If you're gonna take a lady out you should at least make an effort.'

'I'm sort of having a style crisis,' James confessed. 'I think. I've never had one before.'

Carlito fell on the shopping bags and removed their contents with various squeals and exclamations of horror. 'Yeah, I see why *Queer Eye for the Straight Guy* took off. Yeek! Ew! Were you trying to put an image together here or something?'

'I think the stylist had that in mind, yeah.'

'Fire the bitch. Jesus!' Carlito mugged at a T-shirt Darren had described as surfer-chic. 'Who does he dress? *Blue Peter* presenters? Do you still have that in Britain, by the way? *Blue Peter*?'

'Um, yeah,' said James. 'Still going strong, I think. I actually grew up in Dubai.'

'Oh my God! Lawrence of Arabia! Fabulous!' Carlito beamed. 'Right. I'm going to have to do something with you if we're going to show these Limeys the meaning of style. What's in your closet, and what's Mom got in the bathroom?'

James barely had time to explain that he didn't live with his mother and Claire was hardly the maternal type. Carlito ransacked his wardrobe, digging out the camo trousers and tatty jeans that James was more or less forbidden to wear in public. A tight black T-shirt from Darren's collection was strategically torn, flecked with bleach from beneath the kitchen sink and reconstructed with safety pins – 'Because punk's not dead, it always smelled that way.' Carlito then went to town with a box of peroxide Claire had stashed in the bathroom cabinet and, despite James's protests, demanded he wear make-up and a choker that Claire had left beside the sink.

'She'll kill me for wearing her stuff!'

'Honey, it's pure glass,' said Carlito, fastening the necklace around James's throat. 'You only have to bite it to tell. There ain't no harder substance on this planet than a girl's best friend. Head up – lemme do your eyes.'

James struggled not to blink at the unfamiliar sensation of eyeliner being applied. Carlito was close enough to kiss as he applied the make-up, his expression distant as he concentrated on what he was doing. 'You gotta love black eyeliner. Why do you think Fred's so scoped on the stuff? It's got to look fucked though – like you've been wearing it all night. Makes those baby blues just psycho.'

It was so hard to believe that there was a man under Carlito's clothes. Even close up, the only indication of gender about his face was a slight heaviness about the foundation over his jaw and throat. The entire situation was bizarre. He was being made up by a girl from a rock video, who was actually a boy, and they had been introduced to one another in Fred Hill's bed after James walked in on the two of them shagging.

James's perceptions of his world were so skewed that he wouldn't have been surprised to find the floor was no longer beneath his feet. He felt so dizzy he thought the floor would tip beneath his feet and send the furniture spinning like the cars of a fairground waltzer. One more twist and the nuts and bolts of ordinary reality would come loose completely and send him whirling dangerously into the world of the A-list.

'I shouldn't ask,' said James, but did anyway. 'But does Zoe know about you and Fred?'

Carlito sniggered. 'Hell yeah. She was the low-calorie sandwich filling most of last night. Head up – lemme see. Yeah, you're good.' He leaned back. 'So where's this fabulous broad of yours? Where are we meeting her?'

'She's working. She can't make it.'

'She so can. Tell her to play hooky. Now vamoose. Shoo. I gotta pee.'

James walked out of the bathroom and was confronted with his reflection in Claire's mirrored hallway. He was so startled by his appearance that he jumped, not recognising himself. His hair was spiked, with scattershot peroxide highlights. His eyes looked bluer than before with the rings of dark eyeliner and the fake baguette diamond collar gleamed, pleasingly trashy, around his neck. The customised T-shirt seemed to accentuate all the hard work he had put in at the gym. It was ripped and pinned over one nipple, deliberately suggestive, and at once he wanted to see Phoenix and find out what she thought of him like this. He loved it. He felt like he was almost on a glittery par with Carlito.

Carlito came out of the bathroom, smoothing down a stray lock of hair. 'You like it?' he asked, placing his hands on James's shoulders and inspecting his handiwork in the mirror.

'I love it. Thanks.'

'You can thank me later,' Carlito flirted.

James laughed it off. 'I'd just be playing if I did.'

'Nothing wrong with playing. How do you know you don't like it if you've never tried it?'

'I don't,' said James, shrugging. 'I don't know at all. I just know I like women. I mean, I *really* like women.'

'Fred said exactly the same thing.' Carlito flicked his hair and smoothed down his jacket. 'We going out now or do you want to smoke a doobie first to get us in the mood?'

'Dumb question,' James said, unconsciously imitating Carlito.

By the time they left the building they were already laughing like morons at anything and everything. The cab driver raised his eyebrows at James's necklace and asked James if he was 'one of them metrosexuals' – sending Carlito into spasms of laughter. Thankfully by the time he got to pontificating about boys being boys and girls being girls and complimented Carlito on his ladylike attire, they were close enough to Soho to fling the guy his fare and stagger out of the cab in hysterics.

'So what's with the girlfriend?' asked Carlito, as James checked his phone. 'Is she busy?'

'Must be. Hasn't answered my last two texts. We'll go in and surprise her.'

'She'll shit a brick. She'll see me and think you've brought some uber-hoochie.'

'Hoochie?' James laughed. He gulped down his apprehension as they entered the club. The size of the doorman didn't help his nerves whatsoever. He had never been to a strip club before and didn't know how he'd feel about seeing Phoenix ogled by other men. He was determined to be cool about it because he knew she hated it when guys decided they wanted to take her away from it all.

'Uh-huh. Hoochie coochie,' said Carlito, shimmying provocatively as he tossed a couple of twenties at the blonde at the cash till. 'It's OK, baby,' he said, when she double-taked. 'I have a fifty per cent controlling interest in naked ladies. I can show it to you if you want.'

'Oi,' said the doorman, in a warning tone.

'No need to be jealous, honey. You'll get your turn.'

'In.' The doorman rolled his eyes and pointed them through the door.

It was dark and smoky inside the club, the music so loud that the bass thundered up through the soles of your feet and vibrated your guts. On a catwalk with a pole at the end, a topless blonde in jewelled heels was gyrating to a Kylie Minogue number.

'Silicone at six o'clock!' Carlito yelled in James's ear over the sound of the music. 'I hope she didn't pay *too* much for those titties.'

'I'm going to go and find Phoe,' James shouted back.

'OK. I'll get the drinks.'

James had no idea where to look, or where anything was, but knowing Phoenix she was probably somewhere where she could smoke a joint and get good and loaded before going on stage. The huge surly bouncers were obviously there to prevent the girls from being molested, but they added to the general air of intimidation about the place. Various tables were scattered about, some with poles mounted in the middle of them. Half-naked girls wiggled, lolled and squirmed around the poles and the men watched them with either slightly bashful grins or beady-eyed leers, which presumably depended on how pissed they were.

This was strictly men's territory and James hated it almost immediately. If that's what made you a man – the ability to stare at tits and stuff banknotes down a stripper's thong – then he could understand why Carlito liked to put on a dress. Anything to escape the brain-dead, dick-led ideal of fashionable masculinity. He wanted to punch the lot of them, conscious that at some point most of these half-drunk goobers had taken a peek at Phoenix's boobs. They weren't even good enough to breathe the same air as her.

In the end he asked the barmaid, because it was impossible to talk to any of the girls or the topless waitresses without incurring fearsome looks from the bouncers. You didn't touch them – he knew the rule of look, but don't touch – but apparently it was as frowned upon to converse with these women as it was to grope them inappropriately. Talking, James supposed, was the business of whores and courtesans, even geishas – the women throughout history and of various cultures who had all had to endure the eternal complaint of men that their wives didn't really understand them.

When he asked the barmaid, her face slammed shut like a door. 'Don't know who you mean,' she said.

'She's about so high,' James persisted. 'Black. Green eyes. Short hair sort of done up in little plaits. Swears quite a lot.'

'She'll be on later,' the barmaid said, sighing, then disappeared out back.

Further down the bar, Carlito was causing quite a sensation amongst the middle-aged male clientele who were obviously fooled into thinking there was a lady in their midst. Even better, a lady who frequented strip clubs and might be game for some Sapphic squirming for their delectation. What a wet dream!

'They so need to watch MTV sometime,' James muttered to himself, sniggering as Carlito lapped up the attentions of his admirers. When he held out a cigarette, half a dozen men offered him a light. When he accepted a light he dipped his lashes low and peeked out from beneath them, cheeks hollowed and lips pouting as he sucked in the smoke. The sheer depth of his deception was staggering. James hoped he wouldn't get into trouble.

There was a hand on his shoulder and he spun round, startled.

'Fuckin' hell. It *is* you,' Phoenix said. 'What the bloody hell are you wearing?'

'I might ask you the same question,' said James.

Her hair was unbraided and stuck up in an impossibly frizzy halo around her small face. She wore a spiked dog collar around her neck and her eyes and lips were painted jet black. She had her red plastic raincoat wrapped around her and high black buckled knee-boots, but James suspected she wasn't wearing much underneath.

'Back here,' she said, peering furtively around and tugging him through a door at the end of the bar into a shabby narrow hallway. 'I thought it was you, but I couldn't be sure when Sadie said.' She pulled at his diamond necklace and laughed. 'What the fucking hell is all this?' she asked, and kissed him, smothering him in black lipstick.

'I ran into the Queen of New York City. Long story,' James said, when she let him breathe again. She had just a black thong on underneath the raincoat. Her skin had been dusted with some dark, glittery powder to make it look even more like velvet and her nipples stiffened under his fingers when he touched them. He was sure he shouldn't be touching her in this place, but she encouraged him.

'Tell me,' she said. 'I'm not in any hurry to get back to work.'

He told her. She proved to be a rapt audience, all wide eyes and shrieks of delight, punctuating her performance with expressions of incredulity: 'I don't believe you', 'You're taking the fuckin' piss!' and 'Nooooo!'

'I'm not joking!'

'You walked in on a tranny fucking Fred Hill up the bum?' Phoenix gawped. 'You've got to be fuckin' joking.'

'Don't tell anyone!'

'Can I tell my sister?' Phoenix asked. 'Please? She'll go mental. Isis has got this thing about boy porn – writes it on the internet or something.'

'Your sister's name is Isis?'

She raised her eyebrows. 'Jimmy, my name is Phoenix. You didn't think I'd have sisters called Jane and Mary, did you? Well, I got my sister Mary-Jane, if you know what I mean, but Mum likes ancient stuff – historical, like. There's me, Isis, Cassandra, Lilith and Paris.'

'All right, tell her, but don't you dare mention any names.'

'Cross my heart.'

'I can't believe I'm practically flogging true-life porn to your sister.'

'You like porn?' asked Phoenix, with a wolfish grin.

'Depends.'

'You're a man. You love porn. Admit it.' She opened one of the doors off the hallway and pulled him into a stock room. There was a trestle table and a plastic chair but no other furniture aside from shelves and shelves full of video cassettes.

'Is this the porno lounge or something?' he asked, laughing.

'No. This is where they keep the security tapes,' she said, and pointed to the corner of the ceiling. There was a camera winking a little red light back at them. 'And that's to make sure they don't get half-inched.'

'Why would anybody want to steal security tapes?' asked James.

Phoenix perched on the chair. 'If we have any interesting punters then they hold onto the tapes. Politicians and stuff.'

'Isn't that illegal?'

'Nope,' she said, fishing a joint out of the pocket of her raincoat. 'Legitimate business surveillance. If they're not anybody special the tapes just get wiped and re-used, but if it's footballers behaving like fuckin' arseholes then they usually wind up in the papers.'

'Should you be smoking that in here?'

'No, but I'm trying to get fired,' she said, passing him the joint.

'I'm going to have to ask. Why?'

'Because I don't want to quit,' she said, blowing smoke at the camera. 'I don't want to be one of those ex-strippers who give it up and bang on about what fuckin' exploitation it is. I'd rather get chucked out for being too much of a dirty bitch for a Soho titty bar. Looks better on a CV, don't it?'

James laughed. 'Depends what line of work you want to get into, I suppose.'

She turned the chair around and straddled it like Christine Keeler, her raincoat coming open and her breasts only just hidden by the back off the chair. 'Wouldn't mind giving Madonna a run for her money,' she said, peering thoughtfully into the camera. 'It's not been the same since she hung up her pointy bras and S&M gear.'

'Madonna?' James whistled. 'Nothing like big ambitions.'

She handed him the joint and one of her nipples peeked out from behind the chair back. 'You ain't seen nothin' yet,' she said, peering up at the camera and peeling her coat from her shoulders. It dropped to the floor and she gave him a dirty, knowing look. 'You want a private show, Jimmy?'

'There's a camera. It's not so private.' He thought she must have been quite spectacularly stoned. Yet another piece of her patented lunacy – an attitude that scared him shitless and yet turned him on so much he couldn't think straight.

'I love the camera,' she said, pouting. 'And the camera loves me. We can make it a threesome.'

'No way. I've seen the bouncers out there. They're the kind of people I go out of my way to avoid pissing off.'

She ignored him. She lifted her feet from the floor, put her hands on the chairback rode the chair like a horse. She played entirely to the camera, confident of him reacting sooner or later. Her eyes were unfocused and elsewhere as she stood up and turned the chair around the right way. She stood astride the seat and stared into the camera, playing with her nipples so that they stood up stiff. Her muscled legs looked fantastic in the high black boots, her crotch only covered by the skimpy thong.

'Stop it,' said James, his mouth turning dry at the sight of her.

She smiled and shook her head. 'Told you,' she whispered. 'I fuckin' love the camera. So much. You should be jealous.'

'Put your clothes back on, Phoe,' he said, already beginning to feel dizzy with fear and excitement. 'Don't make me come over there.'

'That's the idea, stupid.' She swayed her splayed hips and settled her hands on them – a provocative and confrontational stance made all the more enticing by the way she hooked her thumbs into the waistband of her thong.

'I'm not going to manhandle a lady,' he said, with mock primness.

She stuck her tongue out at him. 'You've done it before. If you won't handle me I'll have to handle myself.'

She meant it. Her fingers slid down to the crotch of her thong and pulled it aside, flashing a sliver of hair as her fingers found their mark. She closed her eyes and shuddered, her leg muscles straining visibly.

'Phoe!' James attempted to interpose himself between her and the camera. 'Someone will see!'

He tried to grab her and reached for her coat to cover her, but he had nothing on her when it came to strength and agility. She jumped nimbly up onto the trestle table, kicked aside a stack of video cassettes and stood on the table, legs apart once more, her hips swaying tauntingly.

'I might want someone to see,' she said. 'I might get off on it.'

'You might?' He didn't want to risk trying to pull her down off the table. It looked unsteady, and besides, she was ferociously strong and her heels could have inflicted damage if she had a mind to.

'I might,' she said, hooking her fingers into her thong again. 'Sometimes I take everything off on stage. You have to keep your legs together and just flash a little bit. Enough to keep their dicks hard. But sometimes I just want to give them something more. You know what I really want?'

'What?'

'One day, I want to go out there in nothing but my pointes. You know the arabesque, Jimmy? The ballet position? It's like a standing splits, one foot *en pointe*. It fucking hurts.'

'Come down. Please.' He could see right up between her thighs and the view was both tormenting and entrancing.

She shook her head. 'I used to practise it for hours. It hurt, but it spread my pussy wide open. When I practised it in the nude it was even better, and I'd just hold it and hold it for as long as I could. Just to see how wet I could get myself. Till it was running down my thigh . . .'

'Jesus . . .' The word rushed out of him in a kind of desperate exhalation. He hadn't even realised he'd been holding his breath until he spoke. 'Oh my God. Please.'

'All in good time,' she said, sliding her knickers down. She kicked them off and stood with her feet apart. Her body was almost more than he could stand. Small breasts, an athletic, muscled torso and then the tender shell of her exposed to his view. She tipped her hips forwards and parted the glistening flesh for his delectation. The very core of her sex was a deep, dark pink, lighter than the brown outer folds. The contrast was intensely erotic and James could feel his own heart thundering in his guts, pounding out the muffled bass from the club behind his eardrums, pulsing through his confined and aching cock.

'All in good time,' she said again, to nobody but herself. She stared directly at the camera and moved her hips to the distant beat. There wasn't a pole, but she didn't need a pole to dance. She squirmed with snakelike movements, the rolls of her hips as fluid as those of a belly dancer. She crouched side-on to show what little curves she had to best advantage. Her knees were demurely drawn together until the beat sped up and then she opened her thighs wide and pistoned her hips back and forth with primitive, tribal movements.

He thought that was sweat running down the inside of her leg but he could have been wrong. When she got down on her hands and knees on the table top she let out something like a moan and couldn't resist slipping one hand between her thighs to touch herself.

'Come on,' James pleaded, reaching out to touch her leg. He no longer cared that the camera was watching. He'd never seen her so turned on before and he had to know what would happen if he touched her, even if it meant some huge hairy bouncer coming in and hurling him out onto the street.

She swivelled onto the edge of her table with frenetic movements that had none of her usual grace. She wound her arms round his neck and kissed him with a fierce intensity. Her legs were open and he reached between them. She was soaking wet and his fingers slid in so effortlessly that he thought for a brief, crazy second that she had somehow sucked them inside of her. She moaned and pushed her hips against his hand, fucking his fingers and making a weird, mewly noise when his thumb found her clit.

His dick felt like it would explode but he wanted so much to make her come. He rubbed her faster and she wound her legs around him and whimpered. Her juices were trickling down his fingers and into his palm and her sweat was all over his T-shirt, her lipstick all over his face. She swore and panted and scrabbled for his fly and he helped her with shaking hands.

'Fuck me,' she whispered. 'Quick. Just fuckin' do it.'

'Condoms,' he said, wishing to God he didn't have to argue at a time like this. She was wet and welcoming and his body tingled and his brain boiled at the possibility of more. She was sensitised and begging for it, her cunt clutching and slick whenever he penetrated it with his fingers.

'It's all right. It's safe. Come on.'

'Are you sure?'

'I'm sure,' she said, turning around with her hands on the table and her bum facing him. 'Don't make me fuckin' beg, Jimmy.'

She didn't have to beg. Not looking like that with her arse in the air and her feet apart and her sex a wet slash beneath her buttocks. There was no way he could have said no.

He pushed, she moaned and he was in, and he had never felt anything like it before. He'd dreamed of doing this without a layer of latex in the way and he could feel every little muscle and groove inside her, his dick bathed from root to tip in glorious wetness. He had to bend his knees because even in her heels she was shorter than him, but he could reach around and touch her clit and feel her jolt and shudder when he did so.

'Do it hard,' she said, in a strained little voice like she'd forgotten how to breathe.

If it hadn't been for the thought of the camera putting him off he wouldn't have lasted five seconds. She made the most incredible noises and arched her back and raised her arse to take more of him. His balls swung and slapped gently against her bum, the weight of them tugging at the root of his cock in a way that was surprisingly exciting. He was sure he was going to lose it but then he felt her tense and he could feel the muscles inside of her clenching sharply – once, twice, three times and she said, 'Ohfuckyes,' in a rush and he realised she had come. He thrust deep inside her, clutching her waist to hold her there as she drooped with exhaustion and held tight, riding out the last shivers of her muscles as his cock spurted inside her.

When she stood up and pulled her coat on she looked completely debauched. Her eyes and lips were smudged, her pubes wet and tangled. She hadn't bothered to put her knickers back on and her inner thighs were noticeably damp. James had never felt so smug in his life.

'I can't believe you did that,' he said, kissing her on the mouth. She was leaning back against the trestle table and he was still hard enough to slip back inside her through the folds of her coat.

She ground her hips and grinned. 'Believe it or not, we did. You've got a fuckin' lovely cock.'

'Have I?'

'Oh yeah.'

He didn't get to ask what she liked about it. The door opened a little way and the woman called Sadie asked if Phoenix was planning on dancing tonight. She didn't look in, as if she knew what had been going on in there and James pulled up his trousers and left the room sheepishly. Phoenix didn't. She strutted out, still half naked, and ordered a drink from the bar.

'Aren't you at work?' asked James, as Carlito sashayed up.

'Yep,' said Phoenix, downing a double vodka.

'No need to ask what you two have been doing,' said Carlito, knowingly. 'So you must be Phoenix, right?'

'That's me,' said Phoenix. 'And you must be Carlito. I hope those blokes you were talking to know you've got a willy – else they're going to be well fucking upset.'

'You see the one with the grey at the temples?' Carlito said, indicating one of his admirers. 'He won't. He offered me two hundred of your English pounds to nail his ass through the mattress and call him Elsie. Go figure.'

James blinked. 'I was going to introduce you to one another but I see you're way ahead of me.'

A man came up and put his hand on Phoenix's shoulder. It wasn't a nice hand – being covered with gold signet rings – and it didn't appear to belong to a nice man. He was a heavy-set bloke wearing an expensive suit and with his thinning grey hair carefully combed forwards. 'Well, well, well, Miss Brooker,' he said. 'What have we here? We laying on a wet bar for you or something, princess?'

Phoenix shrugged. 'Call it industrial action if you want, Guy.'

'Seen enough of your action for one night, you dirty little bitch,' he said, eyeing James. 'This ain't a fucking brothel, you know.'

'I see you finished watching *before* you came out to tell her off though,' James said, amazed at himself for having said it in a nightclub full of scary-looking bouncers. Maybe Claire was right. He *was* too outspoken. And now he was probably going to die for it. Great.

'He won't be in a position to see anything if he keeps that up,' said Phoenix, standing up and pulling her coat around her. 'He'll go stone fucking blind if he doesn't stop playing with himself.'

'Right,' said the man called Guy, and grabbed Phoenix by the collar of her coat, pushing her towards the door by the scruff of the neck like he was trying to put a cat out.

James rushed after them, adrenaline tying his gut in knots. Carlito tottered behind on his high heels and shrieked theatrically in protest as Phoenix was unceremoniously flung onto the streets of Soho. Feline to the last, she managed to land on her feet, although her coat had become obscenely disarranged in the scuffle.

'You're fucking fired!' shouted Guy, his face scarlet.

Phoenix laughed and took a bow. 'Thank you. I never fitted in anyway, since I could actually fucking well dance.'

'Leave it,' James said, pulling her away from the open doorway. 'Please.' He would have loved to have punched Guy but the bouncers would have killed him. Phoenix didn't seem to be hurt. It just seemed part of her policy to go out with a bang.

Carlito was yelling that he was going to sue and Phoenix was giving as good as she got, swearing and shouting back at Guy.

'Get out, you slag,' Guy shouted back at her. 'You'll have to blag your drinks somewhere else, you fucking lazy black bitch.'

Phoenix's mouth fell open and James thought for a terrible moment that she was going to go for Guy's eyes or balls and they would all be obliged to join in and get creamed by the bouncers. But she didn't. She just smiled wryly, as if pleased she'd got the real measure of Guy, and went to walk away from the brewing fight.

James hadn't spotted them before but opposite the club entrance was a bar that seemed to be packed to overflowing. A bunch of young black guys were drinking their pints on the pavement. They wore gold and expensive trainers and they all looked lean, muscled and very, very angry. They were all looking at Guy.

'Well,' said Phoenix, primly, addressing her audience. 'Wasn't that rude?'

'Oh man,' said Carlito.

The menace hanging in the air was palpable. Phoenix grinned broadly and trotted off down the narrow street. 'Stick my P45 in the post, Guy,' she called over her shoulder. 'Once you got out of the hospital, that is.'

12

James couldn't imagine there was anyone on the planet who wouldn't want to see Shade play live, but Tosh seemed unsurprised that Claire would plead a migraine.

'She's not really very rock 'n' roll, is our Claire,' she said.

'Right,' James said, shifting from foot to foot and watching the auditorium fill up with boys and girls in black PVC, spikes and eyeliner. 'She's a closet classical fan?'

Tosh grinned. 'Ah. You looked at her CDs. And yeah, you're right. She's one of the few human beings I know who can actually survive a Wagner opera. *The Ring* thing . . . you know? Goes on for about a fortnight.'

James whistled. 'And they said "Bohemian Rhapsody" was too long for radio.'

'I know! And this in the era of prog and the three-minute guitar solo.'

'Prog?'

'Progressive rock. Seventies. Before your time. You didn't miss much. Concept albums about wizards and magic pixies. Could never get the hang of it, myself.' She sniffed and buried her hands in the pockets of her tatty leather coat. It looked weathered but wasn't covered in patches or studs and the only thing that made it really stand out was the word GONZO painted across the back like a Hell's Angels insignia. Even then, it wasn't entirely visible because she had unravelled the braid of her hair for a change and her jet-black tresses fell all the way to her waist. She wore faded hipster jeans, a plain white

T-shirt and had her glasses perched on the end of her long nose. James thought she looked effortlessly cool.

'I wish Claire had said she wasn't coming,' James said. 'I could have brought Phoe.'

'Maybe she meant to come,' said Tosh. 'Maybe she really did have a migraine. How many tickets did she have anyway?'

'Four, I thought.'

'Four?'

James shrugged and waited impatiently for the show to start. He'd been looking forward to this. There was no sign of Carlito and James wondered if he was part of the act following the success of that now infamous video. Mentally James tallied up the tickets he had seen on the kitchen table. Definitely four, and the two seats beside them were empty. It wasn't like Claire to hang onto an unwanted freebie that someone else, someone useful, might covet, so James was as surprised as Tosh looked when Daniel came and claimed the seat beside them.

He hadn't seen Daniel for weeks. 'How's it going?' he asked. 'Natalie's not here, is she?'

'Not as far as I know,' said Daniel, vaguely, staring at Tosh. She looked like she'd seen a ghost.

'Well, this is a coincidence,' Tosh said, eventually, folding her arms.

'You two know each other?' asked James.

Daniel ignored him. 'You don't waste time, do you?' he said, looking at Tosh in a way that James realised meant they had probably known each other in the biblical sense. Which was ... bizarre. And awkward.

'We're not together,' James clarified. 'Me and Tosh – if that's what you were thinking. So, were you two ...?'

Tosh nodded and pushed her glasses up onto the bridge of her nose. 'Er, yeah. Quite a lot, actually. Daniel, what are you doing here?'

'I got a ticket,' he said, thrusting forwards the ticket

with the seat number. 'Freebie from some blonde I met in a lecture. I'm not gonna knock it, am I? I love this band.'

'Random blondes give you tickets to the biggest gig in London and older women love you?' said James, incredulously. 'You lucky bastard.'

'Random my arse,' Tosh snorted. 'She wasn't wearing Jimmy Choos by any chance, was she?'

'Claire?' James's mouth fell open. The woman was everywhere.

'Yeah. That was it,' Daniel said. 'I think she gave me a business card somewhere. I had it somewhere, anyway.'

He meant that it had usually met the fate of any cardboard that wound up in Daniel's pockets and had been ripped up for roaches.

'I'm going to kill her,' Tosh said.

'What was she doing at your lecture?' asked James, puzzled.

'Oh, she's got the hots for your tutor,' Tosh said, in an offhand way. 'And I feel strangely good about betraying that confidence, actually. Perfectly within my rights.'

James shook his head. Claire? And Doctor Mulholland? At their age? 'OK. I need to go rinse my brain with bleach,' he said. 'Back in a moment.'

He went to the toilets and texted Claire a warning that Tosh was planning her imminent death, but when he came out again, Daniel and Tosh appeared to have resolved their issues to the point where Daniel was barely visible under a tangle of hair and trench coat.

OK. 'I, Gooseberry,' he muttered to himself.

He rather envied Daniel. It wasn't like Tosh was a bad-looking woman, even if she was a lot older. And she was probably really bendy with all that yoga. He wasn't sure if he didn't envy her either, because Daniel was seriously handsome. He definitely envied them each other because he would have done anything to be with

Phoenix right now – with her wild shrieky laugh and revealing clothes and her *banzai* willingness to do anything, no matter how insane or filthy.

James watched the show from the sidelines, avoiding Tosh, who appeared to have forgotten the existence of anyone else in the world besides Daniel anyway. The way Fred commanded the stage was superb. He'd amazed James with his normal concerns about cups of tea even when caught in bed with a transvestite but on stage he was anything but ordinary.

He danced until his shirt was dripping and his hair whipped around his face in sweaty strands. He writhed and screamed, bellowing the lyrics like a mad, half-naked hellfire preacher. If he slowed to catch his breath, the way he threw back his head and clung to the microphone stand made him look like he was recovering from some violent, full-body orgasm. He teased, he played. He threatened and frightened and then flirted to show he didn't mean it and he loved them all really.

James clutched his free backstage pass in a sweaty hand and felt more excited about meeting Fred Hill the Rock Star than he had even felt about meeting Fred Hill the man. The screams of the crowd formed a hysterical counterpoint to the grind of guitars and hammer of drums. They finished with 'Anyone But You', the crowd chanting 'mea culpa, mea culpa' in a way that would have given a cardinal a coronary, because it was more of a scene from Sodom and Gomorrah than St Peter's Square.

Backstage pass. Who would have believed it? Certainly not Natalie.

He flashed the pass at the huge security guards with a sense of coolness so intoxicating that he was sure his ego couldn't possibly get any bigger than it was right now. Skinny, shaggy-haired groupies were offering sexual favours to anyone they thought would get them close to the band. One offered to suck his cock. A second girl offered a full-on lesbian show with her friend, followed by a threesome. Another said he could do her up the arse, but he just laughed and carried on his way, not realising they were serious.

And then, there they were. Shade. In the flesh. Names he knew from album sleeves: Matt Sorenson (drums), shirtless and chugging water from a plastic bottle; Dan Actually (bass), lighting up a cigarette; Paul Oliver (lead guitar), peeling off a sweaty T-shirt and discussing some kind of sound problem with a roadie; and then Fred Hill (guitar, harmonica, vocals) turning towards him, James Bowden (no one in particular), and breaking into a broad grin.

'Jimmy! You made it, you sick fuck!'

James found himself grabbed tight in Fred's sweaty embrace, hands clamped over his ears and lips pressing down full on his in a far too friendly kiss. While still riding the adrenaline high from the stage, Fred Hill was something like a boisterous, over-affectionate dog.

'Enjoy the show?' Fred asked. He was shirtless, drenched, leather pants riding low on his narrow hips. His pupils were so dilated his eyes looked black and he was so skittish he didn't give James time to answer. 'Have you heard from Zoe? Nah, you wouldn't have – she's a fucking bitch and you're better off out of that gig, my dearest. I'm getting the fuck out of here before the press pack sharpens their pencils. Wanna come to a party, Jimmy?'

'Try and stop me.'

'Let's go then,' said Fred, eyeballing a couple of brick shithouse-sized security guards so that they moved aside for the superstar and opened the doors to the back exit. There was a car parked outside. 'I had every intention of fucking legging it,' Fred continued, stomping shirtless into the bitter winter air without even wincing. 'I could see it coming – fucking twenty questions. All about *her*, as bloody usual.'

The driver opened the car door and Fred and James piled in. It was a nice car, but not the limo James would have expected. 'Down in the back,' Fred said, and ducked down behind the passenger seat as the car rounded a corner into an epileptic fit of flashbulbs.

Once they were past it, Fred surfaced and sighed. 'Jesus. Fucking nightmare. Your boss must be freaking out.'

'Why?'

'Zoe's dumped me and checked herself back into rehab.'

'Oh,' said James. 'I thought Claire was in a bad mood. That explains the migraine. She was going to come tonight.'

'Migraine schmigraine,' said Fred. 'She knows she doesn't want to be consorting with the enemy if she wants to keep hold of Zoe. Shrewd little bitch, that one, isn't she?'

'You're not wrong,' James said, cynically, peering at the time on Big Ben as the car swept through Westminster.

'Never know what's up with Zoe,' Fred sighed. 'I don't get her. One minute she's walking down a catwalk with nothing on and the next she's emptying a drink over my head for making a pussy joke at her fucking fashion awards party thing. It wasn't me that made her get her kit off.'

The car pulled up in the courtyard of one of London's plushest hotels. Fred explained it would be best to make a run for it and so they did – through the pale-cream lobby, up the stairs and then through to a palatial suite where champagne had already been placed on ice.

'Home sweet home,' said Fred, picking up an ice cube from the bucket and popping it into his mouth. 'Not what I'm used to, but I heard a rumour you can even get a cup of tea round these parts, which is a start. 'S'cuse us a second. I need a shower. Have a drink. Make yourself comfortable.'

James looked around him, dazed. It didn't look like there was a party anywhere around here, unless there were a bunch of people lurking behind the couch. He checked and there weren't. So it was just him and Fred. Weird. And possibly not cool. He wasn't sure if Fred realised that he was straight – as far as he knew. It wasn't something that had ever come up in James's mind until he'd walked in on Fred and Carlito. He didn't know if he could do that, although it was kind of exciting, kind of different. It wouldn't have been a good idea to experiment with flirting with a man, but some niggling impulse at the back of his brain kept telling him to give it a go, try it on for size.

No. That would just be shitty, duplicitous and potentially dangerous. Not to mention he had no idea what Phoenix's idea of a 'bit of fun' entailed. She might take tremendous exception to his batting for both teams.

James poured the champagne and decided to be direct with Fred when he emerged wrapped in a thick white hotel bathrobe.

'I don't see a party,' said James.

'No,' Fred said, sitting down in the cream-coloured armchair opposite. 'I lied. Sorry.'

'So why did you bring me here?'

'You might think this is weird,' said Fred. 'And I don't blame you if you do.'

'Uh-huh.' James nodded, worried.

'I liked your aura.'

James sputtered a mouthful of champagne. 'My *what*?' he asked, laughing.

'Your aura. I can see 'em. My mother was a gypsy.'

James looked sceptically at him, although some part

199

of him wanted to believe it. With his gold-capped front tooth, wet jet-black hair and dangling earring, Fred could easily have been a little bit Romany. As for the second-sight stuff, the jury was so out. 'I knew someone who said you'd been at Harrow with his cousin,' said James.

Fred flashed a gilded smile. 'What? Gypsy women can't marry up? Actually my dad married beneath himself. She was a princess. Romanian gypsy king's daughter.'

'That's . . . wow.'

'No bullshit,' said Fred, gulping champagne and lighting a cigarette. 'Everything else about me is, more or less – but that's true. How'd you get on with Carlito?'

'He's officially losing his touch,' James said, triumphantly. 'Where is he, anyway?'

'Gone. Back to New York to defend his crown for the third year on the trot. That's what I really love about that boy, you know. He doesn't need me. Not in the slightest. Doesn't need anyone. He takes what he wants and moves on and doesn't try to fool you into thinking it's anything else. It's kind of refreshing when everyone's got their lips attached to your arse while they're secretly working out the best way to fuck you over.'

Fred refilled the champagne glasses and sat back. His eyes had returned to their usual pale grey as his pupils shrunk back to normal. He peered shrewdly at James and blew out smoke. 'Do you want to know how many women I've slept with?'

'Tell me.' James was happy to let him talk. There was very little he could say about himself that wouldn't sound horribly mundane compared to the stories Fred could tell. He was glad they didn't go to a party. It was a privilege to share one-on-one time with a big rock star. The charisma of the man was such that he filled the pale, decorous rooms with his presence – a flash and glamour so potent that it transcended gender and James didn't know if he'd want to resist if Fred led him to the bedroom.

'Hundreds. Maybe a thousand or more. Absolutely swimming in pussy. Up to my eyes in it. Models with long legs, glamour girls with big knockers, groupies who'll do any damn thing and then some, rich bitches who want to rebel against the daddies signing their trust fund cheques.' He curled his lip in a trademark smiling sneer. 'Had 'em. Banged them raw. Listened to them moan and groan – stuck it in their mouths, up their twats, in their arseholes, ate them out, persuaded them to screw one another ... done it all.'

'You moving onto boys or something?' asked James, crossing his legs to conceal the effect that dirty words, delivered in Fred's carefully cultivated cockney tones, had on him.

'Nah,' said Fred, smiling like an alleycat. 'I've always liked boys. They're shyer than women, so it's more fun to loosen them up. More of a challenge. My father always told me not to chase girls – scared I was gonna knock one up and disgrace him – so I said, OK, Daddy. I won't chase girls. But I didn't tell him I was chasing boys instead. They were all gob at school. Didn't want to be the dorm poof, but once you got them alone for the few minutes you could grab they were completely different. Pretty little posh boys with their drawers round their ankles and their little pink cocks sticking up, begging the bad boy to stick it in his mouth.'

James furtively licked his dry lips. 'All this dirty talk,' he said. 'Anyone would think you were trying to seduce me.'

Fred laughed. 'Jimmy, Jimmy, Jimmy ... come on. I'm telling you a story. And I couldn't seduce you. Let me tell you a thing about seduction. You can't seduce someone who doesn't want to be seduced.'

'Right. Totally true,' James laughed, relieved and slightly

disappointed that the atmosphere had lightened. 'Sorry – you were saying?'

There was a knock on the door of the suite and a woman's voice crooned, 'Room Service!'

'What the fuck?' Fred yelled, looking suddenly furious. He leapt out of the armchair and stormed over to the door, then laughed again when a tall, breathtakingly shaped blonde was revealed.

'You bum, Fred. Is that any way to treat a lady?' she asked, in a rich American voice, flipping her shaggy mane of peroxide hair. She wore low-cut snakeskin trousers, a tight black corset through which scraps of tattooed skin showed and she moved like Jessica Rabbit.

Fred watched her ripe, undulating bottom with a leer plastered to his lips. 'Sorry, Diamond – got the press on my case. And I didn't know you were in town. What a pleasant surprise.'

'Here I am,' she said, nonchalantly, grabbing a glass of champagne and tossing herself down in an armchair. 'Hey,' she said, nodding at James. She had a surprisingly fresh, innocent-looking face, given the opulence of her figure. That, or her lips had been so discreetly pumped with collagen that they gave her a natural, pure-looking pout. Her eyes were a clear light green, the bridge of her nose very lightly dusted with freckles and slightly sunburned in a way that suggested she'd come from far away, somewhere a lot warmer than freezing London.

'Diamond, this is Jimmy,' said Fred. 'Jimmy, this is Miz Diamondback – the wildest woman to come out of the lone star state since Janis Joplin.'

'Pleased to meet you,' James said, wondering what on earth she was doing here. She raised her glass to him in a salute, obviously a woman of few words. He noticed her hands as she raised her glass and saw that her inch-long fingernails were painted with an elaborate snakeskin design that Donna would have killed for.

'You should have told me you were coming,' said Fred, standing behind Diamondback's chair and playing with her long hair. 'I would have arranged something for you.'

'I didn't know myself,' she said, leaning her head back into his touch. 'I just heard you'd quit humping that model's bony ass and thought you could use a real woman. Spur of the moment thing.'

'I'm glad you did.'

She turned around and knelt on the armchair, facing Fred and with her back to James. Her arse was succulent and so rounded that her hipsters were under some strain. A band of tattooed flesh showed just above where the crease of her bottom must have begun beneath her trousers. 'So you *are* pleased to see me?' she said, pulling open Fred's bathrobe and peering downwards. 'Good to see I can still charm me some snakes.'

'You mucky reptile,' said Fred, fondly. 'Why don't you show Jimmy why they call you Diamondback?'

Diamondback peered over her shoulder at James, glancing up from under her hair like a movie vamp. 'You sure he's old enough?' she asked, her accent thick as honey.

'I'm nineteen,' said James.

'There you are,' said Fred. 'He's nineteen.'

'Honeychild, he couldn't even get a beer back home.'

'Less of your pilgrim prudery, Miz Diamondback,' said Fred, playfully. 'You didn't come all this way to play Scarlett O'Hara did you?'

She poked her tongue out at him and then held up her hair. 'C'mere,' she said, inviting James to peer at the nape of her neck. He got up from his chair and looked. Down the nape of her neck, along the line of the vertebrae, she had what looked at first glance like a squat string of beads of some sort, tattooed on the skin. As he followed it down through the strands of her thick, unruly hair, he saw that it connected to the body of a snake tattoo and realised what it was on the back of her neck. It was the rattle on the tail of a rattlesnake.

'Eastern diamondback rattlesnake,' Diamondback said. 'Most dangerous snake in America, bar a few in the White House, maybe. You like snakes, Jimmy?'

'You'll like this one,' said Fred, adjusting his bathrobe and sitting back in an armchair, drink in hand with the air of a dissipated Roman Emperor anticipating some new and perverted diversion.

'I don't know much about them,' James admitted. 'Can I...?'

She let him touch the bobbles of the rattle over the nape of her neck. Her hair was amazingly soft. 'The rattles used to be the tips of their tails,' she said. 'Adds a new one every time they shed their skin.'

'Fascinating,' James murmured. Her back was almost bare in the top she wore and he was intrigued by the way the tattoo snaked down her spine and towards her armpit.

'It's a warning, mostly,' she said. 'When a rattlesnake rattles it's 'cause it's fixing for a fight.'

'You're not rattling,' he said, tentatively moving his hands lower.

She smiled at him over her shoulder, green eyes glinting. 'Maybe I like you,' she said.

'Don't tease him, Diamond,' Fred prompted. 'Come on. He's hardly seen anything yet.'

'I might wanna take my time,' she said, but she turned around anyway, unfastened her top and let it fall. Her breasts were so large and firm they couldn't possibly be real. The tip of her left breast was pink and perfect, but the nipple on the right was completely tattooed to merge with the snakeskin pattern that curved over her breast. The snake had been tattooed so that it coiled beneath her arm, across her breast and down across her torso to wind around her waist and disappear somewhere down the base of her spine.

'It's beautiful,' James said, sincerely. It really was a work of art. The scales were painstakingly drawn, the diamond pattern rendered with such loving care that it seemed to gleam like real snakeskin. 'Did it hurt?'

'Like hell. But I didn't pass out. Not once. The artist had never seen anything like it before, but he'd never done such a big tattoo on a woman. Big strong men pass out the whole time, he said, but I guess they're not built to stand pain like a woman's built to stand it, else the human race'd come to a standstill.'

Fred rolled his eyes. 'We know you're the superior sex. Come on.'

'Ooo, the big rock star wants his floor show,' teased Diamondback. 'Whaddaya reckon, Jimmy? You want to give it to him?' She took his hand and guided it to her tattooed breast. He was about to say, 'No, I can't, I'm seeing someone, I shouldn't be here', and a million things that were bound to sound gauche and stupid and *nineteen*, but she was beautiful and her nipple stiffened under his fingers and her tongue flickered so adeptly between his lips he was sure he heard a snake rattle.

Her body was nowhere near as doll-like as it looked. She was muscled and firm fleshed for all her curves. She groaned underneath him in the armchair as he took her snakeskin nipple in his mouth and sucked it gently.

'That's more like it,' he heard Fred say, and glimpsed him sliding off the armchair and crawling on his hands and knees to divest Diamondback of her boots and trousers.

Her mouth tasted of champagne and chewing gum. That pout was as tasty to kiss as it promised – with that sensual crumple of lower lip and long, sumptuous upper lip. He could have lost himself in her hair. There was so much of it – a great tumbling palomino mane of it – the shade of sun-baked dust with the texture of gossamer. She pulled off his top and moaned her approval.

'Oh God damn ... What do they feed you English boys? Y'all got skin like girls.'

'It's probably the weather,' Fred said absently, his hand creeping up James's thigh and over the waistband of his jeans to touch the small of his back.

'Oh God,' James shivered, the ache in his cock redoubling at Fred's touch. This was just fucked – insane. He wanted Fred. He wanted Diamondback. He was definitely not as straight as he thought and Phoenix was going to kill him. Although there was no way he could stop. Fred had negotiated Diamondback's hipsters and James's hand slid inevitably downwards. He was surprised when there was no hair where he expected to touch hair and pulled back enough for Fred to prompt once more: 'Show him!' and for Diamondback to extricate herself and present her back to him again.

He knelt next to Fred. The tattooed snake coiled around her waist from the front and appeared to be sunk in the crease of her buttocks. She stood bent over in front of them, her hands on the seat of the armchair, then her legs opened and James saw that the snake coiled right down between her buttocks. Satisfied that they'd had a good look, she turned round and sprawled on the edge of the armchair, legs spread wide.

James gawped. The tattoo ended just where the lips of her sex met at the top and rounded into the pubic mound. That was the top of the snake's head. She was shaved completely smooth, the better to show her tattoo. The pink flesh of her inner lips was the snake's spitting, wide-open mouth. Around it the fangs and face of the snake had been cunningly, and no doubt excruciatingly, tattooed.

'Y'ever kiss a rattlesnake on the mouth, Jimmy?' she asked.

13

James woke naked in a hotel bed to the sight of Diamond-back's tattooed arse retreating towards the bedroom door. Fred was sprawled a decent distance away on the king-size bed, face down and apparently unconscious.

'Miz Diamondback?' James said, quietly.

'Honey, I think you know me intimately enough to drop the Miz, don't you?' she said, turning around and running a hand through her blonde mane, which had turned into an epic case of bedhead during the course of the night's festivities.

'Sure. Are you ... are you going?'

She nodded and put a finger to her lips. 'I always thought it was kinda tacky to be around for breakfast. An' I got a lunch date in Paris. Paris France, mind, not Paris Texas. It was a blast though. See ya later.'

James sank back onto the bed, head spinning with the memory of last night. It was just a total trip and he wouldn't have believed it himself if it hadn't been for the naked rock star sleeping about three feet away from him. He heard the door of the suite slam shut and Fred stirred.

'She gone?' he asked, as if he'd been feigning sleep.

'Likes to exit the crime scene early, that one.'

James wound the sheet around himself. It was one thing being in bed with another bloke when there was a blonde between you, but this was uncharted territory. 'Do you want me to go?' he asked. 'I'm sort of ... in your bed.'

Fred peered reproachfully at him. 'We were in the

same woman last night, Jimmy. At the same time. You're not gonna go all morning-after on me, are you?'

'I don't know. I've never done this before.'

'What do you usually do when you wake up in bed with someone?'

'I haven't really had much experience of that, either.'

Fred pulled a face. 'Oh my God. I really have corrupted an innocent, haven't I?'

'Not that innocent!' James protested. 'And you have to admit you're quite a pervert by anyone's standards.'

Fred raised his eyebrows. 'I've never been so insulted in my life!' he said. 'This coming from the man who strolled into my bedroom and my life while I was being taken roughly from behind by a transvestite.'

James laughed. 'Look, I don't know, all right?' he said. 'Like, a month ago, I was just another student in a city full of students. Now I'm doing all this lifestyles of the rich and famous stuff and I seriously don't know what the fuck I'm supposed to do or say most of the time. It's like, be smart, be dumb, say something, say nothing, go here, be seen there, don't you dare be seen dead at that place, look pretty and shut up, look angry and say something, wear this, wear that, meet so-and-so ... it's bizarre. What? What's funny?'

Fred was staring at him with an intent, amused expression. He lay propped on one elbow in the big, crumpled bed, the sheets tangled around his long legs. His skinny body was all planes and angles and tattoos and his expression seemed distinctly mocking to James's acutely self-conscious perception.

'It's you,' Fred said, sounding fascinated in a way James would never have imagined Fred Hill could have ever sounded fascinated about someone like himself. 'Just you. First time you've ever really told me anything about you. You're not this blank slate waiting for someone to chalk FAMOUS across it. You're ... fuck, you're what, nineteen? You know, you'll look back at yourself in ten years' time and think: Who the fuck was that? and you'll think you didn't have the first clue about who you really are, but I'll tell you this for nothing – right now, you're so young and you are more yourself than you'll ever be for the rest of your fucking life. You'll never be so much of *you* as you are now.'

James pulled the covers up to his chin, shivering. He wasn't sure if it was the cold or the intensity in the way Fred was speaking. It sounded like a prophecy of doom. 'I don't know if I want to be me,' said James. 'I think I'm sort of fucked up or something.'

'You're not even close, darling.' Fred grinned, somewhat bitterly. 'You're talking to a bloke who has to jump around on stage and scream like a nutter because he'd be locked up for doing it in the streets. When you get to a certain age – different for everyone I suppose – you realise you've got to . . . I dunno. Apologise. Adapt. Make yourself palatable by remembering your manners and not pissing people off. I think it's called growing up and I never wanted to be a part of it. Don't do it, Jimmy. No compromise. No apologies. No surrender.'

He sighed heavily and the cold morning light caught a single silver hair at his temple. He smiled and looked back with colourless eyes still smudgy with clogged eyeliner. James smiled back, uncertain of what to say or do. He wanted to move closer, the way you should be with someone who had just spilled their guts to you, but he was naked and unsure of how he'd proceed if a touch shaded into sex.

'This isn't it, by the way,' Fred said, breaking the silence.

'Isn't what?'

'The morning after thing. Long, intense conversations. Not usually the done thing.' He didn't sound bitter any more, merely rueful.

'Why not?' James asked. 'I don't mind it at all.'

'Yeah, well.' Fred stretched out and leaned a little closer. 'There's a reason I usually hold off on the long intense conversations until I'm off my face at three o'clock in the morning. 'Cause then I don't have to remember the incredible amount of bollocks I talk.'

'You don't talk bollocks.'

'Oh, I do.'

'Don't.'

'Do!'

'Don't!' James laughed, nervous now he realised they were flirting in earnest and they were already naked in bed together. Fred reached out a hand and touched James's cheek with the back of his hand, knuckles hard against his face, palm curled and facing outwards. As caresses went, it was masculine, almost fraternal, so James found himself compelled to test the waters by leaning into the touch. Fred's knuckles were knotty. Their solid hardness drew James's mouth to their shape. The childlike instinct to taste their shape was so strong that his eyes closed as his lips pursed to suckle on skin and bone. He mouthed at a knuckle then the back of a finger and he heard Fred breathe in deeply.

He opened his eyes and Fred was watching him with such a velvety, purposeful look in his eyes that James thrilled at the spark of fear and lust that pricked the back of his brain. But he was not going to lose his nerve – no way. He was too curious to back off now. He caught Fred's hand by the wrist and clumsily sucked on each fingertip in turn, feeling the texture of calluses under his tongue and tasting lingering traces of Diamondback on the skin.

Fred was breathing raggedly already, his eyes darkening and his lips apart. James realised that, however unintentionally, he was teasing Fred, possibly conveying the impression that he knew more than he did.

'I don't know what the fuck I'm doing, by the way,' he managed to say, the words coming out in a breathless rush.

Fred smiled and shook his head. 'It's easy,' he said, quietly. 'I promise.' He wrested his hand back from James, curled it around the nape of his neck and adeptly closed the gap between them.

James realised he had had preconceptions about what being kissed by another man would feel like. He'd expected roughness, aggression even. He would never in a million years have expected this – this slow, deliberate touch of lip to lip, mouths barely open, tongues discreetly furled, so controlled it verged upon being chaste. He closed his eyes and leaned into the kiss, fighting down trepidation as Fred increased the pressure and gently nudged the tip of his tongue against James's lips. Then Fred made a quiet moany sort of noise, a sound so erotic that James's mouth opened in a small, surprised exclamation. A slip of the lip too far and then there was the incredible realisation that that was Fred's tongue, darting inside his mouth and swirling against his own in a way that seemed to scramble his brains.

It felt like the most natural thing in the world to move closer. If he was out of his depth he was out of his mind, so it didn't matter any more. With a rustle of sheets and an intake of breath they were in one another's arms and the liberty to touch him was exhilarating and terrifying all at once. The cognitive dissonance of touching muscle where he would usually have found breasts and feeling a hard, hard cock bumping up against his own wore off almost immediately. There was nothing but sensations – the texture of skin and hair under his hands, the taste of Fred's mouth, the sound of sighs and kisses against the hiss of London traffic moving over the slushy roads outside.

'See? Easy,' Fred whispered, his hands moving over

the spikes of James's hair, down to the nape of his neck, sweeping down his back, cupping and cradling his arse. Fred squeezed and James eagerly pressed against him, crushing his cock pleasurably against Fred's bony thigh.

James nodded in response – a stuttery, gaspy sort of nod, but it was all he could manage. He sprawled on his back with his dick rising hard between his hip bones, the tip pointing towards Fred, who was leaning over him. The poor thing was swollen and looked and felt as though it was begging for attention, inflamed by Fred's stories of public school cock-sucking, pleading to be taken into his mouth.

'Do you trust me?' Fred asked.

James nodded again. 'Anything. Please.'

He let Fred push his thighs apart. Fred kissed each thigh, kissed the underside of his balls, making James buck and whimper, then teased with a long, deliberate lick up the length of his cock. He settled on top, instructing James to wrap his legs around him, then shifted so that their cocks lay against one another between their bodies. When he rocked his hips, James understood perfectly what was required of him because the friction blazed sparks down into his balls and up the length of his dick.

It *was* easy – beautifully easy. He just had to move and kiss and moan, arching his back into each stroke and burying his tongue deep in Fred's mouth. 'Make a noise,' Fred prompted, between kisses, his laughter tickling James's ear.

James let out a self-conscious moan which shaded to a deeper, more sincere sound as the sweat gathering between their bodies made his dick slither and slide against Fred's. When he moaned, Fred held him tighter and thrust harder against him, making him cry out loud.

He had had no idea what to expect, but he hadn't expected so much kissing. He supposed maybe he'd thought men touched each other in a perfunctory, embarrassed way, rather than the way that Fred was touching him and kissing him. Fred was revelling in him, hands everywhere, coming back for more kisses and whispering words of encouragement and lust.

James knew this was out of control when he felt Fred's callused, guitar-playing fingers stroke the length of his cock. Fred's touch was so adept that James knew he'd be back for more of this. Better still that he could test his strength against Fred's without fear, so that they tussled and crushed and ground hard into one another. It was rough and tender all at once, and so fucking good.

'Come for me,' Fred whispered, his breath fanning the inside of James's ear, his hand working smoothly, skilfully. James twisted in his grip to find Fred's lips and kissed; kissed deep and wet and messy as he came, gasping his pleasure into Fred's mouth. He moaned and rocked against the last shudders, his fingers wound into Fred's hair, wet skin pressed to wet skin.

'I want to do that,' he said, when he could catch his breath. 'I want to do that for you.'

He had no idea what he was doing but he supposed the principle was the same as if he were doing it to himself. Fred's cock was slimmer and longer than his own, strange and familiar to the touch. He wanked it experimentally, then his stomach flipped and swirled with excitement as he saw Fred's face. Fred was flushed, his mouth open, his eyes bright and brilliant and looking at him – at James – with this incredible hunger.

The thought that he was making Fred Hill look like that made James's confidence rocket and he curled his fingers tighter, moved faster. Fred moaned and came in a couple of hard, sharp little spurts that made his hips buck under James's body. He sprawled back on the bed, sweaty and panting, and pulled James back down to lie close beside him.

Kissing was good. Post-coital cuddling was even better.

'What did you think?' Fred asked, eventually. His voice was quiet and the question seemed shy, which was funny coming from him.

'I think there's probably a lot more to it, isn't there?' said James, luxuriating in the warmth of the bed. 'That was just the entrees, right?'

'If you want, yeah,' said Fred, smiling and nudging James's toes with his under the covers.

'I want.'

'Good.' Fred looked conspiratorial, elated. James wondered why they couldn't stop staring at one another across the pillows, and why he couldn't do it without some mad desire to scream and laugh welling up inside him. Every time Fred smiled at him he felt a strange bursting sensation beneath his ribs and he couldn't stop smiling back.

'I don't want to go,' James admitted.

'Then don't.'

'I can't stay. I have to go to this stupid premiere tonight. It's sort of important.'

He stayed until Claire called and he couldn't delay the inevitable any longer. She was running round making all her preparations for the big night. This was the acid test, after all – to see if James could pass muster on the red carpet. He'd been building up towards this for so long but now it was here he felt strangely hollow. He sat and submitted to being moisturised, exfoliated, soaked in hot towels, smothered in lotion and shaved with a cut-throat razor. The hairdresser dyed his hair a tasteful ash blond to hide the peroxide splashes and styled it into fashionable asymmetrical planes.

When he emerged from all this pampering it was like looking at a handsome stranger in the mirror. Nice hair, good cheekbones, sensual lips, carefully tinted contact lenses to side-step the glasses and deepen the blue of his eyes. Buff, toned body, fake tan. A fucking Ken Doll.

'Wow,' Claire said, when she saw him. 'I have to say, James – I never imagined you'd scrub up so well. Well, smile! You look a million dollars.'

He smiled. He felt like the change from a bag of chips.

'Claire,' he started to say, wanting to tell her that this wasn't right, this wasn't who he was. He'd spent the morning in another man's arms and it had shaken his whole perception of who he was that it couldn't be healthy to be playing dress-up like this.

'No, no,' she said. 'Don't thank me, darling. Don't you fucking dare make me cry. And I could. You look amazing. It's all been worth it.'

'Thanks,' James sighed, his heart sinking. He had to take the compliments where he could get them where Claire was concerned.

'Now, Sarah will be here at seven and we'll have the car to take you the—'

'Sarah?'

'Sarah Riley. She's been dying to meet you.'

'Sarah fucking Riley?' James demanded. 'That moron?'

'We all have to start somewhere, darling,' Claire snapped, lighting a cigarette. 'Sarah may not be the sharpest crayon in the box but right now she's incredibly good copy.'

'She's a talentless parasite!' James protested, and then exhaled when he realised what he'd said. If she was a talentless parasite, what did that make him?

'I know, but for some insane reason the great unhosed appear to like her. Girl next door appeal. Now, I think the boob job has settled, but for God's sake, if you get drunk, don't go below the waist because I think she's still in one of those compression garments from the lipo – so don't try to fuck her, all right?'

James shook his head. 'I wouldn't worry about that, Claire. Really.'

'Not your type?'

'Oh, you have no idea.'

Santosh was delighted to be able to give the premiere a miss, since it would entail putting on a posh frock, trying to wear heels and wandering up the red carpet while the paparazzi collectively muttered, 'Who the fuck is she, then?'

She'd be the woman who risked life and limb secretly filming inside pre-war Iraq. Now *that* was a photo-opportunity, not some dimwit dolly's new dress. Besides, she had told Claire that she was confined to bed, which was partially true and Claire's own damn fault. If Claire insisted on playing matchmaker she was going to have to accept the consequences of her actions. In this case the consequences meant that Santosh was only prepared to get out of bed to use the bathroom or mix ever more ridiculous cocktails and then crawl back into bed to drink them with Daniel or spill them deliberately over various parts of Daniel's body, where they would have to be licked off.

Daniel was sprawled half drunk and naked on the bed, flicking through a book about cocktails he had found in a pile of books. The pile of books had been knocked all over the living-room floor the night before when they had crashed into the flat pulling one another's clothes off and in no mind to consider the niceties of bookshelves. Santosh finally surrendered in the Battle of the Bookshelves, beaten but still victorious, because it no longer mattered. It didn't matter that she was getting carpet burns and a battered A-level copy of *The Mill on the Floss* was getting even more battered under Daniel's left knee. Nothing at that moment had mattered like Daniel's cock moving sweetly and sleekly inside her, hitting just the right spot and making her come while Daniel reverentially groaned 'Oh my God, I love you so much,' before shuddering to his own climax.

Afterwards, when they were lying shell-shocked on the floor, he had picked up the cocktail book, blown the dust off the spine and crawled into bed with it. So far it had yet to lose its fascination, especially since Santosh had just done the usual festive alcohol shopping.

'I didn't realise there were so many ways to get pissed,' he said, turning a page. 'Would you drink something called a "Concrete Coffin"?'

'What's in it?' she asked, putting two snowballs down on the bedside table and climbing onto the bed beside him.

'Pernod and Drambuie.'

'Sounds absolutely disgusting. Here. Get this down your neck.'

'What's this?'

'Snowball.'

Daniel flipped to the index and looked it up. 'Gin?'

'Vodka. And advocaat.'

'This says it's gin.'

'Then it's wrong,' said Santosh. 'My Great-Auntie Lakshmi was crazy about them and she always made them with advocaat and lemonade.'

'Is that what this is?' Daniel asked, surreptitiously sniffing the frothy yellow contents of his glass.

'With a little something extra. I make it with a finger of vodka, dash of lime and then advocaat and lemonade. And a cherry.'

'Tastes like ice cream,' said Daniel, appreciatively. 'Where's the cherry?'

'Gets bogged down with vodka sometimes. Sinks to the bottom. You might have to dive for it.'

He grinned like a schoolboy. 'Diving for the cherry? Try and stop me.'

'You're so dirty,' she said, happily, kissing him on snowball-sweetened lips. He put his drink down and submitted to more kisses.

This was much more like it. Much better than worrying about not being able to put shelves up or wear heels. She didn't care if she couldn't cook. She could mix a mean snowball, put together a documentary, headbang in front of a computer while listening to snotty music and get drunk off her arse and hump Daniel into a babbling, gibbering heap of lust-soaked goo. That was good enough.

'You'd really rather be here with me than at a West End movie premiere?' Daniel asked, earnestly.

'Definitely. Don't even know what the film is about.'

He disengaged and reached across the bed to roll a joint. The skin of his back was smooth and still held traces of his summer surf-tan. In the middle of a London winter where everyone looked their worst, Daniel still managed to exude good health. She had accidentally nicked his back with a fingernail over the course of the night, to match the carpet burns on his knees.

'I thought it was some kind of romantic comedy,' he said, rolling industriously. 'Some secretary with a love life like a train wreck, you know?'

'Great. Another Bridget Clones,' sighed Santosh, flipping over the channels on the TV set to the 24-hour news channel she knew would be trivial enough to consider live coverage of yet another premiere newsworthy. She read the ticker on the bottom of the screen and was perversely pleased to discover that an overpaid footballer was being disciplined for behaving like a tantruming five-year-old on the pitch and that a Tory MP had been caught with his hand in the till and unceremoniously deselected.

'More Tory sleaze,' she muttered. 'They can't shake that label, can they?'

'They'll shake it when they stop being sleazy,' said Daniel, flopping down on his stomach beside her and lighting up.

'All the more reason to push the vote out next spring. Kick them while they're down.' She nudged his ankle with her toes, meaning she meant him to push the vote.

'Hmm. I dunno,' he said. 'I don't know if I want to stay the course, to be honest. It's not very Zen, is it? Politics, I mean.'

'Zen?' She laughed and gulped her drink. 'God, no. If you want Zen you want Siddhartha, not Machiavelli. Worlds apart.'

'That's what I mean,' said Daniel. 'I think I prefer Zen.' He sucked on the joint and frowned, the light from the TV flickering on his face. 'It's like surfing. When you're catching that big wave you just have to sort of surrender yourself to it. You're on your own and you can't always predict what the wave is going to do, so you have to like, I dunno, go with it. It's totally Zen.'

'Zen and the Art of Surfboard Maintenance?' she asked, sceptically.

'Why not? I've got an A-level in business studies. Whole bunch of people thicker than me have set up their own businesses. It'd be like a surf school with a side order of enlightenment. Go down a bomb in Cornwall, I can tell you. There's like, this real lunatic fringe element back home. You get people in London being all off-beat and a bit weird, but you can tell they're trying, you know?'

'Big city. Everyone wants to be a beautiful and unique snowflake.'

'Yeah, but they're not,' Daniel said, passing the joint. 'Ninety-five per cent of them are just wankers trying to make themselves interesting. You go to a place like Cornwall and people aren't trying to be interesting – they're just bonkers because that's the way they are and they don't think anything of it. Just take it for granted that everyone's into Zen Buddhism or legends of King Arthur or raising llamas and seeing fairies at the bottom of the garden. It's very cool. You'd fit right in.'

'*I'd* fit right in?' she asked, her stomach giving a funny little lurch.

'Yeah,' he said. 'If you're freelance you can work pretty much anywhere, can't you?'

Santosh couldn't quite believe what she was hearing and her credulity was further tested by the part of her brain that told her she liked the idea. 'Wait – are you asking me to move to Cornwall with you and set up a Zen surf school?'

'Kinda,' he said, looking hopeful. 'What do you think?'

'How long have you been thinking about this, Daniel?'

'Not long. It's just an idea. We can have an idea, can't we?'

'Yeah,' she said, trying not to grin like an idiot. 'Ideas are good. Definitely happy with ideas, yep. We'd have to think about it for a lot longer, but yeah. It's an idea.'

It was a good idea. When you found war zones preferable to London it was long past the time you should have gotten the hell out of the godforsaken city and moved somewhere that wasn't going to stress you into an early grave.

'You'd have to teach me to surf,' she said.

'I can do that. Get you into a wetsuit. Did I mention that I'm really into rubber?'

Santosh laughed but the moment was interrupted by the newscast cutting to 'our showbiz correspondent' at the premiere of the movie. She shouted into the microphone over the screaming of fans and the chatter of camera shutters.

'Yeah, hi, Alicia – we're live in Leicester Square at the London premiere of *Single Girl*.'

'Inspired title,' said Santosh. 'Can't believe Stephanie's still doing the rounds.'

'You know her?' asked Daniel.

'Oh yes. Great gossip columnist. Barely literate, brain of a mollusc and no gag reflex whatsoever.'

Stephanie Hayes had gone to town with the fake tan and sun-kissed highlights, meant to make her look as though she hung out in Cap Ferat, rather than living the nocturnal vampiric existence of the paparazzi. The result was neither pretty nor convincing. She nodded and smiled as Alicia the news-anchor asked questions.

'Yes, that's right, Alicia – we're expecting the stars any time soon. There's been a lot of excitement generated by this premiere and, as you can see, the fans are out in full force '

Behind her, people roamed up the red carpet. A pin-up girl posed and pouted for the camera in a next-to-nothing dress, implausible tits and inflatable lips offered to the very same paparazzi she was always threatening to punch the next day. Santosh wished she didn't have to breathe the same air as some of these creatures.

There was a huge storm of flashbulbs and the glamour girl pulled supposedly vampish faces and lapped up the attention, then Santosh noted with amusement that the cameras weren't intended for her. When she realised this ignominy, her expression turned into one of childish petulance. The flashes were going off for someone and behind Stephanie Hayes; Sarah Riley made her way up the red carpet.

'Oh my God,' Daniel groaned. 'Is she still milking it?'

Sarah had lost at least a stone, by the looks of things, gained a cup-size or two and looked glossy, airbrushed, almost attractive. Until she opened her mouth. Stephanie grabbed her, certain of an interview with a Z-lister like Sarah.

'Sarah! Sarah!'

''Allo,' said Sarah, waving at the camera and grinning like a maniac. 'All right?'

'Sarah, you look fantastic! What have you been doing to yourself?'

'Lipo, boob job, ate nothing but liquidised celery for a month,' Santosh heckled.

'Well, you know, Steph,' Sarah giggled, with nauseating fake intimacy. 'When you're a single girl you get more time to take care of yourself and show 'em what they're missing, don't you?'

Daniel shuddered theatrically. 'Please, don't, Sarah. Please.'

'So is there anyone new in your life, Sarah?'

Sarah dragged James into the frame. He was carrying her wrap and looked pouty, polished and suitably bored, dressed to kill in a black tuxedo.

Santosh's mouth fell open. 'Oh my God,' she said, reaching for the phone. This was not part of the plan. James was supposed to be launched as someone famous, not a gigolo for a talentless reality-show tart.

'Well, it's nuffin' serious,' said Sarah. 'We're just friends, aren't we, James?'

'Are we?' said James, looking distracted. He quickly turned back to Stephanie and the cameras and said: 'Yes. Just very good friends.' He managed to infuse the words with sarcastic venom that was perfectly understandable under the circumstances.

There was another flurry of flashbulbs and screams so deafening that Stephanie hurried them along in search of bigger prey, and as well she might. The screams and flashes heralded the arrival of Fred Hill, conspicuously alone since Zoe's latest meltdown.

No tuxedo for him. He wore jeans that hung off his skinny arse and whose bottom hems had trailed in the wet slush on the streets outside. He looked bored and half-stoned but still managed to look absurdly photo-genic from every angle. He was charismatic enough but, in the wake of Sarah's Z-list desperation, he looked like a rock and roll god – a consummate professional. He worked the cameras so expertly that Santosh cancelled the number she was beginning to dial and gawped at him.

Stephanie Hayes was clawing at her competitors in an effort to get a single word from him, but Fred wasn't interested in interviews. He was staring at someone just out of the frame with a come-to-bed look in his eyes.

It was James. James walked back into the frame towards Fred, looking dazed, possessed and (Santosh recognised the symptoms) insanely in love. There were clicks and consternation from the befuddled press pack as Fred stood there and waited for Sarah Riley's escort to come towards him.

'Oh my God,' said Daniel. 'Are they gonna...?'

They kissed, if such a thing could be called a kiss. It looked more like they were trying to devour one another whole. James dropped Sarah's pink satin wrap and stuck his tongue down Fred Hill's throat. If this was Claire's plan then it was going spectacularly well. The kiss didn't look staged in the least. Fred and James were standing there on the red carpet, snogging one another's faces off like two people in a world of their own.

Fred whispered something, James nodded and they ran for it, hand in hand. Off the red carpet, away from the cinema and out of reach of the cameras that were following them. The press pack swarmed over the barri-cades, stormed the red carpet and ran after the abscond-ing couple.

'Well, extraordinary scenes here in Leicester Square tonight, Alicia! Is this a deliberate self-outing by Fred Hill? We'd heard the rumours, but this is totally unex-pected – and more to the point, who's that young man?'

'Genius,' Santosh said, dazzled and appalled by Claire in equal measure once again. She went to punch out Claire's number again but the phone in her hand rang before she had even hit the first button.

Claire babbled on the other end of the line – a string of obscenities and expressions of disbelief.

'What have you done?' asked Santosh. 'I didn't even know he swung that way.'

'Neither did I!' Claire said, regaining some control of her voice. 'He passed the couch test and everything! I don't *believe* that little sod!'

'You mean you didn't plan that?'

Claire groaned. 'Oh, damn. No. I didn't. But fuck, I wish I had!'

14

'Look at this! IS GAY THE NEW STRAIGHT?' Jesus – she's like a one-woman crap factory. Kill it! Kill it with fire!'

'It's column inches, darling,' Claire said, inspecting the newspaper. 'Possibly *feet*. Bloody hell – she does fap on, doesn't she?'

'Started sharpening her pencils and flapping her lip when I was still in nappies. You'd have thought she'd have purged her brain of drivel by now, but the fatuous mare is like Old Faithful. Blows regularly, and literally, I'm told.'

'Tosh – it never ceases to amaze me that a human being so lovely as yourself can turn into such a heinous bitch when confronted with your fellow journalists.'

'I wouldn't if half of them weren't so fucking crap. Look – how much do you think Neil paid her for that priceless piece of copy? Illiterate sod hasn't even spelled Sarah's name right. For that money I'd probably have to bugger off to the West Bank and risk getting my brains blown out.'

'You could always write about Sarah's lipo.'

'No. I really would rather risk getting my brains blown out.' Santosh poured another glass of champagne and negotiated the mountain of tabloids. 'This is phenomenal, though. You'd think nobody had ever seen two guys kiss before.'

'When one of those guys happens to be Fred Hill, it's red top dynamite, darling. Say what you like about the wanker – he's certainly a crowd pleaser. And James appears to like him, don't you, James?'

'Whatever,' James said, and continued playing solitaire on the computer. He was too angry to do anything else. All morning he had been shut in Claire's office listening to Claire answer the phone, talk about the newspapers with Tosh and celebrate her huge PR coup. She'd done it. She had taken a nobody and made him famous for being famous.

They were so busy answering phones and fielding questions that not even Tosh had bothered to ask James if he was all right.

He was far from fucking all right. His kiss with Fred was splattered all over the newspapers and he knew Phoenix would be waking up to the news at some point that afternoon. She was not meant to find out like this.

He hadn't even meant it to happen. He was going to go to the premiere with Frankencunt Riley, smile pretty, play nice and then come back and figure out what to do, but then there was Fred.

Fred – with his broad, off-centre grin and a hint of stubble-burn at the corner of his mouth. His jeans were hanging too low on his bum and the pale skin showing under the hem of his T-shirt was a reminder of how thin he felt to the touch right there where his waist narrowed above bony hips. His eyes were as sleepy and stoned as they always were but this time James knew why he was tired.

And there he was, posing in the flashbulb light, looking like he'd just rolled out of bed with the scent of sex still clinging to his skin. It was never meant to happen like that, but their eyes met and just ... boom. Gone. There was nobody else there.

'No compromise?' Fred said, unheard by the screaming crowd.

James knew what he was talking about. He had remembered every word of their conversation that morning, going over it time and time again to try and decipher what Fred really felt for him. Knowing that Fred also remembered was like seeing a rebel flag raised over the red carpet.

'No apologies,' James replied, meaning, 'I think I'm in love with you.'

There was so little time and it seemed like there was nowhere to go, even though they could have gone to any hotel in London. If they went back to Fred's hotel then the press pack would be there in force. There was a whole huge city and nowhere to hide except for the small, anonymous places where the ordinary people lived out of the glare of the cameras. Claire collared him before he could even think about where they might escape to, and he had spent an uncomfortable night trying to sleep on the couch in Claire's office. Fred was apparently holed up in his hotel, refusing to come out until the press dispersed.

Nobody had asked James if he was OK following the seismic shift in his sexuality. It hadn't occurred to Claire that this might be as much a shock to James as it was to everyone else. The only person who seemed to acknowledge James's existence outside the newspapers was Donna, who looked even more contemptuous than usual of her boss.

That was just Donna's way though. She was a practical creature, a mother of sons and therefore used to tears, tantrums and unreasonable behaviour. 'Neil Savage wants to talk to you,' she told Claire, slouching in the doorway. 'He's called three times already.'

'Tell him,' said Claire, with obvious enjoyment 'That *I* will call *him* when I have *time*.'

Donna shook her head, rolled her eyes and peered over James's shoulder. 'Red jack,' she said, pointing out a card in his solitaire game that he'd missed. She put her hand on his shoulder, the first sign of tactility James had ever seen her display to anyone over the age of six. 'You want a cup of tea, darlin'?' she asked.

'Thank you. Yes. Thanks,' he said, wanting to cry. She gave him a reassuring pat, acknowledging his distress, and went to make him a drink.

'I'm going to have to have to sort these notes,' Tosh was saying, stuffing a backpack with newspaper clippings. 'You will tell Neil I've got first dibs on the interview with James, won't you?'

'It will be a fucking joy, darling,' said Claire, and drained her champagne glass. 'Can't wait to see the look on his face.'

'Take a picture, please.'

'Will do,' said Claire, as Tosh waved James goodbye and left. 'This was worth it, even if it was an absolute nightmare. I mean, I'll lose Zoe, but Zoe's lost her fucking marbles anyway. There's always a possibility I could bag Fred, I suppose.'

James pulled the mouse out of the computer and hurled it at her. 'Fuck you!' he yelled, so angry and hurt he could barely see straight.

Claire turned around and stared at him, looking genuinely bemused. Bitch was so thick she didn't even realise why he was angry. It was about time she found out.

'What on earth is wrong with you?' she asked.

'What do you think?' James shouted. 'An absolute nightmare, am I? All you've done since last night is crow about your fucking PR coup and whine and bitch about how much hard fucking work it was. It's like, hello – I'm here! You wouldn't have much of a coup if it wasn't for me, would you? And you haven't said four fucking words to me.'

Claire blinked incredulously and reached for her cigarettes. 'James, you're famous, you idiot boy. Isn't this what you wanted?'

'That isn't the point!' said James. 'That is so not the fucking point, Claire. I know this is your big social experiment but, you know, you could at least take five minutes out from congratulating yourself to remember that I have feelings, that I'm a person.'

Claire stared at the ceiling and groaned. 'You want a letter of congratulations on your unique DNA structure? Do grow up, darling.'

James shook his head and squashed down the temptation to throw the keyboard at her for good measure. 'Again, the point just sails over your head, doesn't it?'

'You're not making any points, James. You're just flailing around screaming and hurling hardware at me. If you want to make a point, throwing things is usually not the greatest way to make it, you know. If I want hysterics I'll call Justin. I credited you with being a rational human being, at least.'

'I *am* a fucking human being!' James screamed, close to tears. 'That is my point, you stupid fucking bitch! I haven't slept properly in days. I've been told to go here, do this, do that, wear this, don't wear that ... I just ... I don't know. Everyone is talking about me and none of them really know me and I don't know who I am any more. Or what I'm supposed to do now I'm famous. It's all over for you, isn't it? You've pulled it off, fulfilled this little bet you had with yourself. You can sleep safe at night knowing you've done what you wanted to do. But what about me?'

'I don't know,' said Claire. 'Just go to the damn parties, get photographed. You'll pick something up – a celebrity reality show or something.'

'But what will I *do*?'

'You're famous. You don't need to do anything.'

James clenched his teeth and struggled not to scream. 'For fuck's sake. I can't sing. I can't dance. I can't write music. I can't act. I'm not a professional journalist like Tosh. What am I going to *do*?'

'Presenting? Advertising?' Claire shrugged. 'We'll find you something.'

'I'd be awful at it!'

'So is everyone, darling. Doesn't stop them dragging their fifteen minutes out forever.'

James envisioned a life lived on the Z-list and couldn't hold the tears back any longer. Claire stared at him as if she had never seen anyone exhibit genuine emotion, which James was angry enough to believe was the case.

'You're just tired,' she said, patting him awkwardly on the shoulder. 'I'll have a cab come and take you home. You'll see everything quite differently once you've had a good sleep. You'll see.'

'Fine,' he said. 'Fine.' She was right. He was exhausted. He consented to get in the car and go home, but as he was being driven down the Strand he realised he'd never sleep even if he had a bed to lie in, not with the way his nerves were jangling. The cab was stuck in traffic opposite the hotel where he had slept with Fred on a morning that felt like years ago.

James tried the door of the cab. To his surprise, it opened and he ran into the noise of the traffic as the cab driver yelled and the press pack outside the hotel turned as one like a flock of predatory birds. He walked right into them. They crowded and jostled and called his name and took his picture, but he remembered his training. Keep walking, don't engage and, if anyone sticks a microphone in your face, say nothing or 'No comment.'

He got through the cold, dark scrum into the warm, light interior of the lobby, where lurking paparazzi were being politely thrown out by uniformed doormen. He realised he probably looked half mad from lack of sleep and the remains of his evening clothes were pitifully crumpled, but he had to try.

'I need to see Fred Hill,' he told the man at the reception desk. 'Please. I have to see him.'

'There's nobody of that name staying here, sir,' said the receptionist.

'Yes there is,' said James, and told him the room number. 'I was here with him the night before last. Would you call his room, please? It can't hurt you to do that much, can it?'

The receptionist peered down his nose. 'Sir, if I telephoned hotel rooms for every ... fan of popular music who insisted they knew Mr Hill, I'd never be off the telephone.'

'He'll be very annoyed if you don't tell him I'm here,' said James. He spotted a woman carrying one of that morning's tabloids and turned to her. 'Excuse me. Could I borrow your newspaper for a second? Thanks.' He found the relevant page and waved the picture under the receptionist's nose. 'See? Me. I know Fred. I know him very well. Intimately. Now, will you please call his room?'

He handed the woman her newspaper back and she looked what could only be described as starstruck. Oh God.

'You're welcome,' she said. James heard her mutter to her friend what she wouldn't give to be a fly on *that* bedroom wall.

Two of Fred's huge security guards came down to collect James – massive impassive walls of flesh with sunglasses covering their eyes and headsets plugged into their ears. They said nothing on their way upstairs in the lift and simply escorted James to his destination.

The hotel suite was full of people. James assumed they were part of the band's entourage, designed to take care of the rock star's latest tantrum. Fred didn't appear to be there and it was Dan Actually, the bass player, who spoke to James.

'Oh man, am I glad to see you,' he said, chewing frantically on a wedge of gum.

'I don't think we've met,' James said, hesitantly.

'You know who I am, right?' asked Actually. 'And I know who you are? So we're cool, yeah? Listen, you have totally gotta talk to Fred, because he's like, locked himself in his room and won't talk to anyone and I am so not qualified to talk people off ledges.'

'He's on a ledge?' James asked. 'Oh my God, where is he?'

'Don't sweat it. Figure of speech. Just . . . here.' Actually knocked on the bedroom door. 'Fred?'

'Fuck off.'

'Open up,' said Actually. 'Jimmy's just arrived, so you wanna talk to him or what?'

The door opened wide enough for James to slip inside and Fred slammed it quickly again and locked it before anyone noticed it had been open. The curtains were drawn in the bedroom and the place smelled heavily of cigarette smoke and stale wine. Fred looked puffy-eyed and exhausted. He was wearing a hotel bathrobe open over his jeans and, judging by the empty bottles, he'd had a few.

It didn't matter. James was exactly where he wanted to be. When Fred kissed him James didn't care if Fred was drunk or coked to the gills or whatever, because he had been waiting all night to be kissed and hadn't known if it would ever happen again. He didn't care that Fred's mouth tasted bad and his own probably wasn't great – it was enough to be offered a cup of tea, kissed on the lips, talked to as if he were a person and not a commodity to be bought and sold.

He caught his breath with his forehead resting against Fred's, Fred's hand curled around the nape of his neck.

'You all right?' Fred asked, his breath warm and winey on James's face.

'Fine,' James lied. 'Just tired.'

'Don't fancy answering twenty questions about your sexuality?' Fred asked, inclining his head very gently towards the closed door. His body swayed close as he moved and James took the opportunity to burrow a hand under the folds of Fred's robe and round his naked waist.

'Fuck that.'

Fred smiled. 'Thought you'd say something like that.'

It wasn't even funny but it was enough to wring a slight, bitter laugh out of James.

'Last night . . .' James began, but Fred shook his head and pulled him close.

This had to be love: the way they tugged at clothes and scrambled for one another's skin. It didn't need twenty questions to know that this felt amazing. He loved Fred's hands – those calloused, guitar-playing fingers. He'd never get enough of the way the palms smoothed and fingertips scraped against his skin. Hands that clasped and cradled his arse as he arched his back on the bed to get out of his trousers – silly black dress trousers he wanted to toss out of the window, or better still, burn.

Stupid clothes, stupid hair, stupid face, stupid fucking nobody standing around being famous. Strip it all away, get naked, take solace in skin and hair and muscle and sweat – back to reality in the form of the flesh.

He didn't think his own body could stand it because his eyelids were so heavy, but he couldn't help it when he felt Fred's mouth on his dick. He came humiliatingly fast and felt tears leak over his face as if his climax had jerked the anger loose from his tear ducts.

'Hey, don't cry,' Fred said, gently, lying down beside him. 'This is supposed to be a happy thing, isn't it?'

'I know, I know,' said James, grateful for the touch of his hands, the warmth of his body. This was nice, just being touched, caressed, held. 'I'm just so tired.'

'Yeah, me too,' Fred whispered. His eyes looked heavy as he peered at James across the pillow. 'But it's OK, I promise. We're gonna go to sleep and nobody is gonna disturb us. Just you, just me.'

'Sounds great,' James said, curling closer.

Fred stroked his hair and wrapped his arms around him. 'And we're going to do exactly what the fuck we like,' Fred continued, his voice drowsy and barely a whisper. 'And where we like. And nobody is going to stop us because they're all just jealous that we found each other and we fell in love like this.'

'We're in love?' James asked, opening his eyes. He was so tired he felt deeply drunk. He wished he wasn't. He would never have wanted to cut this conversation short, given the choice.

'I think so,' Fred said. 'What do you think?'

'I think so too.' It was tiring to even smile. 'And I wish I wasn't so fucking tired.'

Fred squeezed him tight beneath the sheets. 'Why? D'you want another go?' he asked, his hand tracing the curve of James's spine with a tenderness that felt complete now that they understood one another.

'I want to. I've had sex, yeah, but . . .' He stifled a yawn.

'You've never made love.'

'No.'

'And I'm the first.' Fred looked so happy that James had to kiss him, even though they both knew there was no point in starting anything. They settled facing one another in the bed, curled up like twins, foreheads touching, sharing breath now that they were too sleepy to kiss.

Fred murmured softly to him as he drifted off. 'Just

you wait, Jimmy. Just you wait until we get to New York. We'll rent somewhere and I'll show you how. Cause we'll need practice. Lots of practice. Because we're gonna be the best. There's never going to be anyone in the whole world who can love one another the way we will. We'll reinvent the whole fucking meaning of love, sex, everything. We'll make the rest of them look like amateurs. Just you wait.'

It was no time to be thinking about sex. There had never been a less opportune moment to think about sex, but Claire found her libido had a horrible habit of popping up when she was in the middle of something important. She needed to find James, immediately.

Anything could have happened to the stupid boy. At first, finding him gone, she had been terrified that he'd gone and jumped off a bridge, but people rarely packed their clothes and their toothbrush when taking a trip to the afterlife. Even so, she was not looking forward to explaining this mess to his parents, so she called someone with more experience of talking to outraged parents.

Graham. And therein laid the problem, with emphasis on the 'laid'.

He agreed to come over and the first thing she thought was that she looked bloody awful. She had a T-shirt and tracksuit bottoms on and she had enormous premenstrual tits that strained even the straps of her most sensible and sturdy sports bra. She had no make-up, a prize zit forming on the side of her nose and her hair needed washing. She had almost reached for the tea tree oil and shampoo before sternly reminding herself that they needed to find James.

This was about James. It didn't matter how she looked, because it was not the time to be having sex with James's ex-tutor again – even if the last time had been amazing. The trouble was that she'd spent so long looking for passion in the form of rough and tumble love 'em and leave 'em types that she'd forgotten it was possible to crave conversation with a man you fancied. She'd never picked her partners for their IQ and hadn't been interested in anything they'd had to say until Graham turned up and introduced her to the concept of talking as an elaborate and exciting form of foreplay that made the payoff all the more pleasurable.

They'd just kept fuelling one another until they ran out of words and fell on each other onto the floor of his office and humped like a couple of lust-crazed beasts. The very thought of it made her knees tremble and her mouth water, so although she managed to hold off putting on make-up and changing her clothes, she still opened the door like a shotgun when he pressed the doorbell.

She didn't know if he had put on that plain blue shirt on her account. It didn't matter if he had because she wanted it off as soon as possible. That little tuft of chest hair had escaped from the open throat of his shirt again and she knew what was underneath. Hairy chest, hairy belly, long lean hairy legs. He was like a bear.

'Are you all right?' he asked, going for a polite kiss hello on the cheek. Somehow he missed entirely, collided with her lips and before she could answer his glasses had gone clattering across the hall floor and his tongue was deep in her mouth.

They were reflected in the mirrored wall of the hall and she saw his hands tentatively hovering over her back as if he was debating whether to grab her arse. She decided to help him make up his mind and directed his hands downwards. He groaned into the kiss and squeezed her buttocks.

'This is probably not a good time to say this,' he said, breathlessly, sliding his hands under her tracksuit bottoms. 'But you have the most gorgeous bottom I have ever seen.'

'You're paying me compliments and you're worried about timing?' The view in that mirror was something else. For all the anti-cellulite body polishing and work in the gym, her arse had never looked ... well ... *happier* than it looked with his hands on it. It looked like an arse pleased that it was being put to proper use.

'It's not a good time, though,' he reaffirmed, although it felt as though the contents of his jeans were very much up for a good time.

'No, it's not,' she agreed, fumbling for his fly.

'Terrible timing,' he said, pulling down her trousers so that they fell around her ankles with her knickers inside them. The view in that mirror was getting more obscene by the second. She stumbled back against the opposite wall, tugging one foot free of her trousers, and saw how his hand reached for her bush before his body obscured the image and she felt his fingers delve inside her.

She managed to get his jeans down far enough to bare his arse to the wall – no mean feat when she was trying to steady herself and rub herself off on his fingers at the same time. His cock was just as she remembered it, big and thick with a juicy red head. She shivered every time she thought about it sliding up her without latex or ceremony, her back and his knees getting a severe carpet burning on the nylon floor-covering of his office, but both of them too far gone to care.

She fondled him and his fingers squirmed inside her in response. The timing no longer mattered because this was so much good filthy fun – grabbing at each other's genitals like horny kids in the back of a car, not even bothering to get properly undressed. She had a perfectly good bed in the next room but there was no question of getting that far. She was not going to disengage for a second for fear that he'd zip up his jeans and she would have to wait. She clung with one hand to the nape of his neck, grinding her hips into his touch. 'Come on,' she prompted. 'Do it. Do it, please.'

He slid his fingers out of her and nudged the tip of his cock against her as a tease. 'Oh no you don't,' he said, slowly getting down onto his knees. 'You've had enough of instant gratification to last a lifetime.'

'Oh my God.'

She shut her eyes, not sure if she could stand to open them and see what would be looking back at her in the mirror. It would send her over the edge too fast and she had already determined that she wanted to come while getting fucked – the way she'd come on his office floor. But his fingers were deep inside and his tongue was teasing her clit so beautifully that she couldn't fight the impulse to ratchet up the sensation one step higher.

She opened her eyes and cried out hoarsely at what she saw. Filthy. So hot. She was naked from the waist down and he was kneeling, his face buried in her pubic hair, one hand steadying her bare, undulating hips. He moaned in response to the noise she'd made and sucked her with a renewed relish that made her jolt and shudder.

She shut her eyes again because she knew she'd come if she saw herself pleading. 'For God's sake, fuck me.'

He let her go. She slid to the floor and spread her legs for him. He wiped his lips hastily on his shirt tail and scrambled over her, and for a second she saw how they looked in the mirror as their bodies came together, his cock seeking its destination between her sprawled thighs. He slipped it in easily with a harsh little gasp of pleasure. 'Is that what you wanted?' he asked, his breathing ragged, his cheeks pink. He teased with slow, steady thrusts and laughed when she gasped for more.

'Oh, you think you're good,' she said, her mouth dry.

'I know I'm better.' She clenched her muscles gently around him and he squeezed his eyes tight shut and moaned.

'Move,' she said, impatiently.

Finally he did as he was told. It was good and slippery and satisfying, his dick darting and pounding right where it felt the best. She watched his face while he fucked her, watched his expression and the drops of sweat breaking loose from his hairline. Whenever their eyes met he ducked his gaze away and bit his lip, as if he was trying to hold back.

'Quick. I'm going to come,' she said, feeling the telltale quivers somewhere deep between her hips in the core of her pelvis. In giving him permission to cut loose, she got what she wanted, because he thrust harder, with little staccato jabs that touched right where she needed him to and brought her off a couple of seconds before he cried out loud when he came.

She caught her breath and stared over his shoulder at the ceiling. The weight of him made her tender, swollen breasts hurt and she wondered if they should have been more careful on both occasions, but it was late enough in the month not to worry. She pushed him off gently and he rolled onto the floor beside her.

'I'm fine, considering,' she said, eventually.

'What?'

'You asked me if I was all right. Before we got ... distracted.'

'Oh. Right. Good.' He sat up and reached for his glasses. 'Did you hear anything from James?'

'No,' Claire said, retrieving her crumpled, inside-out trousers from the floor. She wanted a cigarette and the hall floor was no place for post-coital billing and cooing, even if such things had been her style. 'Drink?'

'Please.'

She pulled on her trousers and went to the kitchen to

light a fag and pour wine. Graham followed sheepishly, tucking in his shirt and politely requesting a piece of kitchen roll to clean his smudged glasses.

'You're not really all right though, are you?' he asked.

Claire sighed. 'I'm waiting for you to say it, actually,' she said.

'Say what?'

' "I told you so." I bet you want to, don't you?'

He shrugged and sat down at the table, accepting a glass of Chardonnay. 'I thought about it,' he said, his face still flushed. 'But I thought it would be prudent not to. Given your terrifying level of proficiency in the martial arts.'

She shook her head and laughed. 'Judo's defensive. I wouldn't attack you or anything. But there. You were right – about James. Ungrateful little bastard that he is.'

Graham peered over the top of his glasses. 'Claire, I don't think it's ingratitude. Not everyone wants to be famous, you know.'

'That's absolute balls. If I could get you a panel spot on *Question Time* you'd jump at the chance.'

He tilted his head in thought. 'Perhaps. But that wouldn't be out of any particular lust for fame. It would just be arrogance. A couple of my contemporaries are MPs now and I always remember them as the biggest arseheads in my year, whereas I, an extremely intelligent man, am stuck teaching politics to idiot students.'

Claire blinked and exhaled. 'You're freakish, do you know that?'

'How so?' he asked, neutrally.

'You seem to go through life with no illusions about yourself. It's very strange. And rather refreshing actually. From my point of view, anyway. I suppose I'm used to people pretending to be something they're not, or wallowing in false modesty. I think that's part of James's charm, really. It doesn't matter how you dress him up he still remains essentially himself – the same silly little rebel without a clue.' She drained her glass and lit a fresh cigarette. 'I suppose I should speak to his parents.'

'Why?' asked Graham. 'He's a grown man. He wouldn't have done any of this if he hadn't wanted to, would he?'

'You were just saying I'd done him a tremendous disservice by making him famous.'

'I said nothing of the sort. You didn't make him come to you in the first place, did you?'

'How could I have done that – short of kidnapping?'

'Exactly. You've given him what he wants. Or what he thought he wanted. That's the trouble with getting what you want. You don't know what it's like to have what you want until it's right there in your grasp and when you have it in your grasp it doesn't live up to all the anticipation.'

'Why are you letting me off the hook like this?' Claire said. 'I feel dreadful.'

'You're not his mother.'

'Oh, don't you start too,' she said. 'He was always saying that. I mean, really. Do I look like the maternal type?'

He shrugged. 'You look like a woman. That's generally a prerequisite for maternity. I've yet to meet a man who's pulled it off.'

She enjoyed his wry sense of humour so much she decided she wanted more. 'I'll tell you what,' she said, leaning across the kitchen table. 'Do you fancy doing something really kinky?'

'You don't mean actually doing it in a bed, do you?' he asked, feigning shock.

'Maybe later. But I know this Italian place in Streatham. We could have that dinner you kept talking about.'

'Shouldn't I change into a more embarrassing shirt?'

'Oh no,' Claire grinned. 'I'll just throw on a pair of

jeans and go without make-up. Might not even brush my hair. That should be embarrassing enough for both of us, shouldn't it?'

'Sounds utterly humiliating. I'd love to.'

15

The celebrity lifestyle was not what James had expected. For a few weeks they had roamed from city to city under cover of darkness, darting away from the ever-present cameras. When the paparazzi stopped pursuing them, that was when Fred really became antsy. He complained about being talked about, but complained even more vociferously when he stopped being talked about and began planning his comeback.

They rented a beach-house in Malibu. James already found that breakfast in bed wore thin when you could have it every single day if you wanted it. The silicone scars under women's breasts became more apparent. The champagne tasted flat. The life of sex and drugs and rock 'n' roll palled pretty rapidly when it was all you had and there was nothing to carry you through to the next day with a sense of purpose. He had begun missing his essays and books in New York and when Fred flung himself back into writing the songs for the next album, James had even less to do and an even greater sense of the difference between himself and Fred.

Fred had talent, and he worked like a demon. He would play the same phrase over and over on the guitar until James was close to screaming at him to stop. The kitchen floor became so smothered with the dots and lines of guitar tablature that James had been tempted to scoop the lot up in his arms and fling them into the swimming pool, watch the ink bleed out and the paper fall apart and damn the consequences. If Fred had turned on him it would have been better than simply acting as a sounding board for music he couldn't read, talent he couldn't touch and an album he was allowed nothing to do with.

'You can't be involved, Jimmy. The lads won't have it. They used to call Zoe Yoko all the fucking time.'

There was nothing to read in the house, except for books about music. James could learn about it but he couldn't use his knowledge for fear of annoying Fred. There was nothing to do and nothing he was really good at besides sex.

He picked fights so that they could make up in spectacular fashion. It was the only time he felt he had any control or influence over Fred – while he was fucking him. James had learned to tease when instant gratification had become boring. He would hold Fred on the cusp of orgasm for as long as he could stand, or tie him to the bed and blindfold him. Then he would just sit on the bed for a while and admire his handiwork, watching the way Fred arched his back for attention so that his stiff cock bobbed under its own weight. James got to know Fred's dick intimately this way – the exact heft and width of it, the tints of deep rose pink at the tip, the pattern of veins along the shaft and the way the hair grew at the base. He liked to just look until it showed signs of wilting from inattention and then James would say something, ask Fred if he wanted to him to touch him and it would obediently stiffen again and be rewarded with the lightest brush from the tip of James's finger or tongue.

They'd been in Malibu for a fortnight when Carlito dropped by, bad tempered about a failed audition in Hollywood.

'May as well do a Tootsie, honey,' Carlito said, contemptuously. 'Pretend I'm a chick because I might as well not have a Y-chromosome as far as fucking casting goes. They hear you do drag and all they want is fucking drag.'

'Tch. Typecasting,' Fred muttered, abstractedly.

'That's me screwed unless they make a sequel to the goddamn *Crying Game*,' Carlito complained. 'And you're not very sympathetic. I suppose you've been keeping poor Lawrence of Arabia here cooped up to attend to your monster ego. God, I hate California.'

Fred grinned and scribbled down another chord. 'It's cold and it's damp. That's why the lady is a tramp.'

'You better believe it,' said Carlito. 'I'm using your pool while I'm here.'

'Go ahead. Make yourself at home.'

'I wasn't asking permission, sweetie. I was just telling you. Come on, Lawrence, let's go work on our tans and I'll fill you in on all the dirt from back in Limeyland.'

Carlito stayed for a few days. He had a habit of sunbathing nude, and the first time James had joined him he hadn't known where to look. Carlito's body was lean, brown and very lightly muscled. Apart from a patch of carefully trimmed pubic hair he shaved his entire body, like a swimmer, so that his skin gleamed in the sun. He had a neat, circumcised cock that sometimes stiffened slightly in the heat while he drowsed.

The first time James took his shorts off too it was less an act of solidarity than a blatant come-on. Carlito's body made him so hard that it was impossible to disguise and Carlito responded in kind. They lay there side by side, toasting their skins and testing their nerve, their cocks pointing up like sundials.

'You know it's inevitable,' Carlito said, in that distant sunbather tone of voice where you were too hot to move so you just sort of aimed your words at the sky and hoped they'd find the person you were talking to. 'We'll end up screwing.' He lay flat on his back, his hands palm down at his sides, fingers splayed to catch every ray.

'What about Fred?' asked James.

'What about him? He doesn't pay any attention to

you. You need to get him the hell out of here. He's not bred for La-La Land. Very few folks are. You need a clear head and a manageable ego to survive this fucking place and Fred's got neither. He's got tunnel vision and a frigging God complex. Get his ass back to London and then you might be able to extract his head from out of it.'

'I'm not going back to London,' James said, stubbornly.

'So you got caught with your pants down with Phoebe.'

'Phoenix.'

'Whatever her name is. It's no big deal. You'll probably get a hero's welcome. You only did what half the guys in London want to do to her. She's hot.'

'She sold her story to the press,' James said, still disgusted. He'd had it coming after the way she had found out about him and Fred, but even so, when the stills of those nightclub security tapes hit the headlines and the full uncut version hit the internet, he'd wanted to throw up. He had thought she was better than that.

'She's milking the infamy. So what?' Carlito yawned. 'That racist asshole she used to work for would have tossed that tape in the trash if you hadn't been gaying it up on the red carpet with a rock star a couple of days later. He was probably grabbing the Kleenex when he realised he was on the verge of whacking off to a potential goldmine.'

James sat up. 'What's that tosser got to do with it?'

'*He* sold the tape,' said Carlito, looking at James as if he were the world's greatest idiot, which right now didn't seem far from the truth. 'Think about it, T. E. Lawrence. How did she get her hands on it? She'd have had to go back into that club and – hel-lo – last time she was there she practically started a race riot. She may be crazy, but I'm pretty sure she's smart enough to know she's gonna be about as welcome as a case of oral herpes at a fluffer's convention, right?'

James groaned. 'Oh fuck. It wasn't Phoenix at all?'

'Oh hell, no. Her agent tried the damage limitation thing, but you know – internet. You can't keep a good celebrity home porno down in the age of broadband.'

James wound a towel around his waist and marched into the house, where Fred was busy restringing his acoustic guitar.

'Fred?'

'What's up, babe?'

'I need to square some things in London. We have to go home.'

Fred looked up, which was progress, after a fashion. 'We? Look, Jimmy, you can see I'm up to my eyes in it here.'

'You can be up to your eyes in it in London. I can't stand it here any more. I'm going fucking barmy.'

Fred raised his eyebrows. 'I'm not relocating on your whims, darlin'. Sorry, but it doesn't work that way. I'm sorry if you're bored, but I've got a fucking album to write here.'

'I'm not bored, Fred – well, I am, but that's not the reason.'

'So what is?'

'Phoenix, for a start. I owe her a shitload of apologies.'

Fred snapped a guitar string at the mention of Phoenix's name and sucked on a bruised thumb for a second while glaring at James. 'Her?' he said. 'No way. She'll have you right back where she wants you in no time. Proper little barracuda, by all accounts.'

'Not by mine. And I actually know her, which is more than the press do. Besides, she wouldn't stand a chance if you actually shagged me once in a while.'

Fred put down the half-strung guitar and rose slowly from the chair. 'Oh?' he said, eyes glittering. 'So this is what it's all about, is it? You want your non-conjugal rights?'

James stood his ground. 'It'd be nice,' he said. 'It's only been, what – three times since we've been here? The alfresco fucking with a side order of paparazzi jaded your palate that much?'

'Not even close, Jimmy,' Fred said, moving closer. James backed towards the bedroom door; an almost Pavlovian response since bedrooms were where arguments ended up being, if not resolved, at least brought to a satisfying conclusion.

'Pretty vanilla by my standards, really,' Fred continued.

'Spice it up, then,' James goaded. His blood was roaring through his veins, his heart thundering. He couldn't wait to light the blue touchpaper. 'Carlito seems to fancy a threesome.'

'Not interested,' said Fred, moving close enough to tug the towel loose from James's waist. 'I've had him.'

'I haven't.'

That did the job. James found himself sprawled flat on his back in the middle of the bed, Fred crawling over him, mad with possessive fury.

'Don't you touch him,' Fred said, his hands tight on James's wrists. 'Don't you fucking dare. You're mine.'

'Prove it, then,' James snarled back, opening his legs wide beneath Fred's body. He wouldn't care if it hurt. He just wanted it all. 'Come on,' he goaded. 'If you want me so much why don't you just fuck me? I'm right here. You just have to unzip and stick it in, or is that too much fucking trouble?'

Fred looked down at him with that look of incredulous lust James had come to associate with New York, where they had spent whole days in bed and James had been ecstatic to discover he could surprise Fred with the things he was prepared to do.

'You dirty little bastard,' Fred whispered, his breathing

ragged. 'That what you want, is it? A bit of cock?' He let go of James's wrists and reached over for the lubricant they kept stashed in the bedside drawer. The rough denim of Fred's jeans chafed between James's thighs, rubbing against his swollen dick.

'About fucking time,' James said, determined to wind him up even further.

Fred put a hand over James's mouth. 'Shut up. You're a filthy, foul-mouthed little slut.'

His other hand was between James's hitched-up thighs and James felt a slicked finger push smoothly into his arsehole. He moaned behind Fred's hand and Fred pressed down harder, crushing James's head back against the mattress.

'And I don't know why I put up with you.'

Another finger, maybe two. Fred pushed deliberately, scraping a fingertip over the tender mass of James's prostate, knowing it made him buck, shudder and beg.

'And I wouldn't. If you weren't so fucking *hot*.'

He took his hand away from James's mouth and reached down to unzip his fly. James hitched his feet higher and watched eagerly as Fred slicked his cock with the lube.

'You want this, don't you?' Fred teased, caressing himself with long, smooth strokes, his eyes fixed on James's face. 'His Lordship wants fucking so I have to drop everything and rise to the occasion, don't I?'

'Please,' James moaned, digging his fingers into the bedcovers and gripping tight in an attempt to resist the urge to touch himself. His cock brushed against his belly when he moved, but he knew it would take the pressure of Fred's body rubbing against it while they fucked to get him off.

'Oh. *Now* it asks nicely,' Fred said, laughing. He nudged his dick into position and gently ground his hips back and forth. 'Is that what it takes, eh? Have to stick my fingers up your tight little arse to make you remember your ps and qs?'

He pushed inside and James heard himself make this weird mewling sound as he felt Fred's cock enter his body – a sound so full of need that it was embarrassing to think it had come from his throat. Fred didn't move for a moment. He held him there, catching his breath, his dark hair falling forwards, onto James's face.

'Oh God,' Fred gasped. 'The noises you make.' He thrust slowly, punctuating each stroke with words. 'The dirty ... filthy ... horny ... fuck noises you make.'

James could never help crying out, panting, moaning and outright screaming. Fred was as voluble in bed as he was out of it, and he said such obscene, adoring things that James was often raising the roof before they had even got to the main event. He rocked and bucked into the jabs of Fred's bony hips, practically sobbing with pleasure as he felt Fred's cock moving inside him and heard Fred's voice, breathless and hot against his ear, whispering words of love and lust.

'Tell me you love me. OK, yes, I love you. Tell me again. Tell me when you come. Look me right in the eye, baby, and tell me you love me right at the instant you come all over me. Right then. In that moment.'

'Oh God, yes,' James moaned, squirming to get into a better position. As he moved he glimpsed Carlito standing in the open bedroom doorway, watching the performance with the air of a connoisseur. He was still naked and his sleek little cock stuck up in appreciation, flooding James's mind with the number of times he had just wanted to reach over to the next sunlounger and fuck Carlito's brains out.

Carlito quirked an eyebrow and walked away, but it was too late. James could feel himself coming, giving him just enough time to look into Fred's eyes and say 'I love you' before he exploded, with the image of Carlito's caramel velvet skin apparently imprinted on the back of his eyelids. His climax was so intense that his muscles almost pushed Fred out, but as if he knew what James was thinking, Fred was not going to be supplanted by a sexual fantasy and pushed deep as he came, clutching James's hips to hold himself in place.

Fred slumped on the floor at the end of the bed, so that James had to hand him up onto the bed like he was pulling him onto a life raft. He collapsed next to James and kissed him, slowly and softly, moistening both their dry mouths.

'I'm sorry,' he whispered. 'I'm sorry, baby. I didn't say it too, did I?'

'It's all right.'

'I couldn't speak. You were too much.'

James smiled, contented. To have robbed Fred of words was something of an achievement. Fred was so nice after sex, all flushed and tender, and James knew instinctively that he'd won the argument. They would go back to London after all. Anything to get away from California, where there was nothing but flat blue skies, flat blue rectangles of water, like a David Hockney painting where the only details were in the intimate recollections of someone's face, someone's cock.

The weeks rolled by and the news got older, headlines fading from memory as they were replaced with new scandals, dirt dished up by people who were more willing to keep the gossip coming than Jimmy – and Phoenix Brooker knew how to keep it coming. Justin Vercoe had been off the books for several months now, because he had sneaked out of his detox and gone on a bender, giving Claire a straightforward excuse to get rid of him. Sarah Riley had another reality show, this time of the celebrity variety, and was currently providing a great deal of amusement to the public, who kept voting for her to eat cockroaches or have eels tipped over her empty head. Zoe Luscombe had checked out of rehab and embarked on a torrid and public affair with a tattooed half-French, half-Vietnamese female French photographer, presumably to show Fred that anything he could do, she could do better. She still wasn't speaking to Claire.

It was no skin off Claire's nose, because Claire had acquired Phoenix and Phoenix was like gold dust. After the mess of Fred and James, James's in flagrante exploits with Phoenix hitting the papers and the internet, Phoenix remained admirably willing to play ball.

'They want you to do a bikini shoot,' Claire told her, after a men's magazine approached her. 'You up for it?'

'Why?' asked Phoenix. 'What's the point? Everyone's seen me in nothing but a fuckin' dog collar wanking myself sore in the fuckin' back room of a shitehouse strip club. Tell 'em yeah, but I'm taking the lot off. They're only imagining the bikini away when they buy these bleeding mags anyway, aren't they? No point in being a hypocrite.'

Phoenix ended up posed like Christine Keeler, with a knowing half-smile plastered on her lips. She photographed beautifully and, strangely enough, women seemed to like her too. It probably had a lot to do with her refusal to supplement her little brown bee-sting breasts with silicone and her cheerful disdain for the hackneyed celeb idea of making an exercise video.

'No fuckin' way,' she had told one interviewer, while she was sitting on the couch in Claire's office, looking enviably skinny in a white pantsuit with nothing underneath and her hair in huge soup-can rollered curls. 'I stay this shape because I work at it. I work fuckin' hard. The ballet ain't for everyone. You gotta watch what you eat, watch what you drink, work your arse off for hours every day, pull muscles, get injuries. We're fitter than any of them fuckin' poncy footballers. We're fit as Olympic athletes, and that's not for everyone, is it? I could jiggle about and do a watered-down ballet workout for house-wives, but I'd be fuckin' conning them if they thought it'd get them the same shape as me. I haven't got four kids, a husband and a fuckin' Labrador. They've got lives, not like me. They ain't got time, love. Story of most women's lives, innit?'

Oh yes, Phoenix more than compensated for the com-bined PR catastrophes of losing Zoe Luscombe and James. Claire had more than a few other things on her mind, but business was good, thanks to Phoenix.

She'd seen James, of course. Everyone had. He'd been spotted hand in hand with Fred in New York, being conspicuously anonymous with a baseball cap pulled down over his eyes and dark glasses on, soda cup in his free hand while Fred held a cigarette and seemed to be whispering something in James's ear. Before that she thought it was the Caribbean, or maybe Acapulco. Some-where where the sun shone all the time, anyway. Long lens snaps of them snogging beside a swimming pool – photos the papers had to blur and censor because both of them were naked.

Donna had got her pay rise and Claire no longer had to put up with little Dwayne Pearce occasionally invad-ing her office space when a childcare contingency fell through. Not that she minded Dwayne that much. She almost missed him turning up at the office. That morn-ing Donna had presented her with a drawing – of what appeared to be a blonde-haired blob with high heels. Dwayne had wanted her to have it – his portrait of Claire. She had been shocked to find that she was strangely touched, but not touched enough to do what she had to do, so when she came back from lunch she handed Donna the pharmacy bag and flat out begged.

'You promote me to webmistress and I'm still dealing with piss samples?' asked Donna, shaking her head.

'Please?' Claire said. 'I can't. I just can't. I'm asking you as a friend. Please. I can't do this.'

'All right,' Donna sighed. 'Normally I wouldn't, but whatever. You've got enough stress for one day when you see who's in your office.'

'Who's in my office?' Claire said, outraged that someone would dare just walk in. 'You let someone into my office?'

'He's been in there often enough,' said Donna. 'Jimmy Bowden. Go see for yourself.'

'That little cunt!' Claire exclaimed, and flung open her office door.

The bastard didn't even have the decency to look repentant. He was sat sprawled on the couch, feet on the coffee table, smoking a cigarette and sipping a glass of champagne. He had a light natural suntan and his once muddy, light-brown hair looked sun-kissed almost to gold. It had grown enough to frame his face and give him a raffish look redolent of Fred Hill. Evidently James had learned more than just cock-sucking, judging by the leather trousers and the ink of tattoos shining through the thin voile of his white shirt.

'Hello,' he said, nonchalantly.

'Jimmy, is it?' Claire said, acidly. 'I thought you hated diminutives.'

'Depends who uses them,' he said. 'Lovely to see you. I thought we could do lunch but I'm running kinda late. Dinner, maybe.'

'What?' said Claire, unable to believe the bare-faced cheek of him.

'Dinner. You know? Food? Nourishment?'

Claire snorted. 'Don't you dare play this fucking game with me. I taught it to you.'

He giggled. 'Headline grabber, aren't I? Real credit to you. You must be delighted.'

'Delighted?' said Claire, incredulously. 'You fuck off to New York without so much as a by-your-leave and you expect me to be delighted? I wasn't ruling anything out, going by your previous standards of silly teenage behaviour.'

James laughed. 'If you will go picking up teenagers in Covent Garden. What did you expect from a nineteen-year-old? The wisdom of ages? I'm a bag of hormones. I'm not the fucking Dalai Lama, dear.'

'That doesn't matter!' said Claire, wanting champagne but deciding to put the kettle on instead. 'I thought you'd picked New York on account of it having even taller buildings than London – in order to throw yourself off of. I had to speak to your *parents*.'

'Oh dear,' said James. 'And what did Mother say? That I was all grown up and capable of looking after myself.'

'That and something about not wanting grand-children anyway.'

He raised an eyebrow. 'You can probably see why I chose to live thousands of miles away, right?'

Some needle of maternal instinct prickled at her gut and she chose to ignore it, but she had to admit to herself that she hadn't been impressed by James's mother, who it seemed had unwittingly and unfairly foisted all the worry about her son's welfare onto Claire's unready shoulders. 'You could have called,' Claire said.

'And say what, exactly?'

'I don't know. That you were all right.'

James shrugged. 'Maybe. We unplugged the phone anyway. Didn't have time to talk.'

'Oh. Well. Must be true love then.'

'I don't know,' James said. 'He says he loves me.'

'He'll get bored of you. Look at Zoe. One of the most

beautiful women in the world and she's gone Seine-side Sapphic with a side order of Ho Chi Min City.'

He laughed again, baring perfectly polished teeth – teeth that Claire had paid for. 'That's the way it goes, isn't it? Find 'em, fuck 'em, forget 'em, as Mae West said.'

'You really have switched sides, haven't you?'

'I'm not sure. I saw Phoe, by the way. She said the same as you. That Fred'll get bored and I'll wind up dumped and pointless.'

'You're not pointless now?' asked Claire. 'Famous for taking it up the arse?'

James gave her a dirty look and helped himself to more champagne. 'Actually it's pretty unusual that he's on top.'

'That is officially far more information than I ever needed to know,' Claire said, holding up a hand.

'Whatever,' James said, obviously amused that she'd taken on some of his vocabulary. 'And I'm not pointless. I have a very clear idea of what to do.'

'Oh really?'

'Yep.' He took a long gulp of champagne and looked unbearably smug. 'PR, darling.'

Claire blinked. 'PR?'

'Learned from the best, didn't I?'

'Oh please,' she snorted. 'You? I'd like to see you land a single client.'

'I've got one.'

'Who?'

'Carlos Ibarguren.'

'Again. *Who*?'

'You always said you'd set me up with a nice Argentinian transvestite. You'd know him as Carlito.'

'Limited range, I would think,' Claire said, and then sniffed.

'Not at all. He's very talented. I think I can get him

the lead in that new West End production of *Cat on a Hot Tin Roof*.'

She laughed. 'You're an expert on the theatre now?'

'I read Stanislavsky on the plane.'

'Oh please. I read *Siddhartha* in sixth form. It doesn't make me a Buddhist. You haven't got a clue.'

'Suck it and see,' said James, standing up. 'Like it or not, you have competition. Are you up to it?'

She was impressed in spite of herself. 'Congratulations. You've actually grown some balls. I'll look forward to the challenge.'

'I always had balls,' James said. 'Stood up to you in Covent Garden, didn't I?'

'All right. I'll give you that.'

He headed for the door. 'Oh, by the way, have you seen Tosh? I tried her number but they said she'd moved out.'

'She's gone off to help run some Zen surf school with a piece of twenty-something almost-jailbait.'

James grinned. 'Tell her I said hello.'

'I will.'

He gave her a sly, knowing look. 'Oh, and pass on my best to Dr Mulholland, won't you?'

She opened the door for him. 'Darling, if I gave him my best on your behalf, he'd get entirely the wrong idea, and he doesn't swing that way.'

'Well, well, well,' James said, as they walked into reception. 'Something I should know about?'

'None of your fucking business.'

Donna, at the desk, was less discreet. 'It's Graham, Graham, Graham,' she said, typing furiously. 'Hope he feels the same way or you can join me up shit creek, girl.' Donna handed her a small white object.

Claire took it without the rising sense of panic she had expected to feel. James craned over to see.

'So, which is it?' he asked, with his characteristic unhelpfulness. 'So it's blank for negative and the blue stripe for positive, right?'

'Yes,' said Claire, staring at the blue stripe on the pregnancy-testing kit. 'She who lives by the urine test dies by the urine test, I suppose. Or something.'

To her intense surprise, James kissed her on the cheek. 'Congratulations. I always wanted a brother or sister.'

'Oh, do piss off.'

He laughed. 'Whatever. See you!' He breezed out of reception and left Claire staring at the verification of what she'd suspected. A baby. She supposed it made more sense than picking up strange kids in Covent Garden and shaping them into red-carpet material, but it didn't seem quite real.

Donna got up from the desk and grabbed her arm. 'Sit down,' Donna said. 'You've gone a funny colour.'

Claire exhaled slowly. 'I'm not surprised. Really. We should have been more careful.'

Donna sighed. 'What are you going to do?'

'Can't do any worse than I have already, can I?' Claire said. 'I've made over James, and well ... Graham – I love him just the way he is. So we'll just see how this one turns out, won't we?'

'That's all we can do, darlin'' said Donna, putting a hand on her shoulder. 'All we can do.'

Visit the Black Lace website at
www.blacklace-books.co.uk

FIND OUT THE LATEST INFORMATION AND TAKE ADVANTAGE OF OUR FANTASTIC FREE BOOK OFFER! ALSO VISIT THE SITE FOR . . .

- All Black Lace titles currently available and how to order online
- Great new offers
- Writers' guidelines
- Author interviews
- An erotica newsletter
- Features
- Cool links

BLACK LACE — THE LEADING IMPRINT OF WOMEN'S SEXY FICTION

TAKING YOUR EROTIC READING PLEASURE TO NEW HORIZONS

BLACK LACE

LOOK OUT FOR THE ALL-NEW BLACK LACE BOOKS – AVAILABLE NOW!

All books priced £7.99 in the UK. Please note publication dates apply to the UK only. For other territories, please contact your retailer.

PAGAN HEAT
Monica Belle
ISBN 0 352 33974 8

For Sophie Page, the job of warden at Elmcote Hall is a dream come true. The beauty of the ruined house and the overgrown grounds speaks to her love of nature. As a venue for weddings, films and exotic parties the Hall draws curious and interesting people, including the handsome Richard Fox and his friends – who are equally alluring and more puzzling still. Her aim is to be with Richard, but it quickly becomes plain that he wants rather more than she had expected to give. She suspects he may have something to do with the sexually charged and sinister events taking place by night in the woods around the Hall. Sophie wants to give in to her desires, but the consequences of doing that threaten to take her down a road she hardly dare consider.

CONFESSIONAL
Judith Roycroft
ISBN 0 352 33421 5

Faren Lonsdale is an ambitious young reporter, always searching for the scoop that will rocket her to journalistic fame. In search of a story she infiltrates St Peter's, a seminary for young men who are about to sacrifice earthly pleasures for a life of devotion and abstinence. What she unveils are nocturnal shenanigans in a cloistered world that is anything but chaste. But will she reveal the secrets of St Peter's to the outside world, or will she be complicit in keeping quiet about the activities of the gentlemen priests?

TONGUE IN CHEEK
Tabitha Flyte
ISBN O 352 33484 3

Sally's in a pickle. Her conservative bosses won't let her do anything she wants at work and her long-term boyfriend Will has given her the push. Then she meets the beautiful young Marcus outside a local college. Only problem is he's a little too young. She's thirty-something and he's a teenager. But Sally's a spirited young woman and is determined to shake things up. When Mr Finnegan – her lecherous old-fashioned boss – discovers Sally's sexual peccadillo's, he's determined to get some action of his own and it isn't too long before everyone's enjoying naughty – and very bizarre – shenanigans.

Coming in December

MAD ABOUT THE BOY
Mathilde Madden
ISBN O 352 34001 O

Sophie Taylor's lazy-girl lifestyle is about to unravel. She's been with partner Rex for seven years, and now he wants more commitment. She never planned for a long-term relationship with him. Since a drunken agreement where he offered to fulfil her sexual fantasies for seven years in return for a cash loan, they've drifted into a cosy partnership. Yet still Sophie has a fascination with paying men for sex. As a birthday treat Rex poses as a male escort in one of Brighton's posh seafront hotels. It's fun, but it's not enough. Sophie needs the thrill of the real thing; the forbidden element that turns her on and is missing from her life with Rex. And so begins her descent into Brighton's sleazier nightlife, where she meets Wolfie, the genuine gigolo article, and embarks on a series of liaisons that spread out to suburbia and beyond.

CRUEL ENCHANTMENT
Janine Ashbless
ISBN 0 352 33483 5

Winged demonesses, otherworldly lovers and a dragon with an enormous sexual appetite collide with spoilt princesses, spell-weavers and wicked ancestors in Janine Ashbless's fantastic tales of lust and magic. *Cruel Enchantment* is a stunning collection of unique and breathtakingly beautiful erotic fairy tales. Seductive, dazzling and strange, with each story a journey into the marvellous realms of a fertile imagination.

Black Lace Booklist

Information is correct at time of printing. To avoid disappointment check availability before ordering. Go to www.blacklace-books.co.uk. All books are priced £6.99 unless another price is given.

BLACK LACE BOOKS WITH A CONTEMPORARY SETTING

☐ SHAMELESS Stella Black	ISBN 0 352 33485 1	£5.99
☐ INTENSE BLUE Lyn Wood	ISBN 0 352 33496 7	£5.99
☐ ON THE EDGE Laura Hamilton	ISBN 0 352 33534 3	£5.99
☐ LURED BY LUST Tania Picarda	ISBN 0 352 33533 5	£5.99
☐ THE NINETY DAYS OF GENEVIEVE Lucinda Carrington	ISBN 0 352 33070 8	£5.99
☐ DREAMING SPIRES Juliet Hastings	ISBN 0 352 33584 X	
☐ THE TRANSFORMATION Natasha Rostova	ISBN 0 352 33311 1	
☐ SIN.NET Helena Ravenscroft	ISBN 0 352 33598 X	
☐ TWO WEEKS IN TANGIER Annabel Lee	ISBN 0 352 33599 8	
☐ PLAYING HARD Tina Troy	ISBN 0 352 33617 X	
☐ SYMPHONY X Jasmine Stone	ISBN 0 352 33629 3	
☐ SUMMER FEVER Anna Ricci	ISBN 0 352 33625 0	
☐ A SECRET PLACE Ella Broussard	ISBN 0 352 33307 3	
☐ THE GIFT OF SHAME Sara Hope-Walker	ISBN 0 352 29935 1	
☐ GOING TOO FAR Laura Hamilton	ISBN 0 352 33657 9	
☐ THE STALLION Georgina Brown	ISBN 0 352 33005 8	
☐ SWEET THING Alison Tyler	ISBN 0 352 33682 X	
☐ TIGER LILY Kimberly Dean	ISBN 0 352 33685 4	
☐ RELEASE ME Suki Cunningham	ISBN 0 352 33671 4	
☐ KING'S PAWN Ruth Fox	ISBN 0 352 33684 6	
☐ SLAVE TO SUCCESS Kimberley Raines	ISBN 0 352 33687 0	
☐ SHADOWPLAY Portia Da Costa	ISBN 0 352 33313 8	
☐ I KNOW YOU, JOANNA Ruth Fox	ISBN 0 352 33727 3	
☐ THE HOUSE IN NEW ORLEANS Fleur Reynolds	ISBN 0 352 32951 3	
☐ DRAWN TOGETHER Robyn Russell	ISBN 0 352 33269 7	
☐ VIRTUOSO Katrina Vincenzi-Thyre	ISBN 0 352 32907 6	
☐ FIGHTING OVER YOU Laura Hamilton	ISBN 0 352 33795 8	

BLACK LACE BOOKS WITH AN HISTORICAL SETTING

☐ MINX Megan Blythe	ISBN 0 352 33638 2
☐ DIVINE TORMENT Janine Ashbless	ISBN 0 352 33719 2
☐ SATAN'S ANGEL Melissa MacNeal	ISBN 0 352 33726 5
☐ THE INTIMATE EYE Georgia Angelis	ISBN 0 352 33004 X
☐ SILKEN CHAINS Jodi Nicol	ISBN 0 352 33143 7
☐ THE LION LOVER Mercedes Kelly	ISBN 0 352 33162 3
☐ THE AMULET Lisette Allen	ISBN 0 352 33019 8
☐ WHITE ROSE ENSNARED Juliet Hastings	ISBN 0 352 33052 X
☐ UNHALLOWED RITES Martine Marquand	ISBN 0 352 33222 0
☐ LA BASQUAISE Angel Strand	ISBN 0 352 32988 2
☐ THE HAND OF AMUN Juliet Hastings	ISBN 0 352 33144 5
☐ THE SENSES BEJEWELLED Cleo Cordell	ISBN 0 352 32904 1
☐ UNDRESSING THE DEVIL Angel Strand	ISBN 0 352 33938 1 £7.99
☐ THE BARBARIAN GEISHA Charlotte Royal	ISBN 0 352 33267 0 £7.99
☐ FRENCH MANNERS Olivia Christie	ISBN 0 352 33214 X £7.99
☐ LORD WRAXALL'S FANCY Anna Lieff Saxby	ISBN 0 352 33080 5 £7.99
☐ NICOLE'S REVENGE Lisette Allen	ISBN 0 352 32984 X £7.99

BLACK LACE ANTHOLOGIES

☐ WICKED WORDS Various	ISBN 0 352 33363 4
☐ MORE WICKED WORDS Various	ISBN 0 352 33487 8
☐ WICKED WORDS 3 Various	ISBN 0 352 33522 X
☐ WICKED WORDS 4 Various	ISBN 0 352 33603 X
☐ WICKED WORDS 5 Various	ISBN 0 352 33642 0
☐ WICKED WORDS 6 Various	ISBN 0 352 33690 0
☐ WICKED WORDS 7 Various	ISBN 0 352 33743 5
☐ WICKED WORDS 8 Various	ISBN 0 352 33787 7
☐ WICKED WORDS 9 Various	ISBN 0 352 33860 1
☐ WICKED WORDS 10 Various	ISBN 0 352 33893 8
☐ THE BEST OF BLACK LACE 2 Various	ISBN 0 352 33718 4
☐ WICKED WORDS: SEX IN THE OFFICE Various	ISBN 0 352 33944 6 £7.99
☐ WICKED WORDS: SEX ON HOLIDAY Various	ISBN 0 352 33961 6 £7.99
☐ WICKED WORDS: SEX IN UNIFORM Various	ISBN 0 352 34002 9 £7.99
☐ WICKED WORDS: SEX AT THE SPORTS CLUB Various	ISBN 0 352 33991 8 £7.99

BLACK LACE NON-FICTION

☐ THE BLACK LACE BOOK OF WOMEN'S SEXUAL   ISBN 0 352 33793 1
    FANTASIES Ed. Kerri Sharp

☐ THE BLACK LACE SEXY QUIZ BOOK Maddie Saxon   ISBN 0 352 33884 9

To find out the latest information about Black Lace titles, check out the website: www.blacklace-books.co.uk or send for a booklist with complete synopses by writing to:

> Black Lace Booklist, Virgin Books Ltd
> Thames Wharf Studios
> Rainville Road
> London W6 9HA

Please include an SAE of decent size. Please note only British stamps are valid.

Please send me the books I have ticked above.

Name ....

Address ....

....

....

....

Post Code ....

Send to: Virgin Books Cash Sales, Thames Wharf Studios, Rainville Road, London W6 9HA.

US customers: for prices and details of how to order books for delivery by mail, call 1-800-343-4499.

Please enclose a cheque or postal order, made payable to Virgin Books Ltd, to the value of the books you have ordered plus postage and packing costs as follows:

UK and BFPO – £1.00 for the first book, 50p for each subsequent book.

Overseas (including Republic of Ireland) – £2.00 for the first book, £1.00 for each subsequent book.

If you would prefer to pay by VISA, ACCESS/MASTERCARD, DINERS CLUB, AMEX or SWITCH, please write your card number and expiry date here:

....

Signature ....

Please allow up to 28 days for delivery.